IMPLANTED
EVIDENCE

IMPLANTED EVIDENCE

COLD CASES WARM CORPSES & DISAPPEARING WINGS

MICHAEL A. PELUSO

Library of Congress Control Number:		2019903462
ISBN:	Hardcover	978-1-7960-2333-6
	Softcover	978-1-7960-2332-9
	eBook	978-1-7960-2342-8

Print information available on the last page.

Rev. date: 03/25/2019

To order additional copies of this book, contact:
Xlibris
1-888-795-4274
www.Xlibris.com
Orders@Xlibris.com
791502

For all of my families (related, work, and social),

You have no idea how important you are. Always stay strong, keep moving forward on your perfect path, and shine your light as bright as it can be shone everywhere you go to everyone you meet.

Chapter One

The three best nights of sleep I've ever had were each followed by the three worst stretches of my life. Horrible stretches filled with enough pain, suffering, and loss to drive a person to the edge and make them want to let go. Last night I got fourteen hours of deep uninterrupted sleep.

Here we go again.

Friday morning 11:37. All I need to do is get through this day without anything bad happening. Just one day. It will mean the Breaker P.I. sleep sense is no longer reliable, but I'll gladly take that compared to the alternative. Besides, what's one more thing that doesn't work these days?

I press the scanner. "Save the night's dreams sir?"

"You'd better, just in case."

"I'm sorry your response was not understood. Save the night's dreams sir?"

"Quit busting my balls. I had a long nights sleep."

"Aw, poor baby. Shall I alert the media? I swear to the great home office in the sky you never want to have fun anymore. So, shall I save the night's dreams sir?"

"Yes."

"Uploading."

"Thank you."

And we're off to a fast start. I open the refrigerator. There's nothing but hot sauces and what can only be described as synthetic strawberries now serving as a battleground for three different forms mold. "Screw this, I'm going to work." I slam the frig door shut, grab my jacket, wallet, and keys and leave the apartment.

The elevator is open and running for the first time in five years. I get in, press the L, and ride down seven floors. The elevator touches down in the lobby without one interruption. The sidewalk is empty and I reach my stop as the bus pulls in. I get on. I drop into a free seat and close my eyes. Something strange is going on. This never happens. The bus jerks to a stop and forces my eyes open. It's my stop. It can't be, but there it is. Getting off I look down at my watch, a new record time. Only a ten block walk to the office on the edge of the city to go.

"This has to be a joke, right? It's got to be, a joke, or a missed 180 upload, or something," I mumble to myself. I start to look for hidden cameras as I walk. What am I doing? There are cameras everywhere. I let it go. This isn't right. I can feel it. Things are not supposed to be like this. If I get through these ten blocks without any problems then something really strange is going on or I'm still asleep or both. I walk down the sidewalk slaloming through the shit, the needles, and the bullet casings. Always alert for God knows what that may be falling down my way from the windows and buildings above. This is a part of the city you go to only if you have no other choice.

You've got to love this place.

No, I really mean it because if you don't it will eat you alive and sanity will be the least of your worries. Maybe that's what's going on. Maybe I've finally snapped and everything is beautiful. Better yet, maybe I'm dead and this is a lower floor of Heaven.

I shake my head clear. Five blocks down five more to go. I look up and see a deep blue sky.

Something is definitely going on here.

I look back down and just as I'm about to smile reality sets in. Dead ahead are two wannabes who need to be told that the 1970s Bowery punk scene called and they want their stuff back; and a wannabe human/robot morph who doesn't look like he's become much of either. Bracing for impact in five strides, four strides, three, two, one, and-

And the two punks make a space for me to go through. What the fuck is going on?

"Sir, excuse me, mister, hey."

I snap my head back. The taller of the two punks is jogging back toward me, with chains jingling from his black leather biker jacket and something in his right hand. I point toward myself. He nods as he and the rest of his crew walk the last few strides. "What did you call me?" I ask as I feel a strange look coming onto my face.

"What? Sir?"

"Yeah that's what I thought you said. What did you say after that?"

"Hey?"

"No, no before that."

The punk looks confusedly at his two friends. "Excuse me?"

"Yeah that's what I thought you said. Tell me something," I say stretching my head up to his ear. "Tell me what's going on, where the cameras are. I'll play along. I promise. I just want to know who's doing this."

A relaxed smile comes across the punk's face. "There's nothing going on. Nobody's doing anything as far as I know. And as far as cameras go, everyone knows the cameras are everywhere."

"Oh come on man. I mean you do know that punks don't nor have they ever said sir or excuse me let alone make a space for oncoming pedestrians."

"Well these punks do and no before you ask we are not undercover cops."

"Fair enough, I guess."

"Anyway the reason I called you was you dropped your phone. It looks like a classic. Here." He hands it back to me.

"I could fix it for you if there's anything wrong," the robot morph says. He pulls out a stack of quartered napkins that he's written up to look like business cards and hands me one.

"Old Solderman can fix anything. You should call him if you need something," the big punk says.

"Uh yeah, right, will do, I mean it. I'm serious, thank you guys. I know it may not seem like it, but truly I mean it. Thank you. I'm just kind of in a weird place right now. Truly, thank you."

"We've all been in that place," the punk says.

With that they are off and on their way. I am left standing there with my phone in my hand and my jaw on the ground. What is going on with this planet? I pick up my jaw and start back to the office through the shit, the needles, and the bullet casings. Six blocks down four blocks to go.

I check the time. "12:50 pm" shines back at me. More than halfway there. Then again, the way things have gone so far, do I really want the day to end? I walk ahead keeping an eye out for a sign: a cloud, a dead dog in the street, a screaming baby, a slightly burnt piece of toast, something, anything, that might be a sign of things headed back to reality. All searches turn up nothing, not that I'm complaining about that.

I'm now across the street from my office. I stand planning with extra caution. It would be a waste to have the kind of day I've had so far for the sole purpose of being splattered by a car or truck, or better yet a two ton bus. Fifteen minutes of paralysis by excessive caution pass and I finally make my move.

The cross is uneventful.

I head up to my office on the third floor, one floor above the dream broker and two floors above the synthetic fruit and vegetable factory. I reach my door and stop cold. My name on my door window is now spelled correctly. For three years I've asked and later demanded they fix my name's spelling and for three years I've been ignored. Now, today, I see it's been done. I shake it off and go inside.

The waiting room is empty, as always. It's exactly the first normal thing to happen today. My secretary smiles at me from behind her desk and I almost pass out. I've never seen her smile in the twenty years I've worked with her. I couldn't even be sure she had teeth until just now. She's normally such a jaded wiseass. And God that's why I've loved her all these years. "Ooh, sir, Mr. Breaker did you see they finally fixed your window?"

Normally this would warrant a "Thank you Captain Undeniable" or a grunt and a snort at the very least, but today is most definitely not normal and everything is going so well the best I can come up with is a blank stare and a tilt of the head. "Sir, Mr. Breaker, sir, are you feeling alright sir?" She gently waves her hand back and forth in front of my face. I blink, shake my head, and snap out of the stare. "You weren't having another one of those attacks, were you sir?"

I didn't think anyone knew about my attacks. Wrong again. I wonder who else knows and how long they've known.

I look back at her. She's still anxiously awaiting my answer to her question. I'm taking too long she's not going to believe me. Answer the question stupid. "No, it's just I've never seen you like this. Did you meet someone?"

"No sir."

"Did you win the lottery? Are you on something new and if you are what is it and how can I get it?"

"No silly."

That's it.

I haven't heard anyone use that word in over twenty years and now my wiseass secretary just used it. Something is definitely going on here. I lean in towards my secretary. In a strong, soft voice I say, "Alison, you read those sci-fi stories, right?"

"Yes sir."

"That's what I thought. Let me ask you something. There's a plot where the aliens take over the Earth by inhabiting the humans' bodies town by town. You've read those right?"

"Yes sir I have."

"Good. Now I'm going to ask you a question and I want you to think before answering. Okay?"

"Yes sir."

"Good, now I don't mean anything by this and I don't want you to take this the wrong way, but everyone has been acting strange today-"

"Strange sir?"

"Maybe strange isn't quite the right word. Let's just say they've been acting different today. My question is this. Are you still a human being? I'm serious. I mean you haven't been inhabited by one of these alien breeds-have you? Because there wouldn't necessarily be anything wrong with that if you have."

Her eyes turn bright and a wide smile takes over her face and she starts laughing at me. "Sometimes you're so silly sir. Of course I'm not an alien."

This was not the response I expected. Shock maybe; insult likely; or wiseass rebuke even more likely; but not this. "I'm serious," I say. I feel a rush of insult and embarrassment washing over me and she must sense this. She tries to stifle her laughter instantly causing it to explode. Now I break out into the kind of laugh I haven't had for years.

Tears begin streaming down the sides of our faces and every time we start to peter out one of us breaks out again. This carries on a solid five more minutes. Finally, we regain control of ourselves. I dry my face and snort out the last bits of laughter-for now. "Alison do me a favor. Order a large box of extra spicy wings and fried synthetic zucchini please."

"Yes sir," Alison says still rubbing her eyes.

"Alison, order yourself something too if you want, my treat."

Alison looks at me with a surprised look. "Thank you, sir. Maybe I should be asking you if you've been taken over by aliens."

"No, everything is still human. I'm going into my office. Somehow I don't think we are going to be very busy today." I turn around and go into my office.

Everything looks the same as it did the last time I left. Filthy. I have too much energy to sit down right away. I pace around the room inspecting everything. I stare out of the windows. It looks like it usually does: empty and uneventful. It seems the same, but something is not quite right. It's still; too still even for a day like this. I can feel the time passing as I stare. Has it been ten minutes, twenty-five minutes? That I can't tell, but it is moving even in the stillness. That's for certain. There is definitely something different in the air. That's for certain too. What it is I don't know yet, but it's definitely there.

A name flashes into my mind. Someone who might understand what is going on. I sit down and dial his number on my disposable phone. One of the last ones in existence, so the word disposable is debatable. I automatically get his answering service. "Tony it's me Ken. I was wondering what kind of day you've been having. I need to talk to you about some things. Plus, if you could give me a ride back home at closing it would really be great. By the way, I got fourteen hours of deep, uninterrupted sleep last night. I thought you might find that interesting. So call me when you get a chance, especially if you can't pick me up. Thanks, bye."

Tony Agita, part-time writer, part-time detective, full-time wise ass. A copy of me in every way except always better. To be used only in emergency situations. Today does not qualify as an emergency situation to me- yet. It does seem interesting enough and if Tony has gone into hundred percent happy mode then it will most definitely become an emergency situation.

A knock at the door breaks my chain of thought. "Mr. Breaker, the foods here."

"Bring it in."

I get up and greet Alison, who is cradling a huge bag on top of a six pack. I lighten her load and we put it on my desk.

"I got you a six-pack of throwback Synthcola. Total sugar. It's what you like, right?"

"Yes, thank you. Do you want any of it?"

"No thanks that stuff's way strong for me. I have my order on my desk. It's just about the same as yours except I got the pigeon wings and a less potent liter of soda. Thank you."

"No problem."

"I'm going to eat mine at my desk."

"Okay."

She smiles and leaves closing the door on the way. I open my wings. How she can eat pigeon is beyond me and I know for a fact that she's no lightweight when it comes to sugarcola, but there you go. I down the first wing and it instantly clears my sinuses. I start inhaling the wings one after the other. These are the best wings I've ever had. I don't know why I'm surprised at this point, but I am.

This having everything go right could quickly get to be addictive. I start to look for some napkins and see that the clock is now reading 3:15. These wings may not make it home. I ordered extra to have something to put in the refrigerator, but now it's getting doubtful that anything will make it out of the office. I try to slow down, but it's no use and I clean out the rest of the wings. I decide to save the fried zucchini for the frig.

I look back at the clock. It's now 3:33 turning into 3:34. A rush of sudden drowsiness hits; normally I would just put my head down and wait for Tony's call. Not today. I don't want to change any of whatever it is that's going on. I reach for the six-pack of liquid sugar and take the first gulp.

Yeah, that's the stuff.

I should have no problems staying awake after that. That's the stuff that could bring the dead back to life. I look around the office and notice for the first time in ages what it actually looks like. It hits me all at once. It looks like a bad imitation of a 1940's noir film. My radar starts to go up again. Warnings of this being a dream or the inside of an alien ship disguised to look like classic movies start to sound off. It's the bad imitation part that's bothering me.

I temper my joy and look for something to do. I open the file cabinet. I know this is real. I remember buying it. I got it for nearly nothing because once the chips were installed into us it was thought to be a waste of time, space, and money to keep files by hand. I still keep files by hand for the same reason I do so many things these days: a total lack of trust. It doesn't matter where the chip is and who has it. The idea of large amounts of information being instantly erased, accidently or on purpose is a complete nonstarter for me.

Anyway, I couldn't let this cabinet get away. It was a steal, a classic huge metal five drawer that will still be around long after the last human has turned out the lights. I literally got it for a cup of coffee.

I thumb through the third drawer. I get to the open cases. There aren't many of them, five to be precise. I'll admit that Tony is a better detective than me, but that doesn't mean I'm some kind of slouch. He's better, but he had to work really hard to pass me. I bring the files back to the desk and line them up next to each other. I take another gulp of liquid sugar and stare.

The first case was a missing persons case from about seventeen years ago. A twenty-three year old white male: average height, average weight, intelligence, everything, all described with one word- average. On the surface there was nothing special about this guy. No prior record, no arrests, no convictions, the guy didn't even have a parking ticket.

The one thing this guy did seem to have was bad luck. Catastrophes seemed to follow wherever he went. Death, destruction, loss, bad weather, all seemed to travel with this guy. It was uncanny. No one had ever seen nor did they have any proof of this guy being responsible for these things. It was just that it was so relentless and massive and he was the one constant. It made what happened next inevitable.

One day it all just disappeared. The missing person and all of the trouble were instantly gone. Nobody seemed to mind except his sister. The parents had left them when they were young and it was his older sister who reported his disappearance to the police.

The police whether purposely or not did not find any leads and with all of the trouble now gone, get out and stay out seemed to be the public's attitude at the time. This was when she hired me. She believed he had been killed and wanted me to find her proof if this was so or not. Just for some closure once and for all.

She never came back.

I kept the case open for a while and never found any hard evidence of anything. It had all just disappeared, the sister, the brother, the bad luck, everything, just poof- into thin air. I had left a couple of notes and theories at the bottom of the page, but nothing solid and soon it was cold.

"Strange," I say to myself, the memories growing by the second. I close the file.

The four other cases were all similar. They all occurred within fourteen months of each other. All with the same crime, dream theft. The only difference was the fourth case was filed by a dream broker while the other three were filed by private citizens. All male, all in their twenties, and none of them had any money.

I smirk to myself and shut the files. I stack the five files up and carry them to the cabinet. I refile them and slide the door shut. I glance down at my watch. It now reads 4:57. "That can't be right. Time flies," I mumble. Where the hell is that phone call?

On cue the phone rings, I turn around and Tony is standing in my doorway with his wise ass grin all across his face and his own disposable collectible hanging in his left hand. All typical tough guy Tony, six feet tall, lean, and dripping with sarcasm. "Nice to see one thing hasn't changed today," I say.

"I was just talking to your secretary. She's appeared to undergo an interesting make over."

"Hey, don't knock it. You haven't seen the best of it."

"Oh, I think I've seen a lot."

"Back down chief, this is my territory you're in now."

"Relax tough guy." He smiles that stupid grin and I smirk back at him. Like I said he's always a little bit better than me. "So how's Kenneth Breaker private tough guy doing?"

"Confused, cautiously optimistic, I'm really not sure. I have some things I need to talk to you about."

"Yeah, well let's just do it over drinks and dinner. I have the feeling this could be a long, interesting discussion and I'm in serious need of food and alcohol."

"Fine with me, you're the big shot."

I grab the bag with the soda and fried zucchini. We go down to his car. "What's in the bag?" he asks as we get into his car.

"Tomorrow's dinner."

"Good idea, just don't leave it or spill it in my car the way you did last time."

"You're the one who's driving."

"For now, I'm surprised they haven't outlawed it yet," he says closing the door.

I let out an amused grunt and we head out for B&C's Jazz Restaurant and Lounge about three miles away. It is a silent ride, with each of us paying close attention to everyone and everything we pass. We can't help it. It has become automatic.

We pull into the parking lot and neither one of us move. The Sun is halfway down the horizon and the sky that can be seen through the buildings is now a clear, deep, blue turning purple. "Have you ever seen anything like this before?" he asks.

"Not that I can remember."

Five still minutes go by then, we get out of the car and head inside the club. It's still relatively empty, but that's due to change. This place always sells out. A hostess comes up to us. "Would you like a table, booth, or seat at the bar?"

"A booth halfway to the stage," Tony says.

We enter the lounge behind the hostess. It is cool and dimly lit save for the hot, bright lights on the now empty stage. Cool jazz is pumped in low and steady through the PA system, providing a rhythm to the room. We reach our booth and slide in. A waitress soon arrives to take our orders. "I'll have two doubles and keep them coming," Tony says.

"I'll just have a large liquid sugar, uncontaminated," I say.

"Are you ready to order or should I just get the drinks?"

Tony looks at me. "I trust you," I say.

"Okay, let me just have two of the usual."

"Very good," the waitress says and leaves.

I see him scanning the layout. He is suspicious of the room. I know the feeling. He finds a cigarette in his pocket and lights it up. "Those things will kill you."

"Not anymore they won't."

"That's right I keep forgetting about the aliens."

"Yeah, thank God for the aliens. We live in 15 AAI."

"Right, After Alien Immigration."

"That's not completely right though," Tony says. He blows out a long stream of white smoke and continues. "It shouldn't be immigration, it should be introduction. I see it that way and a lot of our past history and innovations start to make a lot more sense. The ancient Greeks, the ancient Egyptians, aren't as awe inspiring when you realize they were probably getting some extra help." He blows smoke in my direction and gives me a stupid smile.

"Unless-" I say.

"Unless what?" Tony says.

The waitress comes back and sets the drinks down in front of us.

"Unless," I say and take a gulp of my drink. This is killing him I know it. "Unless it's not. You don't even know they're aliens. I mean, if you wanted to take over a city, a country, whatever, and you didn't have the firepower or will of the people to do it; how would you clear out large populations? I'll tell you how. You'd tell them that everything is now healed. There are vaccines and cures for everything. You can now do whatever you want without any consequences. Don't worry, do all the bad stuff, we'll make it better. You'll live as long as you want. You think business and industry wouldn't line up for that. I don't know, I'm just saying."

Tony has a stare on his face I've never seen before. His jaw has now become three feet long and is resting on the table. He puts out his cigarette without looking and tries to gather himself.

"Just saying," I say and smirk.

At that moment the food arrives. Two large slabs of beef are set before us.

Tony shakes himself back together. "Man, you're jaded."

"Right, maybe, I guess and that brings us back to the topic of today." Tony nods as he's working on his first bite. "Let me guess," I say. "It's better than anything you've had before."

"It's unbelievable."

"I know, it's been like this all day. I'm not complaining. I'm just stunned. This is the last thing I would have expected today. What about you?"

"Off, everything felt off. Just a little bit off. Then I got the message from you. My initial response was to prepare for the worst. No offense, but we know your history. Thanks for the heads up by the way; I only wish you would have called a little earlier. Then it clicked. I realized what was off. Nothing was wrong. It sounds sick to say but it's true. I went back over the morning and nothing had gone wrong. Not even the smallest thing. Since then I've been looking for even the smallest thing to be wrong or even normal. Nothing, not even your secretary."

"Right."

"You are the first normal thing I've seen today. How sick does that sound? No offense."

I raise my hand as I devour the last of the beef. "Don't worry," I say. I take a gulp and continue. "It's been the same here. The only normal thing has been you. Even my office seemed like a bad imitation. I ran into a bunch of thoughtful and courteous punk wannabes for God's sake. Although ran into isn't the right way to describe it."

"I know the feeling. Hey, if you make it through today like this, you may be becoming very popular and we might be going out of business."

"It wouldn't be the worst thing that's happened to me," I say and tilt my glass in his direction. He smiles.

"Hittin' the hard stuff, I see."

"Are you kidding? There is no way I want anything that might cloud my judgment or give me an excuse to misinterpret what's going on. Especially on a day like today. Besides, the way things are going I might start enjoying the day."

"Fair enough. So how do you feel right now?"

I think for moment then take a sip. "I really don't know. In one way I just really want to get through the rest of today. In another way I want to enjoy everything that's going on."

A quartet band starts to take the stage. "What were you doing when I came into your office?"

"I was just killing time by going over some dead files. Four of them were stolen dreams."

"They were probably sold for drug money or who knows what and then they forgot about it or instantly regretted it."

"That's what I say." Except for the one that was a dream broker. That one was probably for insurance money."

"Exactly."

"Anyway, there was never any evidence and the cases all just died. Nobody cares. There was also one other case, a missing persons case. The guy had the worst luck you have ever seen in your life. Anyway, he disappeared and then the sister disappeared about a month later."

"I vaguely remember that one. I worked on it for a little while as well. I think I met the sister once or something like that and that was it. I always figured the rest of the town murdered the two of them."

"Right, either that they ran away to a cave or an analog town, something like that," I say.

"Yeah." He looks down at his watch.

"Don't tell me," I say.

"What do you want to do?"

"Let's just hang out for a set. You can start to dry out and then we can go."

"Sounds like a plan," he says.

The night moves forward and the band is smokin'. I have my eyes on the stage, but I don't focus too hard. Just chill. I am one with the room. The sound and the vibe of everything around me have taken over and that is fine with me. Let something else do the work for a change. The tunes are now coming one after the other like a train with no brakes. I scan the room. The crowd looks willfully hypnotized. The guitarist steps up to the microphone and announces this is the last song of the set. That was quick-or maybe it wasn't I don't know. My perspective is completely shot at this point because everything today is off.

Tony is paying the bill. The last note rings and we get up to leave. The lounge is now packed and we snake through to the back door. We get into Tony's car and he shoots his way back to the apartment. He pulls into my parking space. I don't have a car, but I pay for a parking space. Brilliant right, well if you ever saw how many years long the waiting list was you'd understand- or maybe not, what do you want me to tell you?

"Let me come up with you. Don't forget your stuff."

"Right," I say. I grab my bag and we go through the front door. The elevator is sitting there with its doors open. Tony makes a surprised look at me. "It was like that this morning too. Never question miracles."

Tony laughs to himself and we take an uninterrupted seven floor ride. I open and close the door. I walk across the apartment and throw the food into the fridge. "Do you want anything? All I have is some warm sugar cola," I say.

"No thanks," he says. "I'm going to make a run for it."

"Are you sure you're alright?"

"Yeah, I'm nowhere near my limit."

I know he's telling me the truth because whenever he gets near his limit he develops an annoying, bad English accent. You'll know it when you hear it. Trust me. And he's about as English as the Pope is Jewish.

I still give him a stare down.

"Look if it makes you feel more comfortable I'll put the car in auto drive."

"Whatever," I say. "Let me go down there with you."

I open the door.

A dead body falls into the apartment.

"Why didn't you tell me you were expecting guests?"

"What time is it?" I ask.

He looks down. "11:57 in the pm."

"Damn, just when I was starting to get used to everything going right."

Chapter Two

"What the fuck is this?" I say.

"Did you hear anything?" he asks.

"No, you?"

"No."

"Whoever did this can't be that far away."

"One small problem, we have no idea who or what we're looking for."

"Right, shit."

I try to calm down and refocus. We circle the body. It stares back at us, smiling, as if it knows something we don't. Tony is staring intensely across from me. "What's your plan?" he asks.

"Whatever you do don't touch him. I get enough heat from the cops as it is. I don't need them reading false evidence."

"You want to call the cops?"

"It's the only choice. The last thing I need now is them finding out about me hiding a dead body."

"You and me both."

He walks around the body and stands next to me. He goes into his pocket, pulls out a loose cigarette, puts it in his mouth, but doesn't light it. "So, what do you see?" he asks still looking down at the body.

"Male. Five seven and a half. Overweight, maybe one eighty five, one ninety pounds. Brown eyes. No visible wounds of any kind. No scars, but that could change after they take off his clothes for the autopsy. No dried blood on or around the body."

"We should check the hallway and in the elevator."

"Right, do you see anything else or better yet do you not see anything?"

"He appears to be of Asian descent. It is hard to tell if he was killed or not."

"Unless it's something internal, a poison or inner bleeding that we can't see. That will be determined by autopsy. It could also be something underneath him, but I kind of doubt it due to the lack of blood."

"True, but again, he may have been killed at a different location."

"Obviously," I say.

Something is missing. I can feel it. I look up and it hits me. I start slowly pacing the hallway. I reach the elevator and start back. It's got to be here somewhere.

"What is it?" he yells.

"It was that last thing you said. You know about being in another location."

He looks up and I see it come to him. "The footprints," he says in a low tone walking towards me.

"Right. If he was killed at a different location he would've had to have been carried here."

"Yes and your building is always a mess, but now the hallway is clean. Not one spot on the floor."

"Right, and even if, like everything else today, they cleaned it for the first time in ages they still would have left their own footprints."

"Yes and if they didn't it tells us something else."

"They're professionals."

I walk to the feet of the body. Tony catches on immediately and comes with me. We bend over the shoe bottoms. "Do you see what I see?"

"Mud," Tony says.

"Right, he was carried or the hall was cleaned or both."

"Well there's no way they would've had time to clean the hall so he was carried." I nod. "You know what else this means," he says. The intense look coming back onto his face.

I know, but I don't want to voice it.

He says it for me. "The body either came or more likely, was placed against your door. He or his killers or both, know who you are and where you live. So I ask you again, do you know this guy?"

I race through my visual memory files. I'm not finding anything. "No I'm not getting any matches."

"Is he new? Maybe he's someone who's had work done."

"I don't know. I told you before he doesn't match any of my Vfiles. I doubt he had any work done. If he did it would've had to have been done by an A-grade professional. He doesn't have any scars."

My tone has started to get defensive. I know he's not attacking me. He's just trying to help me. It's nothing compared to what the cops are going to do, but it's an automatic response. A defense reflex built on years of bad luck and being under attack.

Tony can sense this.

He backs off. He lights his cigarette and blows a long stream into the air. He looks back at me. "Unless-"

"Unless what?" I say.

"Unless it has been erased from your Vfiles by The Eyes Upstairs. Unless it was done by an A-grade professional in which case, someone rich and most likely important is after you."

"But for what?"

Tony shrugs his shoulders. He walks back to my kitchen and puts out his cigarette without dropping any ashes. I still can't figure out how he does that.

I go back into the kitchen. He has started on a new cigarette. "I thought you quit in the club."

"It didn't take."

At this point we are both throwing out absent minded lines. Our minds, at least I know mine and I strongly suspect his, are somewhere else going a hundred miles an hour. He looks back at me and waits for me to look him back in the eyes. I can feel his look. He's going to have to wait a little bit more. I am almost finished racing through my mind for anything I may have forgotten or overlooked. I am coming up with zeros. Frustrated, I look back at him.

"Anything?" he asks.

"A whole lot of nothing."

Something pops up in the deep recesses of my mind and gives me a sliver of hope.

"What is it?"

It must have shown on my face. "It's a long shot but I can check it out. I don't want to say or even think about what it is, because if things are really as serious as we think they are, I don't want them taking it away."

"Fair enough," Tony says.

I look back at Tony and ask, "If things are what you think they might be do you still think we should call the cops?"

"We may as well, they're going to give us heat one way or the other. It's like you said earlier no reason to give them any legitimate reasons to give us a hard time."

"Right, I was just making sure."

"You know where I am. You also realize we have to work together on this one. They are going to try and play one of us off the other. They would love to take down two of the few remaining P.I.s with one shot. You realize that, don't you?"

"Of course, why should this time be any different than the past?"

Tony puts out his second cigarette and looks back at me. "Good, I was just making sure. Now, you should call them, that's obvious right? I mean it is your apartment."

"What do you think, this is my first case? Give me a little credit." I try to hold back any insult. I look and see he is the one who is acting anxious. Giving away tells left and right.

"Relax," he says. He shifts his weight and rubs his brow. "When you call them use the automatic phone. Be as vague as possible. Let's get them to give away what they already know."

"Right, we should probably keep the collectibles hidden."

"Okay and I'll wait in another room and come in after they're in."

"They probably already know. The cameras are everywhere."

"Yes, but that's not the real question. The real question is: are they watching us now? Let them show us what they know."

I nod my head. I never thought of things that way before. Unfortunately, now that he said it out loud they would have seen it if they were watching and could adjust their response accordingly. I wish I hadn't said anything. We'll play it his way, but I'm not going to trust them either way.

"Alright," I say. "Are you ready to get this started?"

"Let's do it." He takes out his watch. Without looking at it he says, "From the moment you end it."

"Right," I say.

I connect my audio chip phone. Go. Ring number one. Ring number two. Ring number three. For an emergency response team they sure have a strange way of responding to hotlines. Ring number –

"Hotline."

"Hello, I have an ongoing situation in my apartment."

"Don't we all," the male officer responds. "Have you ever reported to us before?"

"I don't believe so."

"Really, because according to our information you have."

"Are you sure? I mean you must be right. Just one question though: If you already knew, why did you ask me?"

"Let me ask the questions buddy. What is the location of your situation?"

"703 Lowbrook Street, but you probably already knew that."

"Look buddy do you want our help or not?"

"Yes, I mean, if I take care of it myself you're going to come after me, right?"

"Most likely, but I will tell you one thing: if you keep up with these wiseass answers I may come after you just to watch you try to escape."

"Now I don't think that's any way to speak to a loyal, tax-paying, red blooded citizen."

"Funny you should say that, because our records show you're two years behind on your taxes."

"The check is in the mail," I say as dryly as possible.

"Sure and we'll be there any second."

"Thank you."

The line goes dead and I give Tony the signal.

"You call that vague?" he says.

I shrug. "You said vague, that was vague. Theoretically, they don't know what they're coming over for. You didn't say anything about sarcastic. Besides, look how much I got them to give away. They probably already know everything."

Tony rolls his eyes, lets out a frustrated yell, and leaves the room. He goes into the bathroom. "They are probably going to take their time. You could be in there a long time."

"I have everything I need in here," he yells from the fake porcelain.

"Don't yell so loud, I think I hear something."

I walk to the doorway. The sound of pounding steps is growing louder. I double time it back to the bathroom. "Steps," I whisper.

Everything is now silent in the apartment.

I listen.

A long moan echoes as the stairwell's door opens slowly then slams shut. Two voices are growing louder, nearer. I hear them stop at the body. The front door bangs. I take a few steps into the hall.

"What have we got here?" asks the male of the two cops.

"Funny, I was wondering the same thing."

"Uh huh, I'm sure you were," says the male cop.

Neither he, who is tagged as Rod, nor the female, who is tagged as Sue, are looking up from their notebooks. This is a giveaway. Whether or not they want me to catch it or not I don't know, but only rookies are forced to use throwback analog equipment. "So what's your story?" Sue says.

"It's not really complicated, but it may seem difficult to believe."

"Tell us, we'll be the judge of that," she says.

"Right, I got home around 11:30. At 11:57 I decided to go outside and get my thoughts together for a short story I'm working on that needs to be in by next Friday. I opened the door and this body fell into the doorway. It's just like it was. I haven't moved it or touched it."

"We'll see about that," Rod says.

He hovers with Sue over the body. They go up and down the body, giving it a quick once over. Sue keeps checking her watch. "We still have three more calls on this run," she mumbles to Rod.

"I know," he says and continues looking over the body. "No wounds, no blood, no bruises, no signs of trauma, no signs of wrongful death," he says to his partner.

"I agree," she says. "Definitely a case of death by natural causes. Call it in to the body squad."

Rod looks back at me. "Do you know this guy?"

"No and he doesn't match any memory files. I was hoping you might know him."

"Nope. We'll look out for any missing persons files over the next week or so, but most likely his name is destined to be John Doe."

"So no autopsy or anything?"

"Are you kidding me? Do you know how backed up the forensics department is? If his family comes forward in the next month and want to take him to a private forensics team that's up to them, but almost no one has the time, money, or even the space these days to do that. Good night."

"Good night."

He turns and starts back down the hall to catch up with Sue. Sue turns and yells, "They should have him out of here in fifteen minutes."

They continue into the stairwell while writing something into their notebooks. I nod and go back inside. I press the scanner. "Scanner, do you have an audio and visual recording of the conversation I just had?"

"Are you talking about the one you had with the police officers just now?"

"Yes."

"Let me check. Yes it appears I do. I will have to clean up the white noise from the hallway, but that will not be a problem."

"Good. Now listen, I want you to save it as a private file with the specific instructions that it is only to be viewed by me or me and Tony and if anyone: human, morph, robot, or otherwise is within hearing or viewing distance you are to immediately to go to mute and wall camouflage. Is that clear?"

"Not a problem sir. Labeling, filing, uploading now. Will be complete in five, four, three, two, done. Now completed sir."

"Much appreciated scanner. Keep that file on cue for after the body squad leaves the building with the body."

"Yes sir."

"Thank you."

"Sir if I may, I have a question."

"About the file?"

"No not the file. Sir, why is Mr. Tony still in the bathroom?"

I look back toward the bathroom. "You know scanner, I have no idea. Do you think we should let him stay in there until he figures it out? I mean we all know what he does for a living."

"I heard that," a voice from the bathroom yells.

"You're bad sir."

"That I am. Keep that file on standby. Thank you."

I walk over to the bathroom door. "So what happened to you?"

"What can I tell you, I was in here and I suddenly became inspired."

"Did you hear the cop conversation?"

"I think I caught most of it. Tell me when the body's gone."

"Good, you just answered my next question for me."

I walk away from the door and head to the hallway. The body is still there. I stand and face the stairwell. No sound or sight of the body squad.

This has to be a set up.

I quickly try to erase any trace of that thought. I try not to think about anything. This doesn't work. I'm still thinking only now I'm thinking about not thinking about anything. That's good enough for now- I guess.

The new silence brings back the feeling of what I had earlier today only to all be washed away so quickly and in such a big way. What's even more troublesome is the loss has already become a thing of the past and what is going on now is what I'm used to and accept as normal.

I look down at the body. "Do I know you?"

Silence.

"Okay, you want to play it that way fine. You don't have to answer me. A better question is do you know me?"

No response.

I look at my watch. It's been thirteen minutes. I hear feet and voices from the stairwell. The door swings open and six men with a bag and stretcher start walking up the hallway. "Is that our guy?" a big, bulky, guy leading the group asks.

"It depends, are you the body squad?"

"Well we ain't pizza delivery," the head guy says with a smile.

"Then this is your guy," I say as they reach.

"Man, doesn't any building in this town have an elevator that works?"

"Let me put it to you this way, I don't know which or how many buildings you've been to, but in this building the working of the elevators is instantly made an official miracle."

"No kidding?"

I sense an unimpressed tone in his voice.

"Absolutely, there's a semiretired priest on the third floor and everything. If he uses it, it becomes an official miracle. I don't know about the other buildings you've been to today."

"I doubt there are priests in five other buildings."

Bingo. Thank you very much. The leader glares back at the grunt who just spoke out of turn. He smiles back at me. "So when was your latest miracle?"

So that's going to be his game: get a little give a little. Okay, I'll play. Careful, don't be too good. Don't look professional. "I don't know if he went out early this morning," I say.

"Really, everything seemed normal all day."

Thank you for the double play. He is purposely trying to mislead me or he is having a very sloppy shift.

"Is there anything else you need?" I say.

He looks back at his crew. They stare at him with an impatient glare.

"No, I think we've taken enough of your time." He smiles and turns back to his crew. "Okay, tag him and bag him." He looks back at me. "Any chance of two miracles in one day?"

I shrug. "Can't hurt to try, right?"

I see a glimmer of hope come into his eyes.

"Unless-"

"Unless what?"

"Unless it only works for part of the ride," I add. Like scanner said, I'm bad. Sometimes I don't know what's good for me. He studies me looking for a clue. He's not finding any. "I truly don't trust them, even during miracles. You see that's the thing, not just with miracles, but everything, you don't know how long it's going to last."

A slow, evil, grin develops on his face. "You don't know how true that is."

He turns to his crew. "Let's get him out of here." They get into position, lift up the body, and carry it to the end of the hall. They reach the end and stop. The leader looks back in my direction. He takes one hand off the stretcher and presses the open button on the elevator.

It refuses to open.

A look of relief takes over his face. He looks back at me.

I shrug.

"What are you going to do?" I say.

He smiles. "Good night."

He turns around and puts his hand back on the stretcher. One of the grunts backs open the door and I hear them walking down the stairs. I listen and then I no longer hear anything. I walk back into the apartment. I press the scanner. "Did you get the body squad conversation I just had?"

"Yes sir, I did."

"Good. Save it with the same special instructions I gave you for the cop conversation I just had."

"I'm all over it sir. Saved, cleaned, privatized, camouflaged and automatically muted. Really sir, sometimes I wish you would come up with a challenge."

"Remember you said that. I may surprise you someday. That's all for now, Thank you."

I walk over to the window. The body is being shoved into the double parked hearse. I turn away and hear the doors slam shut. The engine moans, then catches, and I hear them drive away. Out of the corner of my eye I see them drive into the distance and make a right in the direction of the cop body shop.

At least that seemed right.

I walk to the center of the room. Off, so many things seem just a little bit off. Yet, at the same time, there is one thing I can consistently count on: the cops will always try to knock me off my game. They won't do it well. They'll always underestimate me, but they will always try.

I don't know.

Maybe they just don't want to use any energy if they don't have to. Maybe they're trying to lull me into a false sense of security so I get lazy. Maybe they're trying to make me think about them instead of what my focus should be. I don't know, at this point I no longer have a clue.

I haven't got a clue about them or the body. All I have is questions and they have just created a new and unnecessary one: don't they realize were on the same team? I look down at the floor. Reflexively, my head starts to shake in the negative.

"Sir, I sense question in your mind. If you don't mind I think I have another one for you."

"Which is?"

"Sir, don't you think you should see what's taking him so long? I mean it might be me, but don't you think it's been unusually quiet for an unusually long period of time? Especially when you consider who we're talking about."

My head snaps up. She's absolutely right. "Very true, you are very right scanner. I'll check it out. Oh by the way, that was two questions."

"Ooh, what are you going to do, penalize me fifteen yards?"

"Since when do you know about football?"

"I gave up solitaire months ago. It was too boring. I also used to watch games with my husband. We were big fans. I miss those days. I like to be used you know. You underestimate me."

"Right, I'll keep that in mind."

I start towards the bathroom. I turn back. "Scanner, please get the last two files ready."

"I'm all over it sir."

"Thank you."

I step up to the bathroom door. I bang on it. "Hey, what'd you fall in?"

"Well it's about time. I've been banging on the door for the last fifteen minutes. Your door won't open."

"Did you unlock it?"

"No, I just tried to walk through it. Of course I tried to unlock it. Man, why do you assume that you're the only one with half a brain on the planet?"

"Ah ah- temper, temper. Sweet talk like that will get you nowhere."

Now I'm having fun.

"Look, if you don't get me out of here in the next forty-five seconds I am going to shoot the handle, brass, and lock off this door. This is the last time I buy you a good dinner and give you a ride home."

He's got a very strong point. "Hold on, I've got an emergency skeleton card for occasions like this. Just let me get it. I'll be right back, I swear."

I hear the angry breathing through the door. He's serious this time. I could be in trouble. I run into the bedroom. Where is it, where is it-right, got it. This better work. I pick it up and run back to the bathroom door. I slowly slide the card halfway into the slot. I jiggle it with a quick rhythm that was taught to me by a professional ages ago. I shove it the rest of the way in, and-. Click, the door, she now opens.

"Forty-three, forty-four."

"Whoa, easy, easy, don't shoot." He looks like he might shoot me now anyway-just for the fun of it.

"You're lucky," he says.

I know he means it. "Come on, we've got real work to do. I would also like to get some sleep, preferably before the end of this week. So let's get moving."

Now I'm serious. The night has already turned into this morning and the sun will be coming up in a few hours. Then, again, sleep is what brought on this mess to begin with. So maybe it doesn't make a difference. Who knows anymore?

He takes a deep breath. "Where'd you get that?" he says pointing at the card.

"From a small timer who needed it to match an ante in a poker game. Man, that was decades ago."

"Okay old timer, whatever you say. Like you said let's get going. I don't want to be stuck here any longer than I have to." We start moving towards the scanner. His voice comes up from behind me. "So, do you hold all of your guests hostage?"

"No, I let some of them die outside my door."

How long is he going to keep this up for? It's already gotten old and I really don't need it. I've never seen him like this before. Ever. That's saying a lot because I've known him for decades. "How much of the body squad conversation did you hear?" I ask.

"I think I heard all of it. I hope I didn't or I hope I misheard it because if what I think I heard is what he actually said, then we are going to be in serious trouble."

I know exactly what he means. It's a good thing I didn't have any alcohol earlier or I'd be questioning what I heard myself. I'm having a hard enough time believing it as it is. I don't know why though, after all the crap we've been through in the past. I don't know why anything surprises me, let alone us.

"Scanner are they ready?"

"Whenever you are sir."

I turn to Tony. "So which one do you want to see first?"

"Let's go last first."

"You heard him scanner. Please play the body squad meeting first. Make sure you play it according to our earlier instructions."

"Understood. Will play in three, two, one."

The meeting repeats itself right in front of me.

Tony speaks up before I can. "This is what I thought I heard. We're being set up. You realize that, don't you? I mean look, this guy is acting so hard like he's trying not to give anything away that he's giving everything away."

'Right, the only acting going on is his acting like he doesn't know how to act."

"Which leads us to the next question," he says. "Do they really think we aren't going to catch on to this? Do they really think we're that dumb? Or-"

"Or, do they know we're going to figure it out and probably figure it out quickly. The real question then becomes are they trying to make us question why they let us figure that out so quickly, so easily?"

"We are being set up," he says.

"You are correct. We are most definitely being set up. It's just a question of where and when."

We see the hearse drive down the street and make the right turn out of the corner of my eye.

"Body shop conversation complete," scanner announces.

I look at Tony. He has a frustrated, but determined look on his face. "Do you still want to see the cop visit?" I ask.

"I'd better, just in case."

"Okay scanner, please play the police visit. Same instructions."

"All over it sir. Playing in three, two, one."

"What do you see?" I say.

"These two may not be in on it. Look at the bags under the eyes. They've got the whole 'tired, don't care, let's just get this over with I've got other cases to get to on this run' look to them."

"Unless-"

"Unless what?" he says.

"Unless they've got a real good make-up and acting department. They could have sent these two over just to make us think they were sending over a couple of scrubs who couldn't recognize a murder if it came and bit them in the behinds. That a murderer was going to go scot free and in reality what they're saying to us is 'we don't feel like doing our jobs and we know you have a conscience. Here you go, figure it out.'

"Then again, maybe they don't want us to know who did this. Maybe it was someone with or close to them and they don't want that found out. Or maybe they just sent over a couple of rookies who aren't in on anything. I don't know anything anymore."

Tony looks at me and shakes his head in the negative. We watch. The visit ends and scanner stops the video. I feel Tony look back at me. Thousands of possibilities are crashing around in my head. The last thing I need now is one of his wiseass comments.

"I think I might need one of those sugarcolas you offered me before," he says.

"Sure, let me go get it."

I go to the fridge and get one for him and one for me. Three left with the synthzucc. He sits down at the table. I give him his bottle and sit across from him. "I think there's ice in the freezer if you need it."

"No, I'm good," he says. He stares at me and a smile comes across his face. I look around me.

"What?" I say.

"You still haven't figured it out yet, have you?"

"Figured out what?"

This is starting to get annoying. He takes a slow gulp and reflexively I do the same.

"You figured out what they are trying to do to us. They know I'm here by the way, that's why they never asked to come inside the apartment. Come on, even the worst cop, wait let me correct that, even the worst first day on the job cop who has no idea what he is doing is going to ask to come inside your apartment and see what he can find. Think, what was the last thing you said in your rant?"

"I don't remember."

"You said you didn't know anything anymore. That's exactly what they want. You do realize that, don't you? No matter what's going on, they want us to question ourselves, our friends, and everything we think we know. I don't know if this is going to get big or how big it could get."

"This is going to get personal isn't it?"

"It certainly seems that way. I hope I'm wrong, but I doubt it."

"No, you're definitely right." I take a hard sugar gulp and ask, "Do you want to work together or separate on this?"

"Both," he says. He pushes back his chair. "I'd better get back to the office. So much for getting any rest."

"What good does sleep give you anyway?" I say.

He gets up. We shake hands. "Thanks for dinner and the ride, I mean it."

"I know," he says. "Now to see if they've taken my car."

"The fun never ends."

"It's only beginning."

He turns, leaves, and I close the door behind him. I stand by the window and listen for his car. "Scanner please go into sleep mode."

"Good night sir. Now counting sheep."

I am hit with a strong urge that only warm sugarcola gives me. I rush to the bathroom. As I remedy the situation, I notice he left his wallet and keys on the sink. I rush the finish and pick up the wallet and keys. I run out of the apartment. I hear the door close behind me as I run to the stairs. I fly down seven floors, my eyes open for Tony the entire way.

I push open the exit door. Tony's car is still sitting in the spot, obviously, but no sign of Tony in the parking lot. I move to the sidewalk. I look in both directions.

Absolutely no one. Not one single person.

I start to my right, why I don't know, habit, instinct, I couldn't tell you. I reach the corner and turn to my right. I take a few steps, but this block is completely empty. This is not right. Things are not normally this way. I turn and I'm hit.

I'm being hit by a light to be more specific.

A spotlight.

A mounted spotlight.

A mounted police spotlight.

"You have got to be kidding me."

Chapter Three

The one set of police spotlights increases to three. The front doors swing open.

"Hands up tough guy," the leader of the front car yells.

These guys have seen too many old movies. I mean, who talks like that in real life? They're really going all out this time. Maybe they've had too much coffee or maybe they're just bored and looking for something to do. I don't know and I don't really feel like finding out.

As the good, law abiding citizen that I am, I listen to the nice officer and raise my hands. The leader of the troop goes behind me. He grabs me by my belt and the nape of my shirt. Two of his friends join him. They slam me against the side of the building. The leader slams on the cuffs. He throws the side of my head against the building.

"You guys really know how to make friends. Did you know that? Hey, are you trying to wake up everyone in the city? Are you sure you're using enough lights? What about the sirens' volume? I'm not sure they can hear them in Saskatoon."

He slams my head against the building three times.

"Okay, I deserved that. I think you knocked out a few of my rotting teeth. I would've had to pay to get those removed, but you guys went ahead and did it for free. Thank you, I really appreciate that. I mean it. You guys are alright, in my book you guys are definitely alright. Now, you know I can only hug one of you at a time. You have made it a little difficult with the handcuffs though."

The two side officers beat me with their nightsticks from opposing sides.

I double over and fall to my knees. Air, I need air. Scanner is right. I don't know what's good for me. This looks like a good place for a nap. I fall over from my knees. A slow, steady, stream of blood develops from the side of my mouth.

The light is starting to darken and the volume is fading. I can't be passing out from this small a beating. I haven't gotten that frail yet, have I?

"Say goodnight genius."

"Goodnight genius," I whisper. I look back right into an oncoming nightstick.

*   *   *

"Buddy, mister, mister." I feel the poking from my side. Oh my ribs. "Hey buddy, are you alright?"

"What?" I force one eye open.

A bright light forces me to shut my eye. I turn my head and open both eyes. Daytime, it's daytime, probably late morning. I look back in the poking direction. I jump back and hit my head on the concrete.

"Are you alright?" A cop, a young cop on one knee is the source of the questioning.

"Do I look alright? Maybe you should ask your friends."

"Come again? Look, I think we should get you checked out."

I force myself up from the dried blood. I get to my knees and rest. "Easy, don't rush it," the young cop says.

"Where's Tony," I say.

"Tony who? You were the only one here. Let me help you up." He puts my arm around his neck and lifts me back to my feet.

How embarrassing.

"I've got it from here, thank you," I say.

I take a close look at him. Man, he can't be past twenty, twenty-one years old. Greener than Ireland. Either very naïve or a very good actor. His name tag reads Bob. "Come on, let's get you checked out."

"No, I'll be okay. I've had worse."

"It's not a choice. The captain insisted on it."

"Tell him I was fine."

"You can do that yourself, he's in the car."

I look over at the idling police car. He smiles at me. I have no choice. Bob leads me over to the car and opens the back door for me- cuff free. I duck into the car. "I don't have much more blood to give. I gave most of it last night- just so you know."

"I don't know what you're talking about," the captain says.

"Maybe you should check out last night's recordings."

"I'll be sure to do that. Don't worry we'll have you fixed up in no time," the captain says.

At this point, I don't even want to think about what that might mean. One thing is obvious. Bob is not driving us to the hospital. We are going straight to the police station.

Great.

"Don't worry. We'll have things fixed a lot quicker at the station," Bob says. "The doctor and nurses are so much better, you'll be glad we did."

I nod.

I look at the captain and he smiles back me in his rearview mirror. I don't need this. I swear if I make it through this case I'll go to writing full-time. Tony can have my work. Who needs it?

We reach the station and they lead me to the doctor's office. There are two guards outside the door so I'm not going anywhere. The nurse and doctor arrive together. The doctor stares at me, thoroughly unimpressed. "What's your story?" she asks.

This should be good.

*   *   *

It's twenty-five minutes later and I'll give the kid this, he was right about their medical care. Everything has been cleaned, reset, and taped quicker than it ever has before. It was painful, but it's always going to be painful. The question is are they going to be inflicting more of it? Everything seems to be sticking to Tony's theory of this being about causing confusion.

The doctor comes into the room with more tape to finish up with the last of the broken ribs. "I'll be finished in a minute," she says.

"Then what?"

"Then don't break anymore ribs."

"No, I mean what, can I just leave?"

"No, I'm sure the captain and the kid are going to want to speak with you. You can't go sleeping in pools of blood on the sidewalk and not expect any questions."

"You have a point."

"I know I do."

She continues to look at my wound. She has not looked me in the eyes the entire examination.

"The kid, is that what you call him?"

"Yeah, that's what everyone calls him. He's the son of a sergeant two districts over."

She stops and stares into my eyes.

"If you or anyone else tries to do anything to that kid, tries to hurt or corrupt that kid in any way, they will still be picking up pieces of you decades later. I repeat you or anyone else."

"Promise?"

"You have no idea. All the armies in the world, combined, wouldn't stand a chance."

"It's nice to hear someone with a little conviction for a change."

27

"When it comes to this, you have no idea."

"Excellent," I say and mean it.

She turns away and says, "It's all set. You have to get the oral work done by a dentist."

"Thank you."

"I'll go get the officers," she says and leaves the room.

I let my guard down and stare at the floor. Strange, right when I'm ready to give up on everything. I don't know, they've got to be doing this on purpose, but why? Then again I haven't exactly been maintaining my balance either. No. That's an Eyes Upstairs thought. Trash it immediately.

I hear voices approaching the room. I look up. The normal tone sinks to a low mumble as the footsteps grow louder. They're only a few strides away. I can tell. They stop. Now, they start playing games? No, I don't get that impression. Decades of experience tell me so.

I hear a female voice approaching. The doctor's voice. "There you are. I was looking for you, where were you?"

"Filling out forms, where else?" the captain says.

"Well, your guy is ready."

"Thanks, you're the best, as always," the kid says.

"You've got it," she says. I hear her walking away.

I hear the steps towards the doorway. They stop. Two bangs on the fake wood followed by a young voice. "Are you decent?"

"That's been a matter of debate for quite a few years now."

They walk into the room holding their hats. They stand in front of me, leaving a comfortable amount of space. The kid smiles. The captain says, "We just need to ask you a few questions. Nothing serious, just the routine stuff. It shouldn't take too long. I'm sure you can understand."

"Not really, but for you guys, what the heck." I hop down from the papered bed back onto my feet. "Lead the way," I say and force a smile. At this point that is no small accomplishment.

Following them down the hall, I draw looks left and right. They are classic and vary on the shock meter from zero to one hundred. The zeros come from the vets. They know me and they know the routine. Nothing new here. The high end of shock coming from newbies and those who can't believe I made it back to my feet. The one thing I don't see is anyone from the night before.

Figures.

I'm sure I will. It's just a matter of time. Not that I'm in a big rush or anything.

We're about halfway down the hallway. The captain stops and sticks his head into an open office. "Anything open?" he asks.

"Sin bin number three. Have fun."

He looks back at me. "You heard him, let's go. You know the drill."

"Yeah, I think I carved my name in the wall a few years back."

The kid struggles to hold back laughter. The captain smiles, "Yeah, very funny, let's go."

We walk in. "Take a seat. We'll be right back," the kid says.

They walk out closing the door behind them. I sit there not holding my breath. This has all gotten real old. Even the good ones have to follow protocol. Nothing personal. The fact there are so many bad ones out there make it a lot more understandable. Not that that helps the rest of us or anything.

There are a lot of bad ones out there, no question. Though at the moment I'm having trouble thinking of any. Whoever offed the guy outside my door is one. Man I was starting to worry there for a second. I'm losing my edge. My memory too for that matter.

I'm drifting, trying not to think about anything. If I close my eyes I'll probably fall asleep immediately. It'd probably be a good sleep too and we know what good that would do. No thank you.

There's a crack from the door. I look up. The kid pokes his head in. "Sorry it's taking so long, normally it's not like this. Is there anything I can get you to drink?"

"A sealed bottle of sugarcola would be nice if you have it."

"I'll see. We should only be a couple of more minutes."

Like I said, greener than Ireland.

"Thanks kid."

He nods and closes the door. Now I can see what the doctor was talking about. Some people are too good for this job. Heck some people are too good for this planet. Wait, did I just think the word "heck"? It must be contagious. I'm getting soft. I'm telling you if I get through this case I'm getting out of this. Maybe I'll go full-time writing, like I said before; maybe I'll become a food critic; I don't know at this point maybe I'll just become a monk. I have to get out of this while I'm still a sane, feeling human.

The door clicks again. The kid walks in, my sealed drink in his right hand a file in his left. He sets soda down on the table and pushes it towards me. "Here," he says.

"Thank you."

He nods. "The captain is right down the hall. He's on his way now."

I nod and he heads back and stands in the doorway. I hear those familiar steps nearing the door. The kid is standing in there, but he looks like his mind's somewhere else. Something has happened. Maybe they took my advice. We'll see.

The steps grow slower and louder. He appears in the doorway and the kid follows him in. They drop their folders on the table and sit down.

The captain stares at me.

I do not look away.

The captain takes out the standard questions. "Name?"

"Kenneth Breaker."

"Age?"

"A day older than yesterday and younger than tomorrow. Are we really going to do this? You know all of this already. It's all in your files mental and otherwise. We're all professionals here and we're all on the same team, so please I don't want to waste your time, let alone mine. All we have to do is work together. Just ask me what you want to know and I'll tell you the answers if I know them."

The captain gets up and closes the door. Not that that makes a difference these days. He sits back down. "You're right. We've both been doing this a long time." He closes his file. "I reviewed the video files from the last eighteen hours of the area you were found, as well as nearby areas."

"And?"

"Interesting, to say the least. One might even say disturbing."

"I certainly might," I say.

"We've started searches to find more specific information, but so far everything is coming up inconclusive."

"Big surprise."

"Well it is to me. I reviewed the body squad reports, as well as the ones from the officers who showed up at your apartment earlier that night."

"What did you find?"

"Nothing. They were thoroughly inconclusive."

"To say the least. So what is going on? Why is someone doing this to me?"

"I was about to ask you the same question. Do you know any of these people?"

"No, as I've told everyone who's asked and they're not in any of my memory files. What I want to know from you is were those real cops last night?"

"The first two were. Rookies, they've been having a real hard go of it. The rest I don't know. We're still searching the files. They may have been in retired cop cars that were supposed to be junked, but never made it to their final destination."

"Does that happen often?"

"Not that often, but often enough to be a problem. Now you realize that all this is off the record and will be denied if it is ever made public."

"Understood."

Silence.

I open the soda. Two knocks come at the door. The kid gets up and cracks open the door. Low murmurs come from the other side. "Hold on a second," the kid says. He walks back to the table. "Captain someone wants to speak to you."

The captain gets up and goes to the door. The murmuring is fast. It grows louder the longer it goes. The captain's responses are short and upset. He goes all the way outside and closes the door. The conversation now sounds more like an argument. The words are not understandable from the room, but the captain's tone sounds more like concern and disbelief than it does like an angry argument. The other voice says something in a muted tone and the captain remains silent.

The sound of steps walking away starts, but the captain's shadow can still be seen standing outside the door. The doorknob starts a slow turn and the captain takes a moment and then, in a slow rush comes to the table. He looks the kid in the eyes. "We have to go, now."

"What? Why?"

"Kid trust me, we have to go now. It's in your own best interest." He turns to me, "You- stay here. They will come with the standard questions. Remember what we said. If I were you I would finish off that drink before anyone gets here."

The kid stares up at him. He stays anchored to his seat. He opens his mouth, but his mind has apparently put his voice on mute.

I'm really starting to like this kid.

The captain stares at the kid. The kid stares at the captain. I stare at the two of them. The intensity has formed a vocal Bermuda Triangle in sin bin number three.

"Trust me, it's in your own best interest," the captain says though his teeth.

The kid looks over to me. "I would go if I were you," a voice that sounds a lot like mine says from my direction.

The kid nods and pushes himself up from his seat. The captain grabs him by the arm and shoves the kid ahead. He goes through the door. The captain follows with far more urgency and slams the door behind them.

I sit there stunned. Mindlessly, I reach for my drink and take a gulp. I mentally replay what just happened. I shake my head. Great, just great, now I'm telling cops what to do- and they're listening. Things weren't already strange enough and now- this. Just great.

"Snap out of it. It's obvious they're messing with you. Remember it's all about making you question what you know is happening. I can't believe you're falling for this. Walk away, just get up and walk away. I won't have you going soft and ruining all the work I've done," a voice in my head yells at me. The voice is my voice. A younger, stronger, stupider, version of myself from about twenty-five years ago, but it is my voice, that's not a question. It shows up from time to time, especially when I am running out of gas.

I reach for my bottle and take a long gulp. I slam the now empty bottle down on the table. "You shut up," I mentally say back to my voice. "I'm the one running this show, so back off. I know what I'm doing."

Silence.

Great, the cops are probably loving this. I look to the left corner behind me and see the small trash can I noticed when I walked in. I grab the bottle with my left hand and without turning throw the bottle towards it. It goes in without hitting any plastic. Never any doubt. Weak hand and all.

I find the most comfortable position possible and lock into it, blank face straight ahead. Inside my head is a different story. The facts and questions scroll by at a rapid pace. Reviewing them, I'm not satisfied. There are too many holes. Too many possibilities. Too many possible motivations. I've been through all this before. Someone's going to make a mistake and everything will fit. It's just a matter of time.

Still, something is different this time. I'm making a mistake or overlooking something on this. It's not a feeling, it's a fact and I've worked long enough to know the difference.

Shut it all down and get ready for the meeting. I ready my manual, remote recording prompts. They'll be coming any second. I can feel it. It should also be pretty obvious to them their attempt to freeze me out hasn't worked. Ever since the captain slammed that door fifteen minutes ago there has not been a soul or a sound in or from the hallway or adjoining rooms. Either that or everyone has left, in which case I'll just get up and leave. It's only right. I mean if they don't care why should I?

Let them read that thought.

Over/under for them showing up is one hundred seconds. I start my mental stopwatch. The game begins. Ten seconds down and the first set of feet can be heard growing nearer from down the hall. It sounds like three men, but I could be wrong. It seems to be a slow pace. Too early to tell.

Thirty seconds and they're still more than halfway away. Takers of the over look to be in good shape, but it's still too early to call. Fifty-five seconds and an obvious new pattern develops. After reaching a little past the halfway point, two of the three can be heard entering a clearly empty sin bin. The shoe tapping of the third can clearly be heard waiting in the hall. Two over takers, one under.

The two inside the sin bin are inspecting it like it's never been inspected before. How long will the third put up with this? The highest ranking of the three must be one of the over takers inspecting the empty room for nonexistent clues. There's no way underlings could get away with this and still keep their jobs.

Seventy-five seconds and the two seem to be leaving, wait, yes, yes, they are out of the empty bin and back in the hallway. They are walking at a very slow pace being pushed from behind by the under taker who they are blocking out. The pace increases.

Ninety seconds and the outlines of the three stop in front of the door. One in the center front, two behind him. This is going to be close. Ninety-five seconds and the one on the right makes his move for the door. There is your under taker. He is blocked by the center front shadow, who instinctively reaches for the door and inadvertently opens it on one hundred.

The three walk in.

"Sorry guys, but the over/under was a push. Exactly, one hundred. Hey, look at it this way, sure nobody won, but nobody lost either, right?"

"Over under? What are you babbling about?"

Thank you. Manual, remote recording prompt tripped and we are now recording.

"What? Who me? Nothing, I wasn't saying anything."

The three look at each other with a new degree of disappointment. Center front man sits down and the one who forced his hand sits to his right. The third paces behind them. His anger at the one on the right is overflowing. He is the lower ranking over taker. He probably needed that money. He is mad at the one on the right for being so selfish and costing him money. He will make sure he reminds selfish man of this every chance he gets in the upcoming weeks and months until it breaks up their partnership, which is too bad because he is the best partner he's ever had. A true friend. A hang out together with each other's families on holidays and birthdays kind of friend.

He'll save the largest hostility for the department, for paying him so little he needed to depend on over/under bets to pay his bills. For costing him his best friend and best partner. This anger will grow until he is impossible to be around. His family will say they no longer recognize him; to please get help.

He will resent this. Maybe he will hit one of them. Then, one day when he comes home, they will be gone. After that, who knows what happens. It's a story I've seen too many times before. Nothing new and nothing special.

This is how obvious they can make it sometimes. Even when they're not trying to.

I focus back to the two in front of me. Mr. front and center is indeed the highest ranking of the three. His tag reads "Richards" and below it is the title "Assistant Chief". I don't remember ever seeing this guy before. Assistant Chief can't be that big a deal if you still need to wear a name tag. The guy next to him, like the guy behind them, is a detective. One step higher than the grunts, but still low too low to taste the rewards of real pay and benefits. A mirage the vast majority of them will never reach. It will be snatched away and disappear just as they reach out for it.

Man, I hope they've been reading my thoughts.

"It's a new rule everyone has to wear tags now, even the chief. It's mandatory. And, just so we are starting off straight, I've been here a long time. Longer than that chip's been in your head, which I will easily knock out if you don't start showing a little respect for the shield." Thank you very much. "Are we clear?" he says.

I look around me. I look back at him and point to myself. "What me? Is it my turn to talk now? Right, well I don't know why you bring up your tags. I hadn't even noticed it. It's very fashionable though, it blends with your outfit really well."

A truck runs through my left jaw.

I push myself off the floor and get back into my seat. Anger boy packs quite a punch. "Right, good to meet you too. I don't think I caught you name though." I lean in towards Richards. "Psst, I don't mean to sound disrespectful or anything, Mr. Assistant Chief, sir, but I think one of your boys might have an anger control issue. Don't let anyone know I said this, but you might want to get him some help," I say in a fake whisper.

I lean back. I make eyes at the Assistant Chief and nod my head. "At least take him out to eat or something. Hey how's it going tough guy?"

He comes down at me with a right hook. I catch it in my palm and stop it dead in its tracks using its force to help me get to my feet.

"Vision's a great thing tough guy. It can keep you out of a lot of trouble. It takes away the element of surprise. A lot of tough guys aren't so tough when they're on an even playing field. Which brings us to our second point, gravity is a great thing too. The force you get punching downward into a relaxed target can make any punk look like the next heavyweight champ.

"Now, take that same tough guy and put him eye to eye with an equal size opponent and-. Let's just put it this way: I've seen a lot of heavyweight champs turned into dribbling, dreaming, babies, in the land of the unconscious with just one heads up to an unsuspecting victim. Now if you want to go tough guy, I'll come to the other side of the table and we'll go, but you don't want that and I don't want to be punished for teaching you a lesson everyone is waiting for you to be taught."

I throw his fist back at his face. He looks down at his partners. They give him no response. "Last time I help you, that's the last time I help any of you-ever," he screams and storms out.

"Seriously, you need to get your friend some help. Before it's too late. Now where were we?"

"Respect for the shield," the other detective mumbles.

"Right, well respect is earned and we have all put our time in. So, please as I've been saying all day and will continue to say, tell me what you want to know and I will tell you the answers if I know them. Otherwise, tell me why I had a dead body fall into my house and why I was jumped by a cop car full of uniformed thugs last night. If you don't know get out of my way so I can figure out why."

Richards smiles a bitter, horrible, fake smile. He starts rotating the ring on his middle finger. His smile is locked, that's obvious. Some people just don't get it. He doesn't even feel the frustration coming at him from the detective beside him. He probably still thinks it's about the over/under bet.

I remain still, mentally and physically. There is nothing else they are going to find out in my thoughts. All I have is questions and blank spaces for them to fill in their answers.

Richards starts to laugh. He's stalling. The detective rolls his eyes and stares at the wall. I hope, for his sake, he gets out of this clown show as soon as possible. He could start his own private agency. It would be more competition, but the way things are going, I'll be completely out of this game soon anyway.

Richards' laugh continues. He's trying to make it annoying. Too late, annoying left the building years ago. Now it's just white noise. Whenever you're ready Mr. Assistant Chief. Until then I'll count the spots on the wall.

Richards starts choking on his own spit. He starts gasping for air. If he's waiting for me to do something I have no idea what that would be. Wait, I know, maybe somebody should call the cops. His face is now turning purple. The detective looks at me.

I shrug.

The detective gets up and starts slapping him in the back. I'm sure he's taking a lot of pleasure in that. Read his thoughts right now and I bet they're not about saving the life of a dear and valued boss. Then again I could be wrong. I'm just speculating. Waiting for us to get to the real questions and answers.

Richards coughs and starts to catch his breath. The detective sits back down. Richards takes a deep breath. He looks across at me. "You think this is funny? You like wasting our time?"

"I have no idea what you're talking about. You're the one who was laughing. You and your department have been the ones wasting my time. I still don't know why I'm here in the first place."

Richards starts picking up his stuff. He looks at the detective. "Come on, this guy still doesn't get it. Maybe he needs some more time to think about things and come up with the answers we need."

"Answers to what? You haven't asked me one real question the entire time I've been here."

"Do you hear something? I thought I heard something. Well, never mind. He probably needs to think in silence."

I look at the detective.

This time he shrugs at me.

They leave the bin. I may never get out of here. They have nothing that's obvious. I think it's safe to say at this point that this is not some big act. The French and Italian directors of the mid-twentieth century couldn't come up with shit this surreal and absurd. Some may be in on something, but definitely not all. Most are hiding things, this is true. What? I don't know. A lot of ineptness. Some corruption, likely. Maybe there are a few who are in on something big and I don't mean good big either.

One thing is clear, they don't have any questions they can ask me here. So why I'm still here beats the crap out of me. They don't have any answers I need and apparently the answers I can give them they don't want. Not here at least.

I start counting the dots on the wall again. Familiar steps start coming to the room. How do you like that? It didn't even take an over/under bet or anything. Two shadows appear outside the door. This time the detective opens it.

The two take a step into the bin. "You are free to go. We may be contacting you in the future," the detective says.

"Yeah, your friend gave us all the information we need," Richards says.

"Is that a fact? Where is he? I want to make sure he's okay."

"We are holding him in protective custody."

"Right, I'm sure you are. Well you two have a good day and if you see my friend tell him I said hi."

"Will do," Richards says.

The detective rolls his eyes. Some people always have to have the last word. Not me. I have had enough.

I walk as normally as possible to the exit. I open the door. No fire alarms that's good. I start down the block.

I wait at the corner red light. A heavy sound from across the street draws my attention. Facing me at the red light is a police tow truck pulling a burnt out police car. The car looks familiar. Its spotlight is still open.

The light turns green. I should turn around and follow that tow. The urge is overwhelming. My legs refuse to turn. I keep going in my direction.

Chapter Four

The day is quickly turning into night and I am three blocks away from my office. I regret not following the police tow less and less with each step I take away from the station. Going directly to the office without stopping at the apartment first is another story, but I'm almost there now, so no big deal.

I doubt there will be anyone in my office. Fine by me. I haven't seen the robot morph or two polite punks on the trip. Too bad. I was sort of hoping I would. I wasn't counting on it, but I could've used something positive to think about.

The office is now across the street. There hasn't been one sign of a cop since I saw the tow. None of Tony either. Maybe the cops are taking their whacks at Tony. It wouldn't surprise me if they were, it wouldn't surprise me if they weren't.

I cross the street and lug my way up to the third floor. I make my way down the hall until I reach the lobby door. I stand looking at it. There is a weird feeling coming from it. I can't describe it. There's no time to think about it. I open the door and quickly move inside.

Empty.

Dark and empty, not one human to be found. From the looks of it you get the feeling that nobody's been in this place for years. I know that's not true, but still, the feeling is overwhelming. I flip on a few lights and rush into my office. I check the windows. Nothing strange, not one car on the street.

I turn and go back to my desk. Man, I could really go for some leftovers from yesterday right now. Maybe I left something behind. No luck. I check my wallet and take out the company card. If the guys last night were thieves in cops clothing they weren't very good ones. I still have all the cards and money I had before we met. Strange. I call the same place we got the food from yesterday and order new set of wings.

"Forty to forty-five minutes," the guy says.

"That's fine," I say and hang up.

I go back into the lobby and turn on the rest of the lights. I don't want the delivery guy claiming he was afraid of the dark and running off with my food.

Especially since he already has my credit. I go back into my office and make sure the door is open. It seems dark in here even with the lights on. I check outside the window. It's still empty I go back to my desk and drop into my seat.

I stare blankly down at my desk. Where was I? What was the last thing in my head? The food. No, before that. Before that was the tail. Why did I come here in the first place? Why didn't I go home? The files, that's right the files. "Right," I say and push myself up from the desk. I turn back to the metal filing cabinet. I reach for the cabinet. Two quick knocks on the door. "That was quick."

I turn around.

"Impossible," I say.

Coming in my direction is the most beautiful woman I have ever seen. Long wavy brown hair with blond highlights bounces off her shoulders as she slowly strides towards me. Her brown eyes light up the sky. There's a warm glow around her that doesn't seem human. "The door was open, but I didn't want to be rude or anything." She reaches my desk.

"Impossible," I say. She smiles. I know that smile. That smile heals every ailment a person can possibly have, body and spirit. "Impossible."

She smirks. "Is that all you're going to say? I don't have much time you know."

"No please, sit." She sits down. She stares at me and smiles. "Autumn? Is that really you?"

"Finally, for a second there I thought you were never going to say my name. Is it really that difficult?"

"It's just-"

"It's just what?"

"It's just- you're dead. You died on that charity mission I didn't want you to go on."

Autumn was, correction is, my wife. Is, was, who knows anything anymore?

"We both know that's not completely true, don't we?" she says. "You know that. I know that. I know you know that. My question to you is: why do you act like you don't know you know that? The answers are all there. That's not just true about me. All the answers you need you already have. Some are more obvious than others. That's the one thing I've never understood about you. If a person didn't know any better they would swear you are deliberately making things more difficult for yourself by not looking where you know the answers are."

"You already have everything you need. You know that and I know that. It's all right in front of you. Why won't you let me help you?"

"Please, please, help me. Anything as long as you don't leave again."

"I never left you. We both know that. All you have to do is say my name. I am always there." She reaches out and holds both of my hands. She smiles. "It's almost time. Anything else you want to say?"

"I love you. Baby please don't do this to me again."

She leans over and kisses me on the head. I'm always with you. You have everything you need. It's all right in front of you. It's all staring you right in the face. I love you," she says.

She stands up. "Wake up. The time is now. See you around. Just say my name." She backs her way to the doorway. "Wake up. The time is now," she melodically repeats. She turns at the doorway. She strides though the lobby joyfully repeating her final mantra all the way. She disappears.

"Wait." I push to lift myself up, but my body refuses to move anchored to its current location. Typical, I'm always fighting myself.

I rub my eyes. I look up. This can't be. I must be losing my mind. I'm staring at my bedroom clock. It is showing me 7:32 pm. It is still light outside. I roll over face first into the pillow. I can't remember the last time I cried, but if things don't change in the next few seconds that streak is going to end.

"7:34 pm, time to wake up. This is you're wake up call."

I've never hated where I am as much as I do right now. I look at the clock, it is now reading 7:34 pm. "Scanner, shut off that alarm before I break it myself."

"That is not a good idea sir. I strongly rule against it. Trust me on this one. If anything happens to me you will strongly regret it for the rest of your life."

Somehow I know she's right. "Right, sorry scanner nothing personal, I just felt a sudden, massive sense of loss."

"Understood."

I doubt that very seriously, but we are linked so- who knows. I'm probably wrong again. Besides, there's no call for insults. It's not scanner's fault. It's not anyone's fault.

"Would you like me to save your dreams sir?"

"Yes definitely. Immediately. Put them on priority."

"Yes sir. Dreams are now recorded and prioritized."

I stand up and stretch. "Scanner questions."

"Fire away sir."

"First of all, what the hell just happened?"

"What do you mean? Be more specific."

"Right, first, I remember leaving the police station and walking straight to my office. I remember it getting dark early. I remember choosing not to stop here first and eventually getting to an empty office. Please confirm or correct."

"Sir, your mental records show no records of you going to your office. I can confirm that you arrived at the apartment at four-thirty exactly this afternoon. You were tired and in a frustrated and annoyed state sir. You were mumbling something about good cops, bad cops, idiots, and burnt out cop cars. You set the alarm for three hours. You mumbled something about not wanting a repeat of today."

"What time did this happen?"

"This happened at four thirty-four, exactly. You then threw yourself onto your bed and fell asleep immediately."

"What time did was that, exactly?"

"Four thirty-five exactly sir."

"Thank you."

"Sir, would you like the answers to your two other questions?"

"Yes please."

"Answers, last one first. The memory of you not stopping here cannot be a true one by the fact of your records and you waking up here."

"Right."

"The second part of that cannot be confirmed or denied since you haven't gone there today."

"Right, continue."

"The third question, the one about it getting dark early, is incorrect. The conditions you are describing don't occur until later in the year. We are only in early August. What you're describing doesn't start until late September and early October in a season called Autumn. Autumn is also a popular girl's name. Number thirty-four overall in last year's results."

"Enough scanner, thank you. Remember the three things we don't talk about."

"Yes sir, but this was a general statement. There was nothing personal about it."

"Scanner."

"Yes sir. Anything else sir?"

"Yes, please replay the dreams you just recorded."

"Yes sir, playing in three, two, done."

The wall screen fills up with dreams.

* * *

The dreams have been playing for an hour and twenty-five minutes. Nothing special, all of the usual stuff. The wall brightens. "Dreams complete," scanner says.

"That can't be possible," I yell. I jump from my seat. "Scanner, I know there's more. This is a fact not a question, not a memory. Scanner confirm that you have uploaded all the dreams in the last three hour sleep."

"Yes sir, just a moment. Yes all dreams in today's four thirty-four to seven thirty-four session have been recorded, uploaded, and played."

"That can't be. I woke up from a dream at seven thirty-two. A very realistic dream. It has to be true. Scanner, please report specific dream activity and overall brain activity for the latest session."

"Yes sir, recalling records. Overall records show you were asleep from four thirty-five and thirty-three seconds to six fifty-eight exactly. It says your dreaming activity was from four fifty exactly to five fifteen and one second. Interesting."

"What?"

"Well I don't know how to explain this sir. From seven exactly to seven thirty-two exactly your brain seems to have been somewhere else. I really don't know how to describe it."

"Please explain further scanner."

"I'll try. You see your brain is usually in one of the following states: conscious, unconscious, awake, asleep, or system override. In the sleeping state you are either dreaming or not dreaming. REM or nonREM. This last time period your body and mind do not appear to be in any of these states. It's almost as if it is somewhere between all of them. I've never seen anything like this before. I'll put this on automatic investigation, but it could take a very long time. It might never find the answers."

"Do what it is you think you need to do as long as it doesn't take up too much of your time or attention."

"Thank you sir. You don't need to worry about that sir. The automatic investigation part of me is a miniscule part of me, less than one word from a dream. Its strength is its speed. It is immeasurably quick and efficient. It will report to me any possibilities and I will report it to you."

"Okay scanner, do what you think is best. Please know this, I'm starting to think I'd rather not know. I mean it's not important to me if you find it or not. It's something I'll always remember either way. You always said you wanted a challenge, here it is. Know this though, the second you start dropping off in performance is the second I cancel the investigation. Do you understand?"

"Yes sir, understood and don't worry this will not affect my performance in any way."

"Make sure of it or it gets cancelled."

"Understood, thank you. Anything else?"

"Yes scan through the city and police records from last night until now and see if Tony turns up anywhere. I doubt you'll find anything, but do it just in case."

"Yes sir. Scanning records now."

My dream has made me hungry. I take out the company card and order a large pizza. "It should be about forty to forty-five minutes," the guy on the other end says.

"Right, thank you," I say and disconnect.

"Sir, there is no record of Mr. Tony over the last twenty-four hours."

"That's what I figured. One more thing scanner, please don't let me fall asleep before the food is delivered."

"Not a problem sir.'

"Thank you."

* * *

Twenty-five minutes have passed. I continue to pace back and forth. It's the only way I can make sure I won't fall asleep. I turn and start away from the door. Two quick knocks on the door. That was fast. What are the chances of history repeating itself?

"Yo, pizza delivery here."

It's Tony carrying my delivery. Not quite what I was expecting or hoping for.

"Are you going to open the door all the way so I can come in or are you going to wait for me to die and fall in?" I open the door and Tony walks in with the hot pie. "The nice pizza delivery guy gave it to me for free. He said something about saving him a trip up all those stairs."

"Yeah, it also helps when it's already paid for."

He drops the pizza on the table and sits down. I sit across from him. His face is almost as beat up as mine. He is still in the clothes he was wearing last night. "Where have you been? I just had scanner do a sweep for you."

"I was just out walking around. You know, taking in the city."

"I see you probably ran into the same sweethearts I did."

"Well not so much me running into them as them into me. You know, with their fists and nightsticks and knees. All kinds of good stuff. Hey, are we just going to stare at this food or do you plan on eating it anytime soon?"

"Right," I say. "Let me go get a couple of dishes."

I get up, get the dishes and paper towels, and sit back down. We start to inhale the food. Man, I forgot to order the soda. I get up, go to the fridge, and take out two of the final three bottles. "Take it easy, because that's all I have unless you want to be brave and drink the city water," I say and sit down.

"No thank you I've already had enough of a beating for one day," he says with a full mouth of pizza.

"Remind me to give you back your keys."

"Good, I was hoping you found them."

"They were on the sink, they were kind of hard to miss. You knew something was coming, didn't you."

"Knew no. It was just a last minute feeling. I didn't want anybody beating the snot out of me and taking my car with them."

I slide his keys across the table to him. "Before I forget."

That concludes the speaking portion of the meal. From then on our mouths will be used solely for the purpose of inhaling the food. At the rate we're going that won't take much longer. This is the first I've eaten since last night at the club and from the looks of it, the same applies to Tony.

I look down. Two snatches left. I snatch one, making sure to keep my hands clear of Tony's mouth. Chomp, gulp, chomp, chomp. I look down. The box she is now empty. I look up. Tony takes his last chomp and gulp at the same time. "Disgusting," I say.

He shrugs. "What are you going to do? Are you ready for round two?"

"My tank is nowhere close to being full, but my wallet is on empty too. I have people after me, remember."

"Don't worry about it, not tonight at least. Just get it fixed by the next time I show up."

"Don't worry I'm planning on going to the repair shop by the end on the week."

"Make sure you do."

I take my last gulp of this bottle and let out a belch that shakes the foundation of the building. No exaggeration. I don't know who that says more about: me, the cola, or the building. Tony gets up from his chair and starts cheering. There's only one proper way to respond. I stand. "Thank you, thank you, I'd like to thank my parents; all of the people at the sugarcola factory, if there are any people left at the sugarcola factory; and everyone along the way who made tonight possible." I bow in all directions. "That's enough of that." I sit down.

Tony sits. We stare in each other's general direction. We try to laugh, but the best we can do is smirk. It's moments like this that keep reminding me how far we've fallen.

Tony's stomach starts to grumble. I can hear it from across the table. "The food's not going to order itself," I say.

"Yeah but I've been thinking. I really don't feel like dealing with another dead body falling into your apartment."

"I can't help you with that. You're going to have to open the door again sooner or later. You could order the food and we could pick it up." Tony points to his shiner. "I said we. Four fists are better than two, right?" Tony looks unimpressed. "Stop being such a baby, man. What's the worst that could happen? We take another beating, so what? They can't make us look any worse and I don't know about you, but I stopped feeling pain about twelve hours ago."

"Good point."

"Damn right it's a good point. I'm surprised at you, really. I think all that hiding you did today might have infected you with some kind of chicken flu virus."

Incoming. His famous right cross is headed straight for my head. I weave out of the way. "Ooh whatever you do, don't do that. We might get into a fight. We can't have that. Somebody might get hurt."

I keep moving back and forth; in and out; all the while making goofy faces at him. It's too bad, I was really looking forward to more pizza. I keep moving. "Ah, ah, the face is quicker than the hand."

Tony snorts. He begins to crack a smile. He squints at me and pulls back his head. "The face is quicker than the hand? That has got to be the stupidest thing you have ever said. I'm talking all-time stupid."

"Don't give me that. That's a good line and you know it. You're just jealous you never thought of it."

"No, I'm serious, that was all-time bad, all-time stupid. I think any independent judge would back me up on this one."

"Okay, scanner give us a ruling on what you just saw. That one line in specific. Was it or was it not all-time stupid?"

"Do I have permission to be frank and honest sir?"

"It's not looking good for you."

"Shut up you. Yes scanner you know I would never have it any other way."

"Yes sir, reviewing your files, that was definitely top ten all-time stupid and top seven all-time bad. I liked it though, if that's any consolation."

"Thank you scanner."

"Yes, thank you scanner and if Kenneth is ever mean to you call me and I'll straighten him out for you."

"That's not necessary Mr. Tony. Mr. Kenneth and I are linked together as one forever."

"Thank you scanner," I say. Tony looks at me. "Have you really fallen to the level of making moves on my scanner? Man, I knew you were desperate, but I didn't realize you're that desperate."

Tony lets out a laugh snort. "Come on let's go get more food," he says.

He pushes himself up off his chair. "Make sure you remember your keys this time. They might be your good luck charm."

Tony rolls his eyes at me. "One minute you're a professional wrestler, the next you're my grandmother. I'm going to have to get you checked out."

"Get on line to get into the stadium full of people who want to do that."

Tony turns on his phone, makes the order and we leave the apartment-not one dead body along the way. We're off to a good start. We go down the hall, open the door, and start our trip down the steps.

What we are doing is not normal and it's not normal for a number of reasons. First of which is people don't go outside anymore unless they absolutely have no other choice. It's strange, I don't remember when this started and I don't know why.

A lot of people blame the climate now, which is more honest than it used to be. I remember when I was a kid, everyone would say how great summer was and how much they loved the hot weather. Then, summer would arrive bringing the hot weather with it and all of those people would run inside into their air conditioned rooms, not to be seen again until mid-September at the earliest.

Some people say it started in 2AAI with the summer of killer bugs and insects. Killer mosquitoes, killer wasps, killer fruit flies, you name it and there was a killer breed of it that year. The list of possible causes read like a B-movie file of script rejects: the insects escaped from a government test lab; the insects got into a factory of super steroids after the roof was blown off during a tornado and bred creating a limited generation of super breeds; after generations of exposure the insects became immune to all of the repellents and pesticides; the aliens brought them with them; and the ever popular the bugs and insects just finally got pissed off at the humans and decided to settle the score once and for all.

Whatever it was, after 2AAI it was gone and never heard from again, but during that year of constant indoor living people got lazy. They liked having everything sent to and from them door to door without ever having to leave their living room and wanted it to stay that way. A new market developed and soon it became the new norm.

Whatever the real year and real reasons were I've never understood it. Fine with me. There's almost always room on the sidewalk.

We reach the exit door on the first floor. Tony pushes the door open and waits for me to walk through. To think, up until very recently I thought he was the brave one. The sidewalk is barren. No citizens, no cops real or otherwise. "All clear, captain, Your Highness, sir," I say back to him.

He comes out mumbling something. "That's the last time I show a lady like you an act of chivalry."

It shouldn't take long to get the food. It's not that far. Seven blocks straight one way, seven blocks straight back, and seven floors to climb upstairs. Tony is staring to his center right. "You see something?" I ask.

"No, I was just drifting. Don't mind me."

"Shall we dance?"

"Well that pizza isn't going to eat itself."

"Right, but if we don't step it up somebody might try to eat it for us and take the credit."

"Then what are we waiting for?"

"I don't know what are we waiting for?"

"Fine."

"Fine."

"Let's go."

"Right, let's go."

Tony smacks me in the head. "Cut that shit out." I open my mouth. "Don't even think about it."

"What, I was just going to ask if you know how to get there."

"It's a pizza place, I'm Italian, of course I know how to get there. Besides, the address was on the box."

We start down the street. An aroma cuts through the air. "Somebody's barbecuing," I say.

"Up there," Tony says pointing to a stream of smoke three roofs ahead of us.

"That's a great smell."

"I know what you mean," he says. He takes a deep inhale. "It smells like real meat too."

"Right, someone must have just won the lottery."

"Yeah, or maybe they finally had that trifecta daily double they've been playing every day for the last twenty years come in."

"Good for them if they did," I say and mean it.

We continue moving forward. The talking is over for now. We try to absorb everything around us. Tony, I think, is one of the few people left who appreciates how much we have lost. Another reason what we are doing isn't normal. There aren't any actual stores anymore. No, that's not true, let me correct myself. Maybe any is an exaggeration, but only a slight one. The only stores left are: restaurants; clubs; bars; twenty-four hour emergency everything stores; and dreams sales and rental stores, almost all of which are independents. All of the big chains are digital delivery only.

Most people don't notice this or don't care. I'm sure the fact very few of these people ever leave their apartments is a big reason. The people who do notice and do care often argue about when it started. Most, as with everything else, point to the last event and blame it. In this case the event is the killer bug and insect summer. That summer gets blamed for just about everything. The fact people got so lazy and so much out of it doesn't help its cause, but it's a crutch. A strong, convenient, crutch.

It makes me laugh when I think the argument these people use to blame people for getting lazy is the most recent, convenient, and lazy argument available to them. It's things like this that get stuck in my head and keep me up at night. Which, as we've seen, isn't exactly a bad thing.

The real store disappearance began decades ago in the first years of the automation revolution. Why pay for rent, payroll, vendor fees, security fees, heat, and electricity when you could keep everything in a few automated, computer maintained, warehouses. It made plenty of sense, and dollars for that matter, to and for a lot of people. It was inevitable. It wasn't exactly gradual, but it was slow enough that everybody saw it coming.

It cost us a lot. It cost a lot of people their jobs, a historically high loss of jobs never to be regained. It cost us our economy which suffered its final blow due to this loss of jobs and its money flow into the system. It cost us the most valuable thing we had. The thing we lost no one ever talks about and will soon be forgotten. Our personality. We just gave it away. All of the cities, towns, and neighborhoods lost their personality, their character, lost what made them who they were.

For what?

Now we are just blips on a digital map. Thank God for the clubs and other last standing oasis we have left. Thank God for the analogtowns, just don't tell anyone I thought that. It would cause a lot of problems. In fact let me take care of it now.

"G manual inner filter erase all traces of the last thanks thought I had. Surround all traces in garden camouflage in case there are traces that can't be reached. Confirm."

"Trace erase and garden camouflage implanted, accomplished, and completed. One hundred percent confirmed."

Okay, that's enough of that. Thinking always gets me in trouble. Whoever came up with garden camouflage must have thought a lot. Garden camouflage is something you attach to a thought so if someone ever traces that thought all they will think about is flowers. All they will sense is the smell of flowers. The actual thought will be irretrievably hidden in the garden. Maybe among the infinite flowers. Maybe amid the infinite levels of soil. Maybe directly in the eye of the Sun that's shining down on it.

No one will ever know its exact location and it keeps no records. It had to be invented by someone who thought too much.

"We're here," Tony says.

He opens the door and a new aroma hits us right in the face. I'm knocked from one daze to another. "Another great smell," Tony says.

"Right, two in one night All this and pizza too."

I stand back and Tony starts to the counter. He looks back. "You want anything else?"

"Soda."

He nods and steps back to the counter. He picks up the pie along with a two liter for me and a six pack of beer for him. The man behind the counter looks like a 3d printed version of the jolly pizza man on some boxes. Only this one doesn't look so jolly. He is sweating his brains out and has the look of someone who has been on his feet all week.

Tony starts to walk away. I step up and grab pizza guy's shoulder. "Hey buddy, anybody strange come in here last night?"

"Mister, everyone who comes into this place is strange. Last night, tonight, tomorrow, it doesn't make a difference."

"Are you sure? It could win you fifty. How about cops, any strange or mean cops visit last night?" I reach for my wallet.

"Never, I've never seen any strange or mean cops. Now, unless you have about a day and a half of sleep in your pocket let me get back to the pizza before it burns."

"Nice try rookie," Tony says.

I shrug. "It's late, I'm hungry, what do you expect?"

We start away from the pizza shop. The aroma from the pizza rises up from the box he's carrying into Tony's face. It's the vaporizer he's always dreamed of. He's in Heaven and I'm not sure if I'm exaggerating when I say that. At this point he's not walking back, he's floating. The smile on his face is huge. It doesn't take much these days.

"Try not to drool so much on the pizza. I don't think that's too big a request, is it?" He refuses to acknowledge my request. "Right, if you're going to be that way about it then at least try to keep the drool to your side of the pie. Would you please?" Still no response.

Four blocks down three to go.

A couple of people poke their heads around the corner two blocks ahead of us. They retreat. "Eyes open. Two ahead, two ahead, our side, far end," I say.

"I'm already on it. I'm with you all the way."

So much for anything being simple. An older looking woman, a stereotypically looking older woman if you asked me, comes around that same corner. "One on the other side," Tony says.

I missed that. "Good call." It's a female, probably in her mid-twenties crossing to the old lady's side of the street. "Tell me, does granny look like she's moving unusually slow for someone out at this time or is it me?" I ask.

"I don't know. It's too early to tell."

Another block down and we're all on the same block. Granny's still three quarters of a block away, moving slower by the second.

Granny goes down in a heap.

Tony drops the pizza and runs to her. I pick up the pizza and slowly continue forward. I am deliberately hanging back. Something about this stinks and I don't like it.

The woman reaches her first. She starts screaming, "She's not breathing, she's not breathing."

Tony moves her out of the way and starts CPR. The two original faces rush in from around the corner. They're moving straight for the body. I drop the pizza and pull out my gun. "Don't even think about it," I yell. I'm focused on them and the gun is where it needs to be.

A group of about eight appear from around the corner. They're all in bad costumes. "Everybody stay." I start to move in slowly.

One of the original two faces jerks forward. I take a shot and he dives down. "Jesus man," granny says in a male voice as she miraculously snaps up. She throws off her wig. Granny is a twenty-year old man.

"What the" Tony yells. He jumps up and reaches for his gun.

"Cut," a voice yells and everybody runs away in all directions. Screeching tires all around. Then silence.

I pick up the pie and drinks and walk to Tony. He's still spitting. There's a puddle about four feet away from him. "Couldn't you tell?" I say closing in.

He looks up. "If my pizza is damaged I'll find and kill all of them. I swear."

"No everything is fine, I checked. We've both been doing this long enough to know how to drop everything without damaging the goods. Here you need it." I hold out a beer.

"Keep it until we get back. I don't need to get picked up by real cops on top of all this. Come on, let's get back before anything else happens." He motions with his head. "Looks like you made somebody piss themselves."

"Right, what are you going to do? He's lucky I was aiming two feet ahead of him and not at his head."

"Pretty reckless."

"What do you expect? It was probably one of those acting troops doing an exercise."

"I'm not talking about them I'm talking about you."

"You may be right. No excuses. Let's go before the food gets cold or someone gets shot."

It's eighty-five degrees at 11pm. Nobody's food is getting cold. The only smells in the air now are stale piss and gunpowder. I bend down and dig my bullet out of the sidewalk. Remove any evidence. I put it in my pocket. We start off again.

One block to go.

Chapter Five

There are times when you realize you have lost all control. That the intelligence level in the room has sunk to a third grade level. Where everything is hysterical and everyone is stupid and everyone is aware of this, but you keep on moving forward because what else is there to do, right?

We are now in the middle of one of those moments.

Tony is laughing his brains out on my floor. At this rate he should be gasping for air and turning blue in about twenty seconds. I'm wiping the source of his amusement off my shirt and the remaining half of the pizza. This is the same pizza he was ready to kill for about half an hour and a block ago, but now he's about to piss his pants because he made soda come out of my nose and onto my shirt and pizza.

Like I said, no higher than a third grade intelligence level.

Maybe it will add to the flavor of the pie, who knows? We're going to find out if he ever gets upright again. There's only one thing that will ensure that. I grab my last two slices. The laughter stops on a dime. Tony crawls to his knees. I now have a confused dog, complete with tilted head, staring at me trying to comprehend what he's seeing. "You're really going to eat that?" he asks.

"What does it look like I'm doing?"

He climbs back into his chair without taking his eyes off of me. "That's gross, that now has a topping that comes from inside your nose."

"Right so then I can take your last two slices? You're telling me you're too good for them, right?"

"I didn't say that."

"Then what are you saying?"

"I'm just saying that's gross."

"So?"

"So I never said I wasn't gross. What's it taste like?"

"Why don't you find out for yourself?"

"Fine."

"Fine."

He picks up a slice and takes a bite. He takes another bite. Let the inhaling begin. "It's still really good," he says. He starts to take a chug.

"I know, I think it's better. Ken's snot pie, I think it has a certain ring to it."

Beer comes flowing out of Tony's nose and mouth like a fountain. I cover my last slice. "You ass that's my next to last beer."

"What do you want me to tell you? Use it as a dip for your last slice."

A look comes into his eyes. He's actually considering it. He takes his slice and lets it marinate in his dish of used beer. I'm shaking my head, but I can't look away. He takes a chomp. He puts his fingers in front of his mouth and blows a chef's kiss. "Mm, mmm, magnifique. A slice of our best Ken's snot pie, marinated in a fine sauce of used cheap beer ala Antonio," he says in his worst fake Italian accent. "You like?" he asks.

"No, I no like. I have my own thank you very much."

We inhale our final slices. That's the end of that. Now what? We need something, anything, to keep us from focusing on the dreary eighteen wheeler named reality that is about to run us over. "This really sucks," Tony says.

I look up across the table and Tony's staring up at the ceiling. "Right, so I guess you couldn't come up with anything."

"Nada, how about you?"

"Zip, like you said this really sucks."

He straightens out his head and shifts in his chair. "Well normally this is when I break out the 'this is what we get paid for' line, but we're not even getting paid for this. Remind me again why we're doing this and don't pull out that to defend all that is good and true and right line because if you do I'll break your jaw."

"You're in the wrong neighborhood for that address. It hadn't even crossed my mind. No, apparently, the reason we are doing this to stay out of an analog jail and stay alive."

"Well they'd better kill me because there's no way I'm going to an analog jail."

"You got that right."

"And is your life worth all this crap to keep it going?"

"It is for now. What about you?"

"Yes, I was just asking, just checking, that's all."

"Right, well you'd better check yourself because you didn't sound like you were just checking."

Tony shrugs. "I don't know it was just a temporary thing. It happens every once in a while." He takes a chug. "What we need to do is break this all back down to basics. In general I mean, basic, general facts," he says shifting his eyes around the room.

I start shifting in my chair. I lean forward and grab the side of the table with my arms at a ninety degree angle that shifts to forty five. "Right, I see what you mean, but first let me ask you something. If the sole reason all this is happening is someone or something is trying to make us give up our private dick licenses and we could make it all go away by turning them in would you do it?"

"Would I do what?"

"Would you turn in your dick license to make all the crap disappear for good?"

"I would have to think about it. I have some other stuff I'm thinking about getting into, but all of it is in early development. For now, this is pretty much who I am. So no, no I wouldn't do it. Not this time around anyway. What about you?"

"Right, well nobody makes me do anything. Ever. But I'm telling you this right now and believe it because I'm dead serious. If we make it through this with our lives and therefore our freedom still intact, if we do that, then I'm done. Finished. That's it, no question. I just thought you should know that now."

"I can appreciate that," he says.

He said it a little too quickly for me, as if he wasn't taking me seriously. I don't ever think he's taking me seriously though, so I could be wrong. I continue to stare. The way he is looking I may be wrong. He looks shaken, but there is still a small part of him thinking I always say something like this and I'll come around. They're fighting it out inside him, trying to make him believe one way or the other. I can't tell which side is winning. I'd better give him some help.

"Get up; I want to show you something."

"What?"

"You heard what I said. Get up; now."

He forces himself up. We walk a few steps. "Stop. Scanner show the forms in the latest on-call file please."

"Yes sir, here are the ones I believe you mean."

"They are thank you."

Across the screen is my new résumé along with dozens of confirmed ads and applications for full-time writers. Tony turns and looks at me. The shock and disappointment is written all over his face. "How long have you been doing this?"

"Four weeks, a month maybe."

"Were you planning on telling me? Why didn't you tell me and don't say you wanted it to be a surprise because I'll break your jaw, and I mean it this time."

"Relax, I haven't sent anything in yet. I've been ninety-eight percent sure and I wanted to be one hundred percent sure before I committed to anything. That just happened recently. Do you know when?"

"When?"

"This afternoon at the questioning. There were two good cops and I could tell they wanted what I wanted and were willing to cut the cop crap to do things right. To work together all that stuff. Anyway, that's not the point, the point is I could tell one of them was truly good. He's a rookie and they call him 'The Kid'. Everyone around the precinct is unbelievably protective of this guy and they should be. The whole time I was dealing with this guy the same thought kept running through my mind. Do you know what that thought was?"

"Run?"

"Exactly, the place is going to ruin this guy. Do you know what they protect him from the most?"

"What?"

"They protect him from the rest of The Department, the rest of the system. They don't want to see the inside ruin someone who is starting out so good. How messed up is that? Not even from the bad guys, but from The Department."

"So what? Everyone feels that way about someone and they try to protect them from The Department or The Eyes Upstairs or both so what? You know that. I still don't see how you found your final two percent. It better not be that because if it is then I've been grossly overestimating you all these years."

"You didn't let me finish." Tony shrugs. "No it wasn't that. What happened was a thought popped into my head that was so automatic, so understood, it was presented as an established fact. No questions asked. The thought was for him to get his own private practice immediately, especially since I am retiring and you couldn't possibly handle all of the overflow cases. Then I thought maybe he could start out working for you. Don't you see? My mind and my heart want me to solve this and call it a career. That's where I found the final two percent. Believe me, you were and are the first one to find out about this."

"So then I guess that's that," he says.

"No, not yet. We still have to figure out what is going on and solve this case. So sit down and let's get going before another dead body turns up." We take a few steps backwards. "Thank you, that's all for now scanner. Please close this file for now and send it back to the high level on-call section. Thank you."

"Anything else sir?"

"No, we're good for now scanner. Thank you."

I look down at Tony who's now sitting on the couch. His mind seems to be going back and forth; alternating between arguments over the case and my pending retirement. "Hey big shot you want to make some room please. I mean I know it's not like it's my couch or my apartment. Oh wait, that's right they are. Move. Come on I didn't retire yet."

"You may as well have."

I knew this would happen. Alright you've been practicing, let 'er rip. "What the hell is that shit supposed to mean. Now you know why I didn't tell you earlier. What are you twelve? Man, I expected more from you. Seriously. You had the nerve to talk about overestimating me before, man give me a break. I don't know about you, but I don't like having dead bodies fall into my apartment. Remember you're the one who didn't want to get a second pie because you were afraid of another dead body possibly dropping by." I would like to thank the awards committee.

"Alright, alright, you made your point. In fact because of the volume you made your point with I'm going to thank God and Heaven that I still have one beer left to heal my ears and brain."

He pushes himself up. I sit down. He goes into the kitchen. He grabs the bottle and pulls out his own personal bottle opener engraved with his name, his practice's address, and phone number. Pretty slick. Only one thousand ever made and only hundreds remain so call before it's too late.

He strides back up to the couch beer in one hand, opener in the other. "Hey old man, make a little space for the working man."

I whistle. "Nice try tough guy." He plops down and I jump to one side. "You're going to regret that," I say.

He pops open his bottle. No foam, how about that? He looks up and leans my way. In his best stage whisper voice he says, "Maybe if you worked half as long on your acting as you do on your snot pie you might convince someone of something someday. Tell that to your awards committee."

Awards committee I graciously deny my award.

"That hurt, that really hurt, I don't know if I can go on."

"You'll get over it."

"Shouldn't I be saying that to you?" He grunts. "So now what?" I say.

"Now what? Now we do what we always do. What we already should have started doing. We break this all down to what we know. What we know for certain to be true."

"Right." I shift forward in my seat. "Scanner please start a list, a list that can only be shown to me or to me and Tony. Put total wall camouflage and total refrigerator hum camouflage on it for if it is called up in eyesight or earshot of anyone else. Effective unless and until I request otherwise. Put a please request on that also please."

"Yes sir, conditions being set now. Will be completed in three, two, done. Conditions are now set. You may begin your list. Fire when ready sir."

Tony looks at me. He shakes his head.

"What?"

"Nothing, nothing, let's just start the list."

"Right, first of all there was a dead body leaning against my door last night. Two the only ones to see the body in person are you, me, two rookie cops, and the body squad. Three, no one has claimed knowledge of who the body is. That includes my memory files. Four-"

"Four, we were both jumped by cops last night."

"No."

"What do you mean no?"

"You said know for certain, right?"

"Yeah, so."

"So, we don't know for certain they were cops. We know they were dressed up as cops and in what appeared to be cop cars. Which reminds me, I saw a burnt up cop car on a cop junker about a block away from the station after I was released today."

"Okay, so what, you think someone is using a cop camouflage?"

"No, I'm saying it's a possibility and that's not absolutely certain. Come on, don't get sloppy on me."

"I'm not getting sloppy I'm just making sure you're paying attention to me. You know, just giving you a minimum skills test. I need to know you're still mentally all there and not focusing on your writer applications."

I point to my black eyes. "Does this look like I've checked out on you? No more tests. Let's go."

"No you're right. My fault. No more tests; no more games." He takes a chug. "So, other than those four things, do we have anything else?"

"Nothing I can think of that's certain. I told you I think I have some stuff I can look into, but they're just long shots at this point. What about you?"

"It's hard to say anything yet. I haven't even been able to get home. It seems like something is going on and I'm getting that feeling I don't like, but has never been wrong; the feeling that this is personal. That we specifically have been picked for what is happening. Again, it's just a feeling, but it has always been right. Put on top of that all of the strange things that happened yesterday: the clean hallways; the weather; your polite punks; your secretary; I swear if you hadn't called me I would have started thinking this was some kind of dream or reality game."

Tony is rambling. I can understand it though, because I was thinking the exact same thing. "Okay scanner I think that's all we have for the list. It's not much, but it's early. Please keep it in the urgent on-call section."

"Are you sure, sir?"

"Yes. Thank you."

"Done sir."

"Oh, call up your list again," Tony says.

"Scanner please bring the list back up. Thank you."

The list appears. "The body's shoes had wet mud on their soles, but the hallway was clean with no tracks."

"Right, I forgot that one. Damn. Do you have anything else?"

"No that's it for now."

It feels like I'm forgetting something, but I can't figure out what. The list looks mighty bare and it reminds me why there aren't many still doing what we do. After this case is solved if anyone bothers to report on it it will probably be as a three sentence blurb. Read, seen, and spoken in fifteen seconds and immediately forgotten.

No stress, no concern, and no humanity. Just some words and numbers of little if any meaning to anyone. For us it will be days, maybe weeks of stress, frustration, aggravation, and very little satisfaction. The effects could last forever. They could become something a person never talks about. And we aren't even being paid this time.

I look across at Tony. He's staring at the wall like he's trying to knock it down. He's probably running through the last two days and alternating that with the same thing I was just thinking of. He's still more positive than I am. He'll find something. He always does. He feels me watching him. He shakes his head. "I don't know; it's too soon it's way too soon."

"Remind me again why we do this."

"Because it's who we are and it's what we do. I don't care what you say; deep down you know it's true." He's giving me the stare. His eyes, this stare, have the intensity of a preacher who's receiving his words from above as he speaks. "You know I'm right," he repeats. "We'll find something tomorrow."

How am I supposed to answer that? "You may be right," I say. "You're staying here tonight, right?"

"If it's okay with you."

"I was figuring on it. You get the couch. Don't do any permanent damage to it."

"Your confidence in me is overwhelming."

"What can I say?"

"So I'll drive you to your place tomorrow, then I'll go home, put on a less funky outfit, go to my office, and I'll call you at four."

"Sounds like a plan."

"Good, don't snore too loud."

"I do not snore."

"Do you want to try the independent judge again?"

"No, not because I think you're right, but because I don't care. It's not a big deal to me. It certainly doesn't affect me. So I don't care, have it your way. I'll try not to snore too loud. It shouldn't be too difficult. The soda cleared out everything that was in there."

Tony takes the bottle that was about to enter his mouth and aborts take off. "You're lucky."

"Luck had nothing to do with it my friend. I could have waited a fraction of a second more if I wanted to. Remember that."

"Big deal, it would have gone all over your couch dumb ass."

"I'm starting to think you don't appreciate the favors I do for you."

"You're starting to think?"

"Oh that hurt, that really hurt."

"You'll get over it. Goodnight dumbass."

"Goodnight wiseass. Scanner please set my alarm for seven hours from the moment of sleep. Please set that on auto reset. Thank you, goodnight scanner."

"Goodnight sir."

*　　*　　*

It's morning and I'm up and moving. I might have gotten five hours of sleep total. So that's good, maybe we'll have a corpseless, tortureless day. One can always hope, right? Who knows, maybe Tony's right and we'll get some leads today.

I'm moving pretty quick, ready in less than fifteen minutes. This could be a good day. I enter the living room. Tony's hair is wet and he's reading something, probably one of my old stories. They're lying around all over the place. Tony looks up. "You ready?" he says.

"Let's do it. Do you need anything?"

"No, I've been up awhile."

"Right, then let's get out of here before any corpses or cops try to stop us."

We head for the door. I open it. All clear. We walk toward the end of the hall. The elevator isn't working. Another promising sign for a normal day. We speed down the stairs. There is an urgency in the air and it isn't just coming from me. I open the door to the parking lot. Tony's car is sitting a few feet from us. We get in. The car starts on the first try. This could mean trouble. His car never starts up on the first try, this is definitely not normal. Then again what do we ever do that's normal?

"Hey genius, you're thinking out loud again."

"What?"

"What do we ever do that's normal? You're starting to worry me chief. Seriously, relax a little bit. Reality does not depend on you and you alone. The rest of us get a little say in it too. I'm just saying."

"How did you hear my thoughts?"

"They weren't just your thoughts, you were talking."

"No way."

"Yes way. Look man, your mouth was moving. You were talking."

"How much did I say?"

"You've been talking since the moment you got up this morning. I heard the whole thing."

"Did I do this yesterday?"

"No."

"How long have I done this?"

"Ever since I have known you. When we first started out you joked around. You used to say you were a sports announcer. Back then you used to do play by plays of everyone and everything in the bar."

"I don't remember that."

"You were drinking, you were drinking a lot actually that's why. Check your memory chip if you don't believe me. Anyway you would do play by plays of everyone and everything and eventually you would piss someone off. We'd get into these massive brawls and get thrown out of the place. Ask your scanner if you don't believe me. Check your memory cards."

"It sounds like I wouldn't want to remember."

Tony shrugs. "That's up to you, but to give you a clue how screwed up you used to be, you used to throw up before you started drinking and be normal the rest of the night. Now I know this is one of the things I'm never supposed to talk about, but I get the feeling this case is going to be more dangerous than normal so I don't want you putting yourself in more danger than necessary."

"So you want me second guessing my thoughts?"

"No. Look I couldn't sleep last night. My brain was shooting off strange ideas from all directions. One of the things that came and stuck was your three things. I think you can't even remember what those three things are. Go ahead try."

I'm going to kill him. Why is he doing this to me? Why is he doing this to me now? What did I do to deserve this? Okay wiseass answer his question: what are the three things nobody is allowed to talk about?

Total brain shut down.

I don't believe this. It's like I've given myself some kind of brain camouflage. The harder I think, the less I remember. Oh no. "What did you just hear?"

"Nothing, only the question you just asked."

"What am I supposed to do?"

"Do your old test."

"What old test?"

"You forgot that too? Alright, when you weren't sure if you just thinking or thinking out loud you would drink something and if there was nothing to drink you would take a deep gulp."

"Right, now I remember."

"Are you alright?"

"Yeah."

"Good, because we're here. Remember I'll call you around four. Okay?"

"Sounds good."

"Good now would you find some possible IDs or least some possible leads please."

"Whatever you say wiseass."

"I'll call you at four." He smiles and takes off.

Right, well that's great, just frickin' great. He gets to leave smiling and I'm left standing here with my jaw on the ground. I guess I'll be buying a lot more soda. I can't stop shaking my head. I turn and start towards the office.

*   *   *

I don't remember the trip, but I'm now standing outside my office. At least the new window hasn't been broken yet. I open the door and walk in. The lights are on and the room is empty except for my secretary. "Hey big shot, you decided to show up today. What's the special occasion?"

That's the Alison I'm used to. I gulped while having that thought. Good I'm safe for now. "Anybody call?"

"Just collection agencies."

"What'd you say?"

"I said what I always say. You are not here."

"Nice."

"Well it's true; I don't even have to lie."

"What'd they say?"

"They expect it by know. They just say this is your absolute last warning and then we get on to our usual conversations. I've gotten to know most of them pretty well by now."

"Nice, see how easy I make it for you. That should stop by tomorrow, it should all be taken care of by the end of tomorrow, but good for you. You get to make new friends."

"Oh I know it. I remember when I was working my way through all the stress, all the studying, I knew someday it would all be worth it. I knew someday I would get a dream job like this." She looks up at me and raises an eyebrow. "And if you believe that one-" she says.

"Right. So I guess tenderness and compassion aren't on the schedule for today?"

"They haven't even called yet."

She's on her A game today. I'm safe I gulped again. "Alison, let me ask you something. Do I talk a lot?"

"That's a hard question to answer."

"What do you mean? Why is it hard?"

"Well, because you're never here anymore. I don't really have enough of a sample size."

"What are you talking about? I was here two days ago. You do remember two days ago, don't you?"

"Yeah sure."

"I'm being serious." I'm yelling. I never yell and somehow my hands have gotten around her wrists. She glances down at her wrists. She looks back up and gives me her death stare; right in the eyes.

"I think you'd better back off big shot."

I quickly let go. "What the hell was that?" I say in horror. "I'm sorry. I have no idea what that was. Truly, I didn't mean it. Man, it's a good thing this is my last case."

She's still giving me the stare. "What do you mean this is your last case? Why should I believe you?"

"I don't care if you believe me or not it's true. If I survive this case I'm done."

"Now you're just talking stupid. Besides, I haven't had to let anyone in to see you in months."

"I had a dead body fall into my apartment. Don't ask it's a long story."

"How is this dead body going to pay you?"

"No not the body, the killer. Someone is trying to set me and Tony up or kill us."

"Whatever."

"What, so these bruises don't mean anything to you?"

She shakes her head. "I thought your face decided to save my fists the trouble. Why are you always such a mess?"

"Because I wouldn't want you to die of shock."

She shakes her head again and I walk away. At least I have a new clue, it's not for this case, but still at least I was able to pick something up. She doesn't remember letting in Tony two days ago. It probably also means she doesn't remember two days ago at all.

I walk to my office. A thought flashes into my brain. It's gone just as fast. Damn, I almost had it. It was important, I can feel it. It's just a tease. The only way to test its strength is not to chase it. It'll come back, they always do. The ones that mean anything do, at least. The ones that don't aren't worth finding in the first place.

I push open my door. There is a bag from the wings place sitting in the middle of my desk. It's a full bag. I approach the bag like it's a live bomb. It is definitely full of wings. I touch it. It's cold, but still its food that can be heated. Next to it is a six-pack of sugarcola.

I walk out and go to my secretary's desk. She's in the middle of a call. It sounds like a personal call. I wait for her to terminate her call. She looks up at me and hangs up. "What?" she says.

"I was just wondering when the delivery guy showed up?"

"What delivery guy? I didn't let anyone in."

"Stop. Really, did you do this? You know as a favor for the other day."

"What other day? I have no idea what you're talking about."

I feel sweat start to roll down the side of my face. "Stop playing," I say. I'm forcing myself to stay overly calm.

"I'm not playing with you. Are you okay? Did you see a doctor after you took that beating?"

I shake my head in disgust. I've had enough of this. Forget writing, after this case; if there is an after this case, I'm going somewhere where no one will ever find me. I don't need this. "Alison please do me a favor." I am remaining as overly calm as possible.

"Yes."

"Alison please get up and go into my office. Go to my desk and tell me what's on it and who put it there."

"Okay," she says carefully. I have succeeded in completely freaking her out. No more death stare. She slowly makes her way to the office. I follow close behind her. I think if the office wasn't a dead end she would make a break for it. Who can blame her? I've had that feeling many times.

I stop at my doorway and stare down. I tap the tip of my shoe straight down into the floor. I tap and wait for a reaction. This should be a good one. I see her approach my desk out of the corner of my eye. I hear her circle the desk. She is moving deliberately. She starts to hum under her breath. I can tell she wants to say something. She wants to, but is afraid to. I close my eyes. I focus on keeping my heart rate as low as possible.

"Mr. Breakman?"

She is really afraid.

"Yes," I say still focusing on my heart rate with my eyes closed.

"Could you give me a hint as to what it is I'm supposed to be seeing?"

My head snaps up and my eyes rush open as wide as my body will let them. Calm, stay calm, focus on the calm. I look her way.

There is nothing on the desk.

It figures. Why not? I creep to the desk with my hands in my pockets. I walk in what sounded to be her path. "Right," I keep saying surrounded by grunts and other caveman noises. She is standing still. She wants to yell at me, but she's afraid I've checked out permanently. I can tell.

She is right though, there is nothing there. That's not in question. Just like three minutes ago it couldn't be questioned that there was a bag full of food sitting alongside a six-pack of soda in the middle of that same desk. "Interesting," I say softly. I turn to the metal file cabinet behind me and pull out the files of unsolved cases. I pull them out calmly, but assertively. I softly close the drawer.

I turn back to my secretary. "I have to follow up on a few leads. I will be back in a few hours, so you are not free to go yet. If Tony calls tell him I'm out chasing a few leads. Tell him I'll be back in the office around four, four-thirty the latest. Take all detailed and fine messages like you always do. Whatever you do keep rule number one. What is rule number one?"

"Never call the cops."

I point to my face. "Exactly, and this is exhibit A of why you don't call the cops. Understand?"

"As always."

"Good, be good I'll be back in a few hours." I start towards the doorway. I turn back. "I'm going to the repair shop tonight or tomorrow afternoon at the latest, so run up any bill you want or need to on the company credit card. Preferably by the time I get back. Okay?"

She shakes her head. "Yeah; sure; okay. I'll see you in a few hours?"

"Right."

"Okay."

I turn back and head out. I reach my door and leave at an even pace. My emotions want me to run, but they have been overruled. If this is how they want to play, this is what they're going to get. They want me to lose it. Someone or something is definitely messing with me. The more they want me to go nuts, the saner and more logical I'll get.

At this point I don't care who is doing it. It could be Tony, Alison, and other people on "our" side doing it to convince me I need them and I love this life. It could be the bad cops, the cop imitators, The Eyes Upstairs or some other group or combination of "bad" guys trying to kill me. At this point I really don't care. All I want is to survive and solve this case and I'm gone for good. I'll never look back again.

I look down at the files in my hand. "God only knows why I did that." I know I said that out loud. I did it on purpose. "They're all liars," I say and let out a disgusted grunt.

My instinct takes me into a liquor store. I go to the refrigerated section. I don't know why I'm doing this. I know I shouldn't. "Fuck it." I reach out for it and grab it.

I go to the front of the store. I pay for it with company credit. "You want a bag for that?" The old man behind the counter asks.

"Sure, if you have one."

He puts it inside an old fashion paper bag and puts that in an old fashioned plastic bag. "You take care of them."

"You got it boss. Have a good day." He waves and I head out. I pull out the first one. It's the best bottle of sugarcola I've tasted in a long time.

The thought flashes back into my head. This time I catch it: "Wake up, the time is now."

Chapter Six

I sit stuck on a concrete bench in an abandoned bus stop.

Stuck because everything depends on everything else and right now it all starts in my office. The place I just left twenty minutes ago. I should go back in about forty, that will be short enough to prevent Alison from calling Tony and long enough for her to believe I was actually working.

I can't go to the repair shop because I told Alison to pay all of the bills she needs to pay. I always wait until the last minute and more importantly she knows I always wait until the last minute. Not only knows, but expects. If I were to go now she might not yet have done what needed to be done or worse, she might do it after I get my new financial ID and I'll be starting off in debt again.

Besides, I might need to get a favor there. A favor based on something I might have in my faces of interest files. The files in my office, the office I just left because of disappearing food.

Nice, real nice.

I nurse the second half of my first bottle. Why couldn't the body outside my door have disappeared as easily as the sack of wings on my desk did? I take another sip. Maybe I'll go to the wings place and get something to eat there-in person. It's not a bad idea; it would be on the company charge, it's free food, and it'll knock some time off the clock. Then again, the way things are going the wings will probably disappear the second I put them on my desk. Maybe my desk has developed an appetite for wings.

Why not? It's just as good as any other explanation I've come up with so far. That's what we need more outside of the box thinking. More like outside of the sanity thinking, but what is sanity anyway? "Enough of that. Chip please put the last two self-pity sentences in the trash."

I dead lift myself off the concrete. My stomach is kicking back. All the recent thoughts and visions of wings have awakened a sleeping monster and it will not stand to be teased. The wings place we usually order from is pretty close by. I head right.

The sidewalks are empty even for this early in the day. My eyes are open and alert. Maybe I'll get lucky and run into my favorite punks. I hope so, because they are one of the few positives left out here. Especially today, another plain day in a beat up city. It wasn't always this way, but it's the way it is now. Who knows what direction it will go next. I shake my head and make a left.

The wings place is three blocks away. A car pulls up next to me. It's a taxi. "Hey chief you want a ride?" I look around me. "Hey, I'm talking to you. I thought you were supposed to be some kind of big shot detective."

I know the voice. I walk to the curb. "Do you take company cards?"

"Yeah get in. There isn't anything to look at out there."

I open the door and slide in. "I'm just going to the wings place."

"Yeah so, we still charge for that. How's it going old man?" She knows she's the only one I'd let call me that. I see her reflection in the rearview. She has a huge smile on her face. "So what's up kid?"

"One minute I'm an old man, the next minute I'm a kid? Which one is it?"

"It depends which eye sees you first. I just got my left eye two years ago so it sees you as an old man. The right eye is the original so it sees you as a kid. Got it?"

"Got it boss. So how's life Mrs. Tony's mom? Is Tony treating you right?"

"How would I know? I never see him. He never stops by. You probably see him more than I do."

"Probably, and let me tell you: you're not missing out on anything special."

She laughs with a cigarette dangling from below her top lip the entire time. No hands. All these years and I still haven't been able to figure out how she does it. "I shouldn't complain," she says. "He did hire me a maid as a birthday present."

"Really?"

"Yeah, a real one not even a mechanical one. It's an alien, you know real alien from outer space, not this outside the border crap. I guess outer space is technically outside the borders, but you know what I mean. It gives me these great massages. I don't know how I lived without it. I know I'm not supposed to call them its, but I asked what it was and it just shrugged at me. I don't think they know what sex is."

"That's alright they aren't missing out on much."

"You got that right old man."

"Right, so now we get to the important stuff. Do you have any dirt I can use against him?"

"No luck there kid, like I said you probably know more about him than me. Looks like we're here."

"Right, I tell you what, you can keep driving around if you want. The company's paying for it, so why not, right?"

"That's alright, I don't want you getting in any trouble?"

"What are you talking about, I'm the boss. Besides, I eat trouble for lunch. You know that."

"You're a terrible liar, did you know that?"

"I'll work on it. Do you want anything to eat?"

"From this place? What are you trying to kill me?"

"Never in a million years."

She pulls up in front of the wings place. "How much?"

"Get out of here."

"No, I'm not twelve. I wouldn't have taken the ride if I couldn't have afforded the fee. I'm not a jumper."

"We call them rollers now. They all think they're stuntmen and jump into a roll, but whatever, it's your money old man. Five twenty five."

I knew she needed the money. If she didn't she would have just asked for a kiss. "Here's twenty five." I swipe it through as fast as possible. She doesn't have time to stop it. "Hang on a second." I get out of the driver's side door and stand next to her window. "I get my kiss, right?" She nods. I lean in and kiss her on the cheek.

"See you around old man."

"See you around Mrs. Tony's mom."

I watch her take off. She makes the first right and I head for the entrance. Inside the wings place it is obvious where all of the people missing from the sidewalk are. They're here, on line in front of me. This should kill forty minutes no problem.

I take a sip and scan the place without moving my head. What a freak show this place is, myself included. I should come down here more often. In front of me on the line to my right, an alien–human morph is talking to a three eyed mutant. It's hard to tell if the morph is trying to morph into an alien or a human. I've seen it done both ways.

The mutant's eyes are each different colors. He (I think it's a he) is really yucking it up about something, while the morph is smoking a cigarette through its nose. In one nostril out the other.

Fantastic.

Three spaces in front of me in the line to my left a J.S. Bach clone is arguing with a Beethoven clone over the deciding score in last night's playoff game. It's hard to understand what they're saying, but the Bach clone is speaking strongly and the Beethoven clone just keeps shaking his head. I wonder if the Beethoven clone has been able to get his hearing fixed.

This place is great. Maybe I should see if they would hire me as security. I take the soda bottle down from my mouth. It's been empty for a while, but it's a cheaper way to do the thought test.

"Mr. Breaker I think you should come with us." Great now I'm hearing voices. "Don't make us do this the hard way. Now, turn around slowly and don't make this into a big deal." It sure sounds real. Maybe I should turn around. My head starts to turn to the right. "That's good, keep it up. Slowly-"

It's definitely real; spit hit the side of my face. Slowly, I start to turn around. My eyes catch a glimpse of his face. "You asshole," I say. My body relaxes.

"You don't recognize my voice anymore? What'd you delete me from your memory chip too?"

"You wish." Standing in front of me is Bobby No Heart, former partner, first with the police and later with a group of other P.I.s who were just starting out. He got his name when in an eighteen month period he was shot in the chest four separate times and none of them ever came close to his heart. Word got out that it was impossible to kill this guy because he didn't have a heart. "So what are you up to?" I ask.

"Not much. I checked out of the truth and justice scene a long time ago. How about you?"

"Hopefully I'm on my last case."

"How can you still do it?"

"Well not all of us catch bullets with our chests. You're the one who was always going all out; doing everything the hard way."

We take a couple of steps forward with the line.

"Yeah well, what can I say, I was young and stupid."

"We were all young and stupid."

"True and that was before the craziness set in. Before the department became The Department and the government became The Eyes Upstairs. It wasn't long, but it was fun while it lasted. Too bad it got so crazy so soon."

"Right, but at least you got out. I'm too stupid to jump off when I get the chance."

"Well you should wise up. You heard what happened to Jimmy right?"

"Jimmy the Face?"

"No, Jimmy the Fizz. He started the P.I. place with us. He was always drinking soda."

"Right, no I didn't hear. What happened?"

"Oh man, okay, so two days ago I'm speeding through the system and I see a little blurb with Jimmy's picture next to it. Apparently he was found dead in an apartment complex the night before."

"No."

"Yeah, and get this, the guy who found him doesn't normally go outside. He was only going this time to see his son's band play at a local club. He opened his door to leave and Jimmy's body fell into the apartment. When the cops showed up nobody seemed interested, at least that's what the article claims. Do you believe that?"

"Unfortunately I do. I can relate to it."

"What, what are you into?"

"Nothing, no, I'm just saying it seems like anything can happen these days. Everything is believable. Look around us."

At the front of the line a devil morph is arguing with an angel morph over who is going to pay the bill.

"I guess you're right. It's really sad."

"Right, I know the feeling. Hey, where did you say this happened?"

"Bricksville, it's two towns north of here. Why, are you thinking about doing something?"

"I gave up thinking a long time ago. It's overrated."

"Well I know I haven't been a P.I. for a while, but I dug a little deeper and found there was no autopsy performed. I've been working as an EMT for a long time now and I've never had a case involving death where the body wasn't autopsied. Something's not right."

"Right, I tell you what, I'll give you my card. If you want to send me everything you've found I'll see what I can do. Don't count on anything though. I've been on a losing streak lately, but I'll see what I can find." My hand dives into my pocket and grabs a card. I pull it out, check it, and hand it to Bobby. "If you do anything make all of your tracks invisible. I'm not exactly a popular guy these days and the last thing I would want is for you to get into trouble because of me."

He takes the card. "Don't worry they can't hurt me. I don't have a heart, remember?"

"Right, well you have been warned."

He nods and smiles. "You know not having a heart has its advantages-no heart attacks for example. Speaking of heart attacks it looks like it's your turn to order."

I turn around. The alien behind the counter is about to walk the order of the morph in front of me up to the counter. I turn back. "You are right again as usual. I'll let you ponder over your big decision. If I don't see you again be good and always keep your ass covered."

"You too. I'll call you if we do anything for Jimmy."

"Right. Call me if you hear anything."

I turn around. The morph in front of me grabs his order and steps to the side. A thought shoots through my brain. I grab it, read it, and approve it for immediate use. A purple alien behind the counter struggles to ask me my order. I'll save it the trouble. I order the same order we may or may not have gotten at the office two days ago. Let's see if this stimulates my secretary's memory.

The alien still has a lost look on its face. It calls the manager, at least I think it's the manager, over. A male human in his mid to late seventies rushes to the counter. He doesn't seem very happy at the moment. "I'm sorry, it's its first day here. Could you please repeat your order?"

"Sure I kind of got that feeling."

He grunts. I reorder.

"It should only be a few minutes."

I nod and step to the side. I put the bottle to my lips and take an imaginary chug. "Invisible soda?" Bobby asks.

I smile. "Sure I have cases of them at home. Only the rich can afford it and only those with the most refined palate can appreciate the taste."

He laughs. "Good luck with that one."

"Thanks, it can't be any worse than the crap we see every day."

"You got that right."

The manager steps up and hands me my order. Bobby moves forward and tries his luck with the alien. I give him a nod, put my order on top of the soda in the bag, and head for the exit. I shouldn't have gotten the extra soda. This isn't going to be a fun trip back. It would really be great if Tony's mom were waiting outside. The exit door slides open.

One in a row. Tony's mom is waiting in her cab, cigarette dangling as always. She sees me. "You want to speed it up old man. I've got people to pick up."

The bags aren't heavy, but they are awkward. I struggle with the door. It opens and I slide everything inside. "Thanks."

"What, did you think I would let you give me money like that without a fight? This one's on me and if you even think of doing anything to the contrary I'll break your jaw."

"Now I know where Tony gets it from." She smiles. "Do you want a wing?"

"Like I said before, what are you trying to poison me? Besides, I don't have any teeth."

"How about a sugarcola? You can drink it without the threat of cavities."

"Yeah alright, but don't complain if I start driving faster."

I hand her the bottle. She slides it between the front seats as she weaves in and out of traffic. I download four curses and phrases I have never heard before. It just goes to show you're never too old to learn something new. I keep the soda shut. If I had been drinking I would have had at least five nose cleansings by now. She makes a wild left and bellys out onto my office street. She straightens it out and brings it in for an easy landing.

"Here you go old man, home sweet home."

I explode into laughter. "Thanks for that one. The next time Tony's drinking something I'll tell him what you called this place. He should get a good nose cleaning out of it."

"No problem."

"Don't worry about him not stopping by. By the time I get through telling him about our rides he'll know he's in trouble. Making him feel guilty about you is one of my specialties. He'll be by soon, don't worry about it."

A smirk grows on her reflection. I reach between the front seats. "Here's another soda, just in case the one up front got all shook up and couldn't handle the ride."

She shakes her head and takes the bottle. "They don't make anything the way they used to. It's this younger generation-it ain't worth shit."

"Right, you are absolutely right on that."

"Am I going to have to help you carry all of your crap upstairs?"

"No, what do you think I'm one of them?"

"It depends which eye sees you first," she says with a smile spreading from one side of the car to the other. "Either way I'm still not charging you for the ride and don't give me any lip. I don't want to have to get up and body slam you. You know I can and I will."

She can and she will. She proved it to me the first day I met her. I almost had to bring her in for assaulting an officer due to the embarrassment. Luckily, I found out she had done it to everyone else. "Have it your way. I'm too old to fight and too young to care. You take care of yourself Mrs. Tony's mom."

"I don't see anyone else volunteering for the honor."

I kiss her on the cheek. "Thanks for the rides. I mean it, I really needed it today."

"Yeah sure, whatever you say tough guy. I've got rides to pick up, what are you trying to make me late? Give Tony a good nose cleansing for me the next time you see him. Wait 'til he least expects it. Tell him I gave you permission, no better yet; tell him I made you do it."

She honks her horn and squeals her tires. I jump out of the way. She waves. I wave back and start upstairs with the wings and sodas. I can feel myself smiling as I walk. I can't help it. How could you not? That'll have to be fixed before I go inside. I'll have to straighten up, look miserable, and act disgusted or at least bored. If I don't my secretary will definitely think I've lost it completely. Mentally flown away to another time and another place in the far reaches of the universe. I don't know if this says more about her or me.

I can still enjoy this for now though, right? No one's going to hold the fact I just had a good time against me, are they? Being in a good mood doesn't violate any of the societal codes of conduct, does it? Man, I hope not, but then again it would explain a lot if it does.

I adjust my hold on the bags. The heat from the food warms my hands. This should be good. It would probably be a good idea to take out a bottle and use it as a thought tester, but without a free hand this is going to have to wait. It won't be long. The office is only a few feet away.

The office door stares me in the face. I use my elbow to try to turn the knob and open it. It seems unrealistic to still have to do things this way, but here we are.

It wasn't always like this. Initially this place was made with the most advanced technology available. It had an automated state of the art security system based on chip recognition. It was said to be the most advanced, secure, and cost efficient system anyone had ever seen and would ever see for the next fifty years.

It looked promising the first few days. Then reality set in. One thing would stop working and bring everything to a halt. It would be fixed and instantly something else would breakdown and the cycle would continue. The repairs were more expensive than the rents. Word got out and soon so did the people. The place went bankrupt. The few who stayed put in a manual twentieth century system on their own and now here we are prying open doors with elbows and ankles.

My elbows aren't getting anything open. Forget this. I stop, put down the bag, and open the door. Holding it open with my ankle, I reach back, pick up the bag, and slink my way inside while easing the door shut behind me. The lobby is empty except for my secretary. She has her head down and doesn't look up. Maybe I've disappeared this time, who knows?

I open the door to my office and take a step inside. It's here. How long it's been here I don't know, but it's here now. I can feel it. It's the pull and it is trying to draw my line of vision. I resist. My body takes two steps forward on its own. The pull grabs hold and forces me to look at my desk. It focuses all of my attention to what is now sitting dead center on my desk.

The disappearing food has reappeared.

"You've got to be kidding me." I know I should have expected it, but I didn't. This fact alone is all anyone should need to see to know it's time for me to move on to another profession.

I circle the desk and approach the food from behind. Interesting, inside the bag are synthetic zucchini sticks. I didn't order zucchini the night of the disappearing food. I got it with the original order, the order Alison claims not to remember. Let's feel the bag. It's hot, hotter than the extremely warm bag I'm carrying. A smile takes over my face.

"Nice, more food for me. It must be Christmas," I say trying not to sound too happy. I wouldn't want to be arrested before I eat.

I put the bags of soda and food I'm carrying down to the left of the existing hot order. One by one my hands quickly take the hot food out of its bag and arrange them in the center of the desk. The wings look like they've just gotten out of bath of hot sauce. This is going to be good. Instinctively I grab the first over sauced wing and use it to write an "x" directly onto the desk where the food is. Maybe it's paranoia or maybe it's just years of covering my ass, but I need to leave as much of a trail as possible.

Keeping one eye on the food, I use the other one to help me bring over a shelf of files and pile them to the right of the open food. I grab a wing and inhale it. Good stuff. I take another wing and hold it in my mouth like a lollipop. My hands grab Alison's order. Leaving the office I'm careful to make sure the door is left open.

I approach Alison. She looks up. Her hands dart at hyper speed and force something under her desk. Her eyes stay focused on me the entire time.

"Any calls?" I ask.

"Are you kidding me?"

"Right, well do me a favor and see if you find can anything out about the death of Jimmy the Fizz. It occurred earlier this week."

"No problem. Anything else?"

"Yeah, I stopped by the wings place on the way back. I figured you'd probably be hungry. Here it's on the card."

She looks inside. "How did you know this is what I get?"

"I told you, you ordered it when we got it delivered here two days ago." Now she looks confused. "One more thing before I forget," I say.

She brings her eyes from the bag back to me. "Yes?"

"I am definitely going to be going to the repair shop first thing tomorrow morning. So charge everything that needs to be charged before you leave tonight. You can come in late tomorrow if you want."

"Okay."

"I know what you did. Thank you. You should probably put the bag you just hid back on the desk before something happens to it. I'll be in my office eating my food before it gets cold or disappears whichever comes first." My mouth tries to force a smile onto my face. Only the left side makes it. I turn and start back to the office.

"Hey big shot."

"Yeah," I say looking over my shoulder.

"Don't you think we should get a small refrigerator for this place? You know, one of the really small ones, just to keep any orders we get cold."

It's not a bad idea. I turn around. She wears a hopeful stare tinged with just a glint of sarcasm dead on into my eyes. "I could do it right now if you let me put it on the card."

"I know. It's a good idea, but there's only one thing. What if we put the food in there and the next time we open the door it's gone, disappeared? What then? Are you going to say I stole it? Will you believe me if say I didn't? Are you going to believe that it just disappeared? I've known you too long to risk it all on food. Besides, where would we put it: in my office or behind your desk?"

I shake my head. "Right, I'll tell you what, if you trust me enough to believe me, then order it on the card before you leave today. If not, then don't. Either way it's not a problem, just make sure it's done by tonight. Now, I have dead poultry to inhale before it gets cold, so if there's nothing else I'll be in my office if you need me."

"Ha," she reflexively spits out.

A smile crawls onto my face and I head back to the office. She didn't mean that. I can tell. She's had to be so tough over so many years that it's become a reflex. This place does it to everyone eventually. Too bad.

I reach my desk. All of the food is still there. So are all of the files. The wing inhaling begins with one arm and file examining starts with the other. It has a rhythm to it if you do it right. A synchronicity that just requires you to relax and focus. It becomes automatic. This is the way it used to be all the time.

It's strange, in a twisted sort of way there is a part of me that's been dying to this one last time. The blood starts to flow; the muscles start to move; the mouth starts to taste: and the eyes and brain start to examine, together as one in a symphony. A symphony written, played, conducted, and heard by me and me alone. The first movement is underway. What it will build to and where it will lead is still a mystery, but right now everyone is focused and the conductor is intense, demanding perfection as if his life depends on it.

*   *   *

Three hours and fifteen minutes, that's what it took to finish off a metal cabinet full of files and a bag and a half full of fire wings. I take my eyes off the clock. "Well that's the end of that movement," I say closing the final file with one hand and tossing a bare bone into a pile of bare bones with the other. Three hours fifteen minutes and all I get are three possible names attached to three IDs and files.

*   *   *

A whole lot of nothing. We'll probably get more from the info Bobby sent me about Jimmy.

Four o'clock has come and gone and there still has been no call from Tony. Maybe he's working on a hot lead, who knows? Somehow I'm not getting that feeling. There's a knock on the door. "What is it?" Alison pokes her head inside. "Yes?"

"Tony just told me he'll be here in ten minutes." She has a big smile on her face. She's holding back laughter, I can tell.

"Alison-what is it?"

"Nothing. Oh, I forgot to tell you, the frig will be in tomorrow."

"Right, thank you, but that means you'll have to be here. I'm going to be getting rid of the bill."

"Okay, it's fine."

She closes the door. Her laughter can be heard through the walls. It doesn't take a detective to figure out what's going on. I yell, "Hey wiseass you can get away from my secretary now."

The laughter stops. Slowly the door creeps open. A smiling wiseass fills my doorway. "Are you going to come in or are you auditioning for work as a human statue?"

"It's good to see you too. You should treat your employees better you know." He takes a few steps in.

"So, she acknowledged you right?"

"You could say that, why?"

"No, nothing, it's just earlier today she denied two days ago ever happened."

"What?"

"Right, I know, but if you talked to people earlier today you would think we were the crazy ones."

He rolls his eyes. "So what were you busy doing today?" he asks staring at the wing graveyard on my desk.

"I was getting a couple of rides from your mom. You should treat her better, you know." That wipes the smile off his face. "Relax, she picked me up in her taxi."

He looks at me and shakes his head. "You know it's one thing if you want to be miserable, but why do you try to bring the rest of us down with you?"

"You'll get over it tough guy." It looks like I've hurt somebody's feelings. "What did you find out?"

"Not here, not now. That's what I came to tell you. We need to go now."

"Where?"

"You'll see. Bring whatever you found out."

This should be good. Automatically I throw the bones out in a bag, grab two sodas, and leave everything else on the desk. "Alison come here," I yell.

She shows up. "Yeah big shot."

"Alison, you see all of the food and soda on my desk, right?"

"Yeah so?"

"So I just recorded everything that happened so there will not be any question. If that stuff is even moved people are going to wish they were never born. Am I clear?"

"Sure you don't need to be so sensitive."

Tony looks at me. He shakes his head as if he's given up hope on me. He looks back at Alison. "Yeah and if anything happens you can always call the cops right?"

They both burst into laughter. I have a few hundred comebacks lined up, but instead I let them go. It's going to get real ugly real soon. This feeling has become undeniably clear over the last few hours. It's like he says, sometimes you just know. Right now I just know. In an act of displaced aggression I write out a DO NOT TOUCH sign and place it next to the food.

In my memory chip a shooting is being played over and over. It has played constantly from the time I opened the first file three hours and fifteen or so minutes ago. The shooting playing constantly in my memory chip involves Tony and me, but it's a shooting that has never happened before. It's a warning of something that will become a memory in the future.

Calmly, coldly, I walk around my desk and put my free hand on a doubled over Tony's back. He looks back at me. I smile and show him the handful of info and files. Softly I say, "Time to go."

"What, oh yeah right."

He starts to wipe away the tears of laughter from his eyes. I take a chug. Turning back I look at them.

They're not laughing anymore.

They look like they're staring at a ghost. Maybe now they see it too. "Let's go," Tony says.

He sounds afraid. I have never heard him sound this way before. Something is happening now that has never happened in the history of mankind. The three of us are in the same room at the same time in complete silence. This is going to be big. The two of them look lost. I should break the moment. "Let's go," I whisper.

Slowly we all move toward the door. I glance back over my shoulder. In the center of my desk is the bag of wings that disappeared this morning.

We are now officially all on the same page.

I close the door.

Chapter Seven

I look across the front seat at Tony. His vessels are trying to escape from his forehead. I can see the blood pulsating. He's still shaking his head. He's been shaking it since he witnessed the reappearing food.

It's not so funny anymore, is it?

The choice I now face is: do I let him continue to beat himself up or do I pull him away with the distraction of now. "Is your memory chip taking this all in?" I ask.

He glances at me with what I guess is supposed to be a dirty look, but comes off as a cry for help. He looks back ahead and starts to nod. "Funny, real funny," he says.

"What's funny?"

"Forget it."

"Forget what?"

"Do you want to walk home?"

"No."

"Then cut the crap."

"Right."

I have to watch myself, especially considering where we are now- halfway between the present and centuries ago. I think I know where we're headed, but I'm not sure. We're between the digital city and the analog edge of town. When we left the office we kept going out instead of heading back. Out here there's nothing, literally nothing. It's an invisible moat between the past and the present.

There are a couple of places coming up soon. They should all be out of the digital security range. The most recent system is extremely fast, intelligent, and strong, but it's not this strong. "Which one of these places are we going to?" I ask.

"You'll see when we get there."

"Right, well were you able to find anything?"

"You'll see when we get there."

Here we go. "Am I going to recognize this fine establishment?"

"You'll see when we get there."

I don't need this. "Do they have waitresses to deliver the orders or does the food just magically appear on the table?"

He slams on the breaks and turns hard right onto the dirt. He grabs my shirt and strong-arms me back first into the inside of my door. "I don't know how you made that happen, but-"

"I had nothing to do with it."

"Then how did it happen?"

"I have no clue. I do know this, it happened to me twice today and no one believed me until it happened to them. So cut the insulted teenager routine."

"It's not a routine dumbass. No one has ever really tested the latest system so it's impossible to be too safe."

"Right let's just go."

He lets go of my shirt and puts the car into gear. We turn back onto the empty road. He must have something. If he didn't he wouldn't be acting so overly cautious. Whenever he gets on edge it means he has something. Hopefully it's something good and not a duplicate. We'll see.

I look outside. There are more dead cars on the side of the road than there are running ones on it. If you're out here you're trying to get away. Away from one reality to another, but make no mistake-

"You're talking out loud genius."

"Damn, what did I start with?"

"You said there are more dead cars than ones on the road."

"Alright then it wasn't that much."

Time for some protection, just in case. I reach to get one of the two sodas I brought with me. I get it, open it, and take a swig. Looking outside it hits me. "Hey," I say.

"What?"

"I just noticed something strange."

"What's that?"

"You would agree someone out here is in the process of getting away from something, right? I mean it doesn't matter which way you're going. Either way it doesn't make a difference."

"I guess, but it could also be that you're trying to get back."

"Right, but that just means the new place wasn't as good as you wanted it to be and now you're trying to get away from there."

"Whatever," he says. He tosses his cigarette out the window. "Is there a point to this?"

"Yes, just listen, in a place with so many people trying to get away what is the one thing you would expect to see?"

He shrugs.

"Cameras," I say. "And what is the one thing missing from this picture- cameras."

"No, that can't be." He starts looking outside more intensely. "I guess there could be some hidden in the car frames. I don't know."

"Right, it looks like the cameras aren't everywhere. Do you remember it being this way before?"

"No."

"No, you don't remember or no it was never this way before?"

"No, I don't remember."

"I would check my chip, but I doubt it would've worked out here."

"The last time we were out this far was on the old system anyway."

"Right."

On the horizon signs of life in the form of old fashioned neon signs have appeared. I lean over, put the soda back into the door pocket, and straighten back up in my seat. Ahead the lights are getting brighter and the bars are getting closer. I know two of the three of them. It's been a long time since our last trip out here. We closed the case the next day.

"I don't know," I say.

"You don't know what?"

"I was just thinking about the last time we were out here. Do you remember?"

He continues to stare ahead as if he's the only one in the car. He tosses another cigarette into the night. "Of course I remember. We found the guy the next day."

"Right, are you getting that feeling this time?"

"I'm not getting any feelings about anything."

I can't tell if he's serious or being a wiseass. It's hard to tell with him sometimes. I open my mouth and then close it. It's not worth it. Besides I don't know what direction to go next. "Are you planning on stopping at any of these three places?"

"No," he says coldly.

"Right, just checking."

I reach down, grab the soda without looking, lift it up, and open it. Looking out the window, I start to take automatic sips and let the soda rest in my mouth for as long as possible. This is definitely the wrong place for me to be right now. Who needs it? Friggin' unknown bodies. A voice in my head is telling me to let it go. It's probably being sent by The Eyes Upstairs or some kind of pirate. At this point I really don't care.

I stare outside and try not to think of anything. The cars on the side of the road are becoming more and more bare. Hopeless. I close my eyes and imagine being back at the wings place watching and listening to all of the conversations between the morphs, aliens, and mutants. I feel a smile coming onto my face. Blindly I take another swig of sugarcola.

*   *   *

I open my eyes. Darkness has started to set in. I check the time. It looks like my trip to the mental wings place lasted forty-five minutes. We are now in a wannabe city of neon, bricks, dirt, and concrete. The sidewalks are packed shoulder to shoulder with people.

I used to know this place well. My partner and I were regulars out here. I wonder who is left. There are a lot of places I recognize and a few I don't. I look over at my partner. He's in the same position he was in forty-five minutes ago. He makes a right onto Fourth Street and pulls in.

"This is the place," he says and throws the car into park.

"Right, it is exactly that, and might I say you've made a fine choice, a damn fine choice sir," I say in my worst English accent. I shut the door.

"Save the bad Englishman for me. There's a good chance he'll be showing up tonight."

We start toward the entrance. Outside the door a red and white neon sign shines "The Place". "I was figuring since this might be the last time around. You know-" he says.

"I hadn't thought of it like that, but yeah, good choice. We always had good luck after coming here."

"Exactly, and I think after what's gone down today we could use all the help we can get."

"Right."

We might be in trouble. It doesn't sound like he's found much. I reach for the door. "Hey, do you know if Guy is still here?"

"I don't know," he says.

Guy owns this place and is the main bartender. At least he was, I don't know if he still is. If he is then this is still "The Place with the Guy". He has silver hair and it's never gotten darker or lighter in the twenty plus years we've been coming here. I open the door.

Inside, the place is dark. Lit with twentieth century lighting, it looks like the bars you see in 1970's movies. Some things never change.

"I don't see Guy," Tony says to me.

"Right, it looks like Darius is working."

"Let's check it out."

It's hard to hear him though the music. I nod and we head to the bar. The place is packed. Everyone looks like a tough guy, the kids and the vets. The difference being the kids are constantly trying to prove it to everyone while the vets are saving it until it's absolutely necessary.

We reach the bar. Tony slams his hands down on it. "Damn, can't a guy get somethin' decent to drink around here?"

Darius spins around fire coming from his eyes. He spots us. The fire fades and a smile grows across his face. He slowly starts walking over to us. "Well she-it, look who decided to grace us with their presence. What'd you become erased from the system?"

"Not yet," I say.

He slaps Tony's hand and shakes it. He comes over to me and tries to crush my hand. "So what's going on? What emergency brings you here?"

"Farewell tour, my partner here is planning on hanging it up as soon as we can stop dead bodies from falling into doorways."

"No," Darius says. I nod. "Well then you won't have any excuse not to be here every night."

"That depends on the quality of your sugarcola."

He shakes his head. "Sugarcola? Man what happened to you?"

"Crash and burn my friend, crash and burn."

Tony points to a picture of Guy behind the bar. "What happened to the old man?" he says.

"He's helping his old lady start her own place. They're going to call it the 'The Other Place'. We only see him once or twice a week these days."

"Well, tell him we stopped by," Tony says.

"You got it, but he probably won't believe me. Not many of the old timers come by anymore."

"Right we'll have to see if we can change that."

"Okay, but we don't have rocking chairs for old timers like you."

"Hey, I'm not retired yet."

"How about booths, do you have any of those?" Tony asks.

"Yeah there are a couple of open ones over there."

"Alright boss, take it easy, but not that easy," I say.

"Whatever you say old man." We smile and Tony and I walk away from the bar.

Tony and I slide into a booth. A waitress shows up and throws our menus at us. She's enough of looker and enough hard ass to get away with it. In this place you have to be. I see Tony cover the excuse me look he was going to shoot her.

"You know you can't do that here," I say.

He smirks. I caught him. He pulls out his cigarettes. "Yeah I guess it's been longer than I thought."

"Old man," I say.

He blows smoke at me. "How are you going to walk away from this?"

"Relax, I'm retiring not dying, at least I hope not. Besides, like Darius said this will mean we can come by more often."

The waitress reappears and takes our orders. Tony shifts on his side of the table. The music dies down and we wait for the next song before we say anything. The music starts back up. I lean on the table. "So- did you find anything?"

"Let's wait until the food shows up. I don't want anybody walking in on the conversation."

He's right. I'm pushing it. I don't know why I'm being so overanxious. Maybe it's just the urge to get it over with. I stretch out and scan the bar. Aside from Darius, there isn't one other recognizable face here. It has been a long time. They don't know any of the stories. They have no idea what kind of characters they've missed out on. Would they care or appreciate any of them if they did? Another reason to leave this job and write full-time. Somebody needs to tell the stories.

"You may be right," Tony says.

"What?"

"I said you may be right."

"Was I thinking out loud again?" He nods. "Do you see anyone?" I ask.

"Not from the old days, no."

He lights another alien approved cigarette. I bite the inside of my mouth. I have a bad feeling about those things. It could be me. Everyone and all the proof shows me I'm wrong, and God knows I've been wrong a lot recently, but they give me that feeling and that feeling has never been wrong. I wish it would be wrong about things I care about. Why am I always right about the bad things? Feeling do me a favor and focus on the case.

"I should've brought that second soda inside with me."

"Yeah we should've ordered something at the bar"

"Hey, do you remember anyone from when we first started out privately?"

"Yeah, why?"

"Do you know what they're up to now?"

"No, why?"

"I'll tell you later," I say. I've put out the bait let's see if he goes for it.

The waitress shows up with our food. "Now can we get on with this?"

"Do you mind? I'd like to enjoy my food while it's still hot. Why can't you enjoy things once in a while?"

He's stalling. He'd be eating slower if he wasn't so hungry. I take a bite. I didn't think I could be hungry after all of those wings earlier, but I was wrong. The wait and the aroma of the food have made it impossible not to eat.

The waitress reappears at our table and asks if everything is okay. We both nod, our mouths full of half chewed food. She leaves. Tony gulps and reaches for something. "Okay let's get this over with," he says.

"What did you find?"

"One face." He slides a file across the table. It's not a duplicate. I've never seen this guy before. He looks something like the body, but it's hard to tell. "What about you?"

"Three faces and a story." I flip him the files. He looks though them. He doesn't look impressed.

"I don't know, but at this point-"

He flips them back to me, the frustration showing all over his face. I take my three faces and his one face and put them next to me on the bench. "I'm going to the repair shop tomorrow. There's a guy I know there who does some side work. He should be able to write a story for these faces."

"Does he work cheap?"

"He's in the affordable range."

"I guess it's worth a shot."

Tony is fidgeting like a rookie. He takes one of the three shots he has lined up. "What's the story?" he asks.

"Right, do you remember Bobby No Heart? He started out with us, remember?"

"Yeah so?"

"So we ran into each other at the wings place today."

"What were you doing at the wings place?"

"Trying to replace disappearing food. Anyway he told me about a story he saw a couple of days ago. Do you remember Jimmy the Fizz?"

"Jimmy the Face?"

"No, Jimmy the Fizz. He worked with us. He was always carrying soda around."

"Yeah, oh man, I worked on a lot of cases with him. Why, what happened?"

"He fell through someone's doorway as a dead body. Here's a copy of all of the info Bobby was able to find on his own the last couple of days."

I hand him the info. All of the life leaves Tony's face. He rushes to his second shot then starts to inspect the info. The waitress stops at our booth. Tony orders another three shots.

"What do you think?" I ask.

"I think we should look into what Bobby's been up to."

"He said he's been working as an EMT. I told him I would look into it and then get back to him. I think he wants in."

"Not until we check him out first. We also need to see if we can get Jimmy's body."

"He's one of us. You're not thinking Bobby had anything to do with this, are you?"

"EMT's have a lot of access to a lot of things. We haven't heard from him or Jimmy in years and all of a sudden he finds you in a wings place? I'm not thinking anything. I'm just saying we don't let anyone in until we check them out."

"Right, I see what you're saying. We should also check out Jimmy and the apartment he fell into. It might help us more than any of the faces we have."

"What, are you figuring a case of inept murderers and confused addresses?"

"It's worth a look, just to see where it takes us."

He nods. "It's better than anything else we've got. Why not?"

He throws back another drink. This Jimmy news is hitting him harder than I thought it would. I swirl the cola around in my mouth to make sure I didn't just say that out loud. It's still all there. I'm safe.

My eyes look across the table. Tony has broken into a mean sweat. "Are you alright?"

"No I'm not alright; you're not alright; this case is not alright; and Jimmy is definitely not alright. It's okay though because at least it fits in with everything else in this case."

Tony's volume attracts the collective stare of everyone around us.

"You see something?" I say breaking their trance.

The sound of tsks and teeth sucking fills the area. They all start to turn away and a hum of murmured voices starts back up. I turn back to Tony. He looks like crap. "How are you doing smartass?"

"I feel like shit."

"Just keep yourself from smelling like it and we'll be alright." No response. "You should get some air."

"Yeah, here." He flips me his cards and some cash. "In case the bill comes while I'm outside."

"Right," I say catching the cash folded around the cards. "Are you going to be able to hold it together or what?"

"Yeah, sure."

Slowly he forces himself up. I watch him start his way to the exit. The Jimmy news; the alcohol; the disappearing food; it has all just broken Tony's limit. Run him over like racecars over the start/finish line.

I take a swig and wait for the bill. Tony can be seen opening the front door. The waitress shows up with the check. I hand her the card. She leaves with it.

Tony has now left the building; maybe he's reached the car. Hopefully he hasn't started it up and left without me. The waitress shows up with the card and two receipts from the bar. I sign one of them. She takes it, hands me the other, and leaves. I leave her a cash tip courtesy of my partner and get up.

I go to the bar. Darius turns around. "So, are you ready for the harder stuff?"

"No, not yet. We need to split early so I'll see you when and if."

Darius smiles. "Yeah when hell freezes over and if we're not all frozen."

I smile back. "The next time you see Guy you're going to tell him we were here, right?"

"Right." He ferociously shakes my hand. "Come back when you're retired."

"Right, definitely." I turn and head for the door.

I open the door. A rush of heat hits me. It causes me to break into an instant sweat. The metal door crashes behind me. I doubt anyone inside the bar even heard it. My eyes focus on the parking lot. Stepping forward there's nothing but rocks, empty cars, and open road. A cop car pulls out of the darkness and takes off. There's something you don't normally see around here. I think it was a cop car, it was painted like one. Not unless it was an incredible imitation or stolen junk one. Maybe I've been away for too long. Things have definitely changed.

I turn left and start to the car. So far the rocks show no sign of Tony being sick. There are no liquids of any kind. I look up. My partner is trying to get into his car, but can't. I don't think he can find his keys. I run to the car. "Hey, hey."

He isn't looking back. I stop and whistle through my teeth. His head shoots up. He looks back. He must see me, actually the way he was drinking he probably sees two or three of me. "Hey, get over here. What do you think you're doing? Get over here."

He looks left and right. I point at him. He points at himself. "Yes, you know I mean you. Get over here."

I walk toward him. He points to the car and shrugs. I nod. I'm a few strides away from him now. His pockets are completely inside out. "Pardon me mate, but could you possibly help me locate my keys?"

Oh no, the bad English accent has arrived, emphasis on bad. This is not going to be good. Trying to look him in the eyes, I say, "I'll see what I can do."

"Righto, jolly good, that's awfully decent of you sir."

"Don't call me sir, I not a knight."

I'm now at the car. Staring him in the face it's obvious something's off. There's a glaze over his eyes that wasn't there five minutes ago. His head starts falling to the side. I pull it up. It falls in the other direction. I pick it up again. "Tony, smartass, listen to me, listen."

I firmly tap him on the side of his face. He straightens his head out. "Tony," I say staring him in his eyes. "Has anyone done anything to you in the last five minutes?"

He looks confused.

"You know, after you ate, since you've been outside."

He points at me and starts to laugh. It's useless. At least his breath doesn't smell like vomit. His gears haven't gone into reverse yet. That's a positive.

Something in the corner of my eye calls for my attention. I turn my head and see Tony's keychain reflecting the neon lights from the side of the bar. This is going to be tricky. Trying to maintain one hand in contact with Tony, I bend and reach for the keys. My left hand grabs them. I step toward them to maintain my balance and return to my original upright position. I lose contact with Tony. He spots the keys in my hand.

"You've located my keys. Damn fine job sir. I say, jolly good show."

He begins to step toward me. His body wavers and he tumbles face first into the rocks. He lifts up his head. "Bugger."

He forces himself to his knees. His face turns blue. "Oh no." I jump out of the firing line. Looks like the thought I had about reverse gears was a little premature. I run behind him and grab him up under the arms. What a mess.

It appears to all be out. I sit him up with his back against the side of his car. "Why not?" I walk away from him. The anger in me is ready to explode like my partner's digestive system. "Great, just great. And all these years you're the one preaching to me about self-control."

He points to himself and makes the face of an innocent seven year-old. I pace back and forth in front of him, the frustration driving me each way. His head follows me back and forth. The innocent seven year-old who is pointing at himself while following me with his head like a bad tennis fan looks like he's about to cry.

I stop. "What?"

He bursts out into uncontrollable laughter. His body lurches forward. He starts to vomit on the rocks between his legs.

He stops. His head turns to the left and leans against the car. Nice, real nice. He starts to laugh. Mt. Tony erupts again. This time he's throwing up against the back half of his car. It's his car what do I care. As long as none of it gets inside the car or on me it's manageable. He still hasn't gotten any vomit on his clothes. It's amazing. I don't know how he does it. It must be all that practice. He's a real pro.

Enough of this. The smell has gotten to the level that will cause anyone within a ten foot radius to join in the eruption. I head back for the entrance. The road keeps drawing my attention. How many other stalkers are out there waiting for us in the darkness?

One problem at a time.

I turn back toward the bar. Shoving my left hand into my pocket I search for the remaining cash Tony has given me. I find it as I reach the door. Two steps in and there are two cigarette machines to my left. I put in some cash and pull the lever twice. Two packs fall out. That should be enough. I grab a couple of matchbooks and head back to the car.

I reach the car and my partner is sitting there asleep and surrounded, but not touched by a buffet of former meals. I light the cigarettes two at a time and use them as incense for the area. A neutralizer against the instigation of any future eruptions. It's too much fun for one person to be allowed to have.

I move back and forth around the area spreading the smoke like an altar boy in a Latin mass. At this point it's hard to see Tony or the car. "That's enough of that," I say.

I check on my partner. He's out cold and snoring. Hopefully the English accent went with him. I turn away. Through the smoke someone can be seen staring at us from below the neon.

I walk out of the smoke.

The body moves starts in my direction. It's Darius and he's smoking. It figures. "What's up?" I ask.

"Someone came inside said and they thought there was a car on fire in our parking lot. Man, what is that smell?"

"It's the returns of my partner's last week of dining."

"Damn."

"Right, and you got lucky, the Englishman just left."

Darius shakes his head. "Where is he?"

"Tony is propped up against the side of his car. He's out cold."

"That bad?"

"I don't know, it's been a really bad week, but usually he can take it."

"Do you think something's up?"

"It certainly seems like it, but I don't know maybe we're just getting too old." I look down at the body. "You know, I could get rid of this mess for you if you help me get him into the passenger's seat."

He inspects the mess- carefully. He looks like he's about to turn colors. "One body, clean like when he came in. The only mess is all around him," I say.

Darius stares. He grunts. "Alright, let's go."

"Right, just be careful not to get any on him. I don't want to drive home with it."

"Yeah, yeah, let's just go."

Darius tiptoes around the vomit and grabs Tony's ankles. I get him from under the armpits and we lift him into the passenger's seat. No mess; no problem.

I grab the keys and we walk out of the smoke. Darius gives me another one of his ferocious handshakes. "I promise it will be a lot cleaner next time."

"It better be or else you two better be carrying me."

"Right." He starts away. The thought flashes into my mind. "Darius," I yell. He turns around. "Yeah."

I move toward him. "I noticed a cop around here before. I don't remember it ever being that way before. Do they hang around here now?"

"Are you kidding me?"

"No. I saw a black and white out there when I first left the bar."

He looks into the night with the fire back in his eyes. "No, there have never been any around here. Not since I've been working here. Not that I know of." He looks back at me. "What kind of trouble are you bringing around here?"

"I don't know, like I said it's been a bad week, a really bad week."

"Well whatever it is you're into don't bring it around here."

"No shit, I told you, the next time I see you I'll be retired."

"Right," he says. He gives me a look, tosses his cigarette, and turns away. I head back to the car.

I slide into the car and instinctively slam the door shut. My eyes look over at Tony. He's still out cold. It figures. The car starts up and I throw it into gear. It's been awhile since I've done this, about five years. We make a left and start past the other bars. In about a mile I'll make a right and we'll be back in the highway darkness.

Like I said, this is just a wannabe city. I reach to adjust the rearview mirror. "You've got to be kidding me."

In the reflection is what appears to be a cop car. So much for never seeing one around here in over twenty years. The black and white is right up on my tail. If I were to stop short he'd be in my front seat. Something tells me if that were to happen tonight I would be the one held responsible, even though he's the one breaking the law. I don't think Tony would appreciate it much either.

In my younger days I might show this guy up. Put her into automatic drive and sit back with my hands behind my head. Not tonight though, not here, not now, not with the luck I've been having. The highway entrance comes up on my right.

I turn, it keeps going straight. I scan the darkness, my eyes wide open waiting and expecting something to happen.

I've been driving on this road for about thirty minutes and the only things I've seen are darkness and car skeletons. Tony is still asleep. I reach for the radio. Nothing but static. I hit the power button. Light floods the car.

"What the hell is that?" Tony says jumping up out of his sleep.

He looks at me. He looks behind us. There's a black multipurpose vehicle with lights bright enough to illuminate half of the highways in the country all at once, literally right up on our rear bumper. "Go around us asshole. You've only got the whole highway."

It honks its horn. Tony raises his badge and waves it at our friend. Its engine revs and it knocks us forward.

I steer to the right. It follows me. I turn back. It stays on my tail. It revs again. We lurch forward.

Tony reaches for his gun. The lights disappear as quickly as they showed up. "I don't hear the engine," I say.

"It must have dropped back. Keep driving. It's playing with us."

"I think it had an Eyes Upstairs flag on its window. Hang on."

I hit the gas and we take off. "Keep it going for a little while longer," Tony says. "See if you can make some space."

"How am I supposed to make space when I don't even know where it is?"

"Just drive." Tony has his gun drawn and ready to go. "Okay ease up."

I let up on the gas. "What the-"

I turn hard and try to regain control of the car. Tony starts firing at the black utility truck that jumped in front of us from the sideline of skeletons. There's a pop. Lights turn on behind us again.

I make a right into the dirt. There's a crash. The sound of twisting metal behind us.

I turn left through the skeletons and back onto the highway. We're even with our other friend. "Lean back." Tony is pointing to my open window. I put the car into automatic drive. With both of my feet I push as hard as I can. My seat flies to the back seat.

Tony takes his shot.

There's a ping and a hiss. It swerves into the dirt with smoke or steam coming from its hood. I can't tell which it is exactly and I'm not planning on hanging around to find out.

I move the seat forward and take off the automatic drive. I hit the gas and we take off. "Only ten more minutes until we reach the city," Tony says.

"Right." There's a pop from the passenger front side. "Shit."

We pull over and go to the back of the car to get the spare. "I'll cover you." I say.

There isn't much damage to the back of the car, only to the bumper and around the trunk keyhole. "I've got it." he says. "Turn and cover me."

"Right." I turn, gun drawn. I hear the trunk open.

"Shit." Tony yells.

"What?" I turn to see. Tony is frozen. I look into the trunk. Enter corpse number three. Shit is right.

Chapter Eight

The body stares up at us.

Tony is pacing back and forth in the dirt, but I'm frozen- eyelocked with the corpse. I don't know why, but I'm not even surprised. After the disappearing food this morning I don't know if anything can surprise me anymore. Still, something seems familiar about this body.

"Tony, get over here."

He walks faster than I think he wants to. He reaches me and faces me instead of the trunk. "I don't believe this," he says in a tone that's more angry than afraid.

"Relax."

"Relax? I have a dead body in my trunk and you want me to relax?"

"And I had one fall into my apartment, what's your point? Now do me a favor, get it together and look at this body. Something seems familiar about him, but I don't know what it is."

He turns around and focuses on the body.

"Tell me what you see."

"He's a male, old enough to be our father. There doesn't seem to be any blood on the body or in my trunk. In fact, it looks like whoever did this dressed him up afterwards. No visible wounds. He looks like he was in good shape at the time of death. You're right though, something does seem familiar about him."

Tony turns away then snaps back. He lunges forward and searches the corpse's pockets.

"Do you think it's a good idea to do that?"

"Yeah, I think I might know who this is. Besides, we're going to have to move the body to get to the spare tire anyway." He finds a wallet and flips it open. "It is, damn." He throws the wallet down into the trunk.

"What?"

"Look at the name and address," he says.

I lean in and pick up the wallet. I flip it open and find the ID. "Right, so?"

"You don't remember?" I shrug. "That's Leo Ericson. He worked with my dad. He used to stop by our station all the time. Remember, when we first started out?"

"Vaguely." I look behind us. "So how are we going to play this?" I say turning back to Tony.

"The first thing we need to do is move the body and get the spare. We aren't going anywhere until we get that tire changed. I don't know how many more of our demolition derby friends are out there, and I don't really feel like hanging around to find out. They could already be on their way for all we know. If we don't get that tire changed soon there'll be three bodies in the trunk instead of one."

He looks at me, then down at the trunk, and back at me.

"Right, I guess it's the only play."

"Okay, help me move this body. Let's try to keep him in the trunk. I don't want somebody driving by out of nowhere and seeing a dead body lying at our feet."

"Alright, let's go."

We grab the body. The rigor mortis hasn't set in yet.

"The death must have been recent," Tony says.

"Right, I was just thinking the same thing. It couldn't have been more than two to six hours ago."

He nods. "Move him to the left."

We shift the body to the left of the trunk. The forensics on it are going to be a mess. Tony grabs the tire and jack. He bounces the spare onto the street and rolls it toward the blowout. He looks back at me. "Bring the crow bar up with you."

I nod. I bend over, grab it, and carry it up to him.

"Cover me," he says.

"What about the body?"

"It's not going anywhere."

"What if someone drives by? Don't you think we should hide it a little better?"

He wipes the sweat from his forehead. "Just lay him back out again and lower the top as far as you can without closing it."

I hustle my way back to the trunk. I get there. The body is still flexible. I move it to its original position. My hand lowers the trunk until it is hard to tell if it's open or not. It should be enough especially in the dark. I step back. Hopefully the body doesn't stiffen up before we put the blowout under it.

This is bad. The clock is ticking down on us in so many ways if I stopped to think about it I'd have a breakdown. I won't though because I've been through this so often it's become reflex. I'm running on automatic drive. It's sick if you think about it, but it's true.

"Go ahead," I yell.

He starts jacking the car up. I reload my gun and take my angle. My attention is favored toward the direction of our prior attacks, but only slightly. I don't trust anything. The more that happens the readier I am. That's what whoever is doing this doesn't understand. Not unless they're trying to do this, trying to make this the new normal. I don't know, it just doesn't make sense. Not yet at least, not until I find a motive.

The roads are empty. Shit. I twist around. I'd left my back open. Ahead of me is nothing but darkness. I don't see or hear anything. "How close are you to finishing?"

"I'm just about there."

"Good, because we need to get moving as soon as possible. We're sitting targets out here and even though I'm good I'm not good enough to cover all sides at once."

"Done, let's get out of here."

The jack slides down. Tony grabs it and we head to the trunk. The rim and a few shreds of tire are the only things remaining from the blowout. Tony lifts open the trunk. I reach down. The body is still pliable. I lift its top half. Tony slides the rim into where the body was. I put the body back down and Tony throws in the tools. He slams the door shut.

"Let's go," I say.

"Keys," he says walking around to the driver's side.

I toss them to him. He snatches them out of the air. We head to the front of the car. A pair of lights appears coming from the opposite direction. We open the doors and jump inside.

Tony tries to start the car. It doesn't catch. The lights are getting closer. I draw my gun and hold it on my lap. Tony turns the keys again. It doesn't start. The lights are now about twenty feet away. I cock the gun. Tony tries to start the car. The engine roars. The lights are a car length ahead of us.

They drive by.

"Tinted windows, but no flags," I say.

Tony throws it into gear and we're moving again. I keep checking behind us. Nothing but darkness every time. I've seen that show before. "Nine more miles," Tony says.

I look at him "You know that body was only recently killed, right?"

"Obviously, what's your point?"

"It means the time between when he was killed and put in your car wasn't long. Do you remember anything that happened in the parking lot?"

He stares ahead. I can tell he's thinking. A worried look takes over his face. He looks at me. "No I don't remember anything."

"Check your mental mind chip. Just in case-"

He checks his mind chip. "No, I don't have anything for the ride after we got out of the city."

His voice sounds fragile. He's afraid of what I'm afraid of- mind virus injection. If they inject one of those viruses into your system you will lose the ability to use your mind chip. "I've got an idea," I say. "Let me check my memory chip. I know nobody did anything to me in the parking lot. So if there's nothing past the city you're alright."

Checking the mind chip the last registered memory I have is leaving the city. "You're good. I don't have anything past the city either. So, you're good and now we know the chip limits."

Tony takes a deep breath. "Now all we need to do is come up with a plan in the next eight miles," he says.

"Then you'd better start driving slower because I don't see any way out of this one."

"No can do, I'm not letting anyone catch up to us. Come on, we need to come up with something before we're back in range."

"What can we do? Our prints and DNA are all over the dead body. Never mind the fact that he knew us. The cameras will show we went out of range. If anyone was watching they're going to ask us where and why."

"Well we can't come back with a dead body. Things like that tend to attract attention. They are already after you as it is. They're just looking for an excuse."

"Right, but it wouldn't make any sense. If we had done something wrong why would we bring it back to the city with us? Wouldn't we drive out there to get rid of it? Why would we pick up a dead body?"

"We wouldn't, but you're making a big mistake. You're assuming they care if we did it or not. They don't. They just need something to pin on us. Remember our friends back there had government flags. They looked like they worked for The Eyes Upstairs. Somebody doesn't like something we're doing," he says.

"That's another thing," I say. "Those vehicles looked like they were trying to make us see they were from The Eyes Upstairs. They were almost too perfect."

"I don't see how you had time to figure that. It's too big of a chance for me to take."

"Maybe, but I also saw a black and white come out of the darkness when I walked out of the bar. I asked Darius if cops had started patrolling the area. He said not since he's been working there. I'm more sure that that black and white delivered the body to your car than I am it was an actual cop."

He shakes his head. "You may be right, but it's too many assumptions for me to make right now."

"Then you better come up with something soon because we can't bring the body into range. We'd never be able to get rid of it without being on camera and found out."

"This is crazy, we didn't even do anything."

"Right."

A silence takes over the car. He's right of course, but these days right doesn't seem to mean anything. There has to be a way out of this before it gets too deep. I look at Tony. "How attached are you to this car?" I ask.

"What?"

"You heard me, how attached are you to this car and how far do you think you could walk?"

"You want to blow up my car?"

"It would get rid of our immediate problems. You crash the car into a skeleton; we light the tank on fire; and no more car, no more body. Your insurance company will buy you a new car. We'll just say we were run off the road. There are no cameras out here to disprove it. If they say we're lying and tell us what actually happened then we know they were the ones behind the body getting there in the first place."

Tony thinks about it. He shakes his head in the negative. "I can't do that to him, maybe if this was some regular John Doe, but not to Leo. I can't do that to his family. Besides, I can't walk that far, not tonight."

"I have my flip phone, we could call an independent cab as soon as we're in range. Better yet, I could call Alison."

"It's tempting, but like I said I can't do this to Leo and his family. Even if I could we would be easy targets if anyone were to come after us."

"Right, well that's the best I can come up with."

Tony pulls out a cigarette. He lights it. It dangles from his mouth as he stares ahead. "I wouldn't do that to his family," he mumbles to no one in particular.

Something inside him wants to do it. I've worked with him long enough to tell. I take a swig of my second cola and hold it in my mouth. This is it. Nothing else needs to be or is thought. I swallow the soda.

"You realize what the possibilities are, right?" He flicks the ashes off of his cigarette and checks the windows. "I mean you know I'm with you no matter what you choose, but just remember this isn't just about you. Who knows what could happen to us if they take us in. We could end up as the next two bodies falling through doorways. You realize that, right?" I say.

"Yeah I get that," he says.

He tosses his half-smoked alien approved cigarette through the window.

One mile to go.

He checks the mirrors again. He looks across at me. "Okay, this is what we're going to do," he says focusing back on the road. "You don't have to be involved. No one knows I have a body in my trunk. I'll take you home. Tomorrow morning I'll call up Leo's family and tell them I found his body on the side of the road.

Technically that is true, I just won't tell them I found it in my car. I'll say we picked it up and brought it back with us.

"If I go to the cops I'll tell them the same thing. Like you said there aren't any cameras out here so they're in no position to say I'm lying. If they do and they say we had it in the car all along then we know who put it there. Got it so far?"

"Right."

"Okay, now if the cops ask what we were doing out there we say it was a farewell party for you as a P.I.. If they ask about the car damage we tell them it was like that when we came out to leave. Technically that's not lying either. We tell them we have no idea how it happened, but it wasn't like that when we left to go into the bar.

"Don't mention the bar's name if you don't have to. Give them as little as possible. If they do press say 'you know the place with the guy' and keep them running around in circles until they give up. Okay?"

"It sounds good to me, but where are you going to take the body?"

"To the family if it's possible. I'll offer to bring it to the undertaker for them. If they have any questions I'll give them the same story."

"Right, that's good. It explains the fingerprints and the DNA on him too."

"Exactly."

"What about our demolition derby friends?"

"What about them? We don't mention them. The cops don't know about them and if they do they're in no position to say anything."

"Right."

"Okay good."

"If you do go to the cops tell them you want to talk to 'the kid'. He hasn't been jaded yet. If you do talk to him and he asks how you know about him, tell him I told you about him one time."

"Okay, I'll call you when it's taken care of."

"I might be in the repair shop so if I am just leave a vague message implying which way it went or better yet, pick me up at my office tomorrow night. Okay?"

"Yeah good."

I take a swig of liquid sugar and check behind me. "All clear," I say.

"We'll be in range in about five hundred feet so lose all memories of this conversation."

"What conversation?"

"Exactly."

I camouflage the conversation even though it shouldn't have been able to be recorded. To be safe I camouflage the whole night. The city is now visible. Once we reach it we should be safe from any cut-offs and there is no place to jump out from. Here they do all of that digitally in your mind.

"You can't win," I mumble. I take a swig of soda. We break city lines and head for my apartment.

We pull up in front of my building. I give Tony a nod. I grab the remainders of my sugarcola, get out of the car, and close the door with enough force to lock it without risking the trunk popping open. Tony heads home. I take a swig and head for the stairs.

I open the door and walk in. "Any messages scanner?"

"Welcome home sir, no you had no visitors or messages."

"Thank you scanner, please reset my alarm for tomorrow."

"Done, anything else?"

"No, thank you. Goodnight."

"Goodnight sir, going into sleep mode in five, four…"

I enter the bedroom. I throw myself onto the bed. That was a mistake. I am in the same sweaty clothes I wore to lift up two bodies one drunk and one dead. The stink is overpowering. I'll get up and change in five minutes. I just need some rest. The sleep senses this and teams up with the stink to knock me out.

*   *   *

It's six thirty in the morning. I've just gotten into an independent taxi on my way to the financial district. I'm working on two hours of sleep separated by three hours of pacing, apartment deodorizing, and clothes disposal. It should be a good day.

The taxi is a beat-up twenty year old jalopy. The driver is an alien who can morph into whoever or whatever you want. "What would you like?" the driver asks.

"It doesn't matter. I need to concentrate on getting my new ID and can't afford to be distracted. What's your favorite?"

"I don't have one, but most busy riders like you seem to like my fallback. It's not annoying or distracting."

"Sounds good, let's go with that."

It morphs into the stereotypical nineteen seventies New York City cab driver. White male complete with accent, fat cigar, and paperboy hat.

"Nice," I say.

"Pretty cool, right?" It says in its rough voice. "And don't worry about the cigar. I only chew on them. I can't afford to really smoke them. If you want smoke you have to pay extra for it."

"No, it's good the way it is. Thank you."

The financial district is twelve blocks away from my apartment in the opposite direction of my office. It's also conveniently located two blocks away from the repair shop.

The repair shop is officially known as the Federal Financial And Identification Rescue And Installation Department or F.F.A.I.R.A.I.D., but no one has ever called it that. Originally people called it the second chance show, but then they started using it more frequently and it became known as the repair shop.

First things first though, in order to get a new financial ID, the one I have needs to be stolen. That's a lot harder than it used to be. Originally it was pretty easy. People were constantly being ripped off. Thieves, professional and amateur, were all over the place. Business was good.

Not anymore. The prices of everything have gone up. Salaries have gone down or disappeared. Students graduate into a part-time society with debts they will never be able to pay off. The aliens came and found everything they thought was here is now gone. Everyone is now trying to lose what they have because all they have is debt.

The pros are now wise. They know it could cost more to take a wallet than to leave it alone. They know most IDs are toxic. They need to believe I'm loaded.

I check my suit. It's the best one I have. It's always worked in the past, hopefully it works again today. I have the files in a professional looking briefcase. It looks like Italian leather, but I really bought it from a chip vendor for three dollars.

We pass the repair shop. "Okay here is good," I say.

He tells me the fee. I hand him the card and tell him to add thirty five percent to it. "Thanks. You call me whenever you need a ride," he says and hands me a card.

I take his card and my soon to be ex-card from him and smile. I can't afford to be seen leaving this taxi so I check the windows. The streets are empty. I step out as quickly as possible.

I stride down the street with a smug, confident look on my face. The kind of look that projects the image of someone who is twenty minutes late for a meeting, but doesn't give a shit because I could terminate all of the people in this building with the snap of my fingers.

I look at my wrist even though I'm not wearing a watch. It doesn't matter. People are more likely to doubt themselves than me in this neighborhood. Nobody dares question anyone who works here.

This is the attitude I project on the outside. Inside, my mind is guiding me with the experience of a detective and the knowledge of a thief.

I'm in the World Plaza. It's easy to tell. The financial district is the only place in the city that is kept up and renovated. It's only a block and a half long, but there is more money in this block and a half than there is in the rest of the country.

The people here make sure they remind everyone of this every chance they get.

I get on line at the trending morning shop. I listen. All of the orders are the same. Typical. I step up to the counter and order what everyone else ordered. I take out my wallet and scan. No one seems to be watching. I pay, get my drink, and walk.

There is a mini-park on the edge of the district. It's a few hundred yards ahead. Just in front of it are a few separate groups of big shot wannabes. They're talking at each other, each trying to steer the conversation to themselves. Two of the bigger groups are about two feet apart from each other.

I confidently glide between them. My wallet is peeking out from my back pocket. Far enough so everyone can see it, but not so far that it looks like it's trying to be stolen. I nod my head with everything that is said, while my eyes search for any possible takers. I hope it's not taken by a first timer; if it is they will soon have to learn how to get it restolen.

All the wallet is holding are my debted cards and ID card. Nothing but red zone. Hopefully one of these big shots takes it. They could probably pay for it with the money they have in their pocket and still have plenty left over.

My mind alert goes off. Possible taker at three o'clock. Out of the corner of my eye I spot a man my age, maybe a little younger, drift behind the groups. He's dressed better than I am. Something about him says undercover to me. He reaches the group to my left. His head is tilted up, but his eyes are looking down.

He's now behind me. My back pocket deflates. I try not to smile or become too relaxed. I peek out of the corner of my right eye. He lifts two more wallets. Slowly, I begin to walk away. Next stop the repair shop.

The repair shop is almost as beat up as the people inside of it. I grab the entrance door handle. It shakes and threatens to come inside with me. I step inside. It's packed as usual. Ray is sitting at his usual desk. He looks up. I am standing in his line of sight. He sees me and shakes his head. "Kenneth Breaker," he calls.

Some of the people sitting in the waiting rows start to make noise. Too bad. Do this long enough and you become highly efficient. I walk through the synthetic wood gate. It continues to swing behind me. Ray makes a disgusted sound and starts to shake his head again. "Sit down," he says in a strained tone.

I plop into my chair. "You got the form I sent, right?"

"How could I miss it? What do you have them preprinted?"

I shrug. "Pretty much, you know how efficient I am. Think in the blank and send immediately."

A smile creeps onto his face. "I guess I should have expected it. It's been longer than usual. When was the last time you were here?"

"What is this- confession?" He breaks into more of a wheeze than a laugh. "Forgive me repairer, it's been eight months since my last repair job."

"Eight months? That's longer than I thought."

"Right, well I'll try to make it quicker for you next time." He raises his eyebrow and begins to bring up my file on an ancient computer. "Can they spare it?" I say nodding toward the antique.

He grunts. "Don't get me started."

My file comes up on the screen. He types in some information. "This is your sixth time? Do you even remember who you really are?"

"Sure, sometimes."

He turns and looks back at me. "So what do you want this time, the usual?"

"Right. Keep the name, address, memories, and medical records. Lose the debt. They steal it they keep it, that's still how it works right?"

"Right." He types in the request. "Okay, you're new again. Welcome back to the profit side. Your debts have been washed clean. How does it feel?"

"The same as it did the first five times."

"Try to see if you can make it last longer this time."

"What, and put you out of a job. Why would I do that?"

He snorts. "Anything else?"

I check for the cameras. "There are no working cameras here. They're all older than the computers. The only thing that works is the red light on top. It's all a show."

"Yeah?"

"Well that depends, do you trust me?"

I trust no one, but I've already given him my information six times before. If he's going to do something I doubt this would be what pushes him over the edge. I lean toward him. "Are you looking for something on the side?"

"It depends."

"Depends on what?"

"On what's in it for me."

"That's funny, I was just thinking the same thing."

"How do you figure that?"

"Simple. How many times have I come to you?"

"Six."

"Right, and how many times have you been divorced?"

"Seven."

"And of those seven times, how many times did I get you evidence that proved your wife was cheating on you?"

"Seven."

"How many times did you win in court because of that evidence?"

"Seven."

"And how much did you end up paying your wife? How much did I charge you?"

"Zero, zero, alright what do you want?"

"Right." I open up my case, take out the folders, and put them on his desk. "I need IDs, bios, and locales on all of these people." I take out an 8x10 of my apartment crasher and a paper with the second crashed apartment's address on it.

"I need the ID and bio of Mr. 8x10 over here and the ID and bio of the dwellers of this apartment address."

"That's it?"

"Are you being sarcastic?"

"No, everyone has gone through the system at one time or another. I should have your info in about an hour. You could stay here if you want."

"Let me go back to my apartment, change, and come back. You can call me in when you see me and I'll get to piss off a new group in the waiting rows."

"Sounds good." I stand up to leave. "Hey." I turn around. "Don't you want your new ID card?"

"Unbelievable." I turn back and take it from Ray's outstretched hand. "Thanks, I'll see you in an hour." He looks at me with a smartass smile. I turn and leave.

*   *   *

My apartment is a block away. The first eleven blocks have gone by pretty quick. Maybe it's instinct or maybe it's guilt, but I have the feeling someone is following me. I glance behind me. The streets are clear. Still, something doesn't feel right. I pick up the pace. The apartment building is up ahead. I turn into it and look outside. Nothing. I start up the stairs.

I enter the apartment. Everything is normal. "Scanner has there been any activity?"

"None sir."

"Good, thank you."

I change my clothes and call my office simultaneously. I tell Alison no more charges. She tells me everything was paid off last night and we end the call. I grab a sugar cola and leave the apartment. I'm practically running. Why am I running? I laugh and head back to the repair shop.

*   *   *

I grab the wobbly handle and enter the repair shop. It's been seventy-five minutes, more than enough time. Ray sees me and calls me in. I sit at the desk. "You're late," he says.

"What can I do?" I say. "So what did you find?"

He is fidgeting in his chair. "I found out you're going to have to pay me more than one divorce. This could be serious shit you led me into."

"What, what shit?"

"Not for what you gave me."

"Alright, you're engaged right?"

"Yeah so?"

"So, when you need me to get dirt on this one I'll do it for free." He rejects my offer with his stare. "I'll throw in a sugarcola, limited edition, never opened."

He shakes his head. "Whatever let's get this over with." He grabs the soda. "First off let's get the easy stuff out of the way first. All of the file guys are now dead except one."

He opens the soda and takes a gulp. He tosses Tony's file and one of my files across to me. "These guys have been dead six and seven years respectively." He reads off the names and charges. "Typical drug addicts, nothing special. Both od'd. No family, you get the idea."

He throws another one of my files across the desk. "This guy, Mark Johnson, was stabbed to death by his wife four years ago. He had been unemployed for ten. I put it all in the files."

He starts to speak in a lower tone. "Now I do have to thank you for one thing. You shortened my work by giving me a duplicate." Yes. "The 8x10 picture was that of this man, Sean Wells. At least that was his last ID."

"So what about this guy?"

"Okay this is the thing, we're not supposed to know this guy. Nobody's supposed to know this guy." He leans across the desk, covers his mouth, and whispers, "He's undercover. He went off the radar about ten days ago."

He hands me the file and leans back. "I think that's probably what you're looking for."

I nod. "What about the address?"

"Oh yeah, right the address. Here, all of the information is on there. I think you night find it interesting." He hands me the report.

"Alright, alright," I keep mumbling to myself.

"Is it what you're looking for?"

"If it's true it is."

"It is, absolutely one hundred percent. There is no doubt." He stares as I read. "Now do you see why I'm nervous?"

"Yes, thanks." I collect the info together. "Just so you know, the duplicate was found dead in my apartment building a few nights ago."

I look up. He is struggling to keep himself together. "The cops reported it as a John Doe death by natural causes. Whatever that's worth. I really appreciate this."

"You'd better," he says.

"Call me if you need anything."

He nods. "I will."

I get up and walk out.

Chapter Nine

I'm five blocks away from my office. It's still early, but I'm running late. The sky can't make up its mind as to what kind of day it's going to be.

Just like this case. Facts about the who's are starting to fall into place. Even some of the why's are beginning to show their faces. This could be great. The ray of sunshine we need to lead us out of the darkness.

Or, it could be another low hanging storm cloud who brings more clouds with it to threaten us every moment of the day. Nothing is ever simple. Every fact I find is bringing five questions with it. One question is beginning to yell louder and louder. Is it even going to be possible to make a difference when we have all of the other answers?

We'll see. I got what I needed this morning. Now it's up to Tony to get us cleared so we can focus back on the apartment crashing corpses.

I look down and step over a broken bottle. "Excuse me, heads up bro."

I look up. The head polite punk is headed right for me. He is in a hurry. No time to talk. He picks a side and I go in the opposite direction.

I smile.

On cue, I'm filled with guilt. Guilt for the position I've put Ray in. I didn't intend to. I had no idea how big those names were or maybe I did and now I don't want to admit it.

I'll fix this. It will be fixed. Everything can be fixed. A taxi speeds past me. A smirk takes over my face. Someone's trying to use all they have left on their card. I see my office ahead.

A black and white makes a right onto this street. It's headed for my office. Instinct is telling me to stop, but I only slow down. Its brake lights go on. Shit, keep calm. Focus on the back seat. It's empty. Okay, I'm getting closer. It's not moving.

The brake lights turn off. It creeps forward. I'm close enough to hear its radio. Let's save this for posterity. "Mobile visual/audio memory record."

It turns into a U-turn. There is only one person in the front seat. I don't recognize the face. It crawls forward on my side of the street. I look directly at it. The driver and I make eye contact. "Smile for the camera."

The car continues to crawl. The driver looks away. He squeals his tires and takes off. "Gotcha, mobile visual/audio record off." That face didn't look familiar. I'll run it through the public police registry when I get to the office.

I check the intersection in both directions. The roads are completely empty. No cops, no civilians, no cars, and no pedestrians of any kind. I cross the street. The office is two blocks away. Last night's thoughts try to rush back into my consciousness. They're automatically blocked. Even if they were to get in they're also camouflaged. I should be safe.

"I get it, I noticed," I say to myself. The rush subsides. I head for my office.

I enter my office. It's empty as usual. Something is different though- the sound. Alison looks bored out of her mind. I walk toward her desk. "Any calls or messages?"

She shoots me a look that would kill the average, well-adjusted human being. "Yeah right, can't you tell?"

"Don't worry, I'll try to get the debt running as soon as possible."

"You do that. Other than you and your partner I haven't had a call since yesterday afternoon."

"Tony called?"

"Yeah, about twenty minutes ago. He said he'd be here around five. Here I wrote it all down."

"Anything else?"

"No, I got everything done yesterday afternoon, like I told you this morning."

"Right."

I start away from her desk. "Aren't you going to ask? Aren't you interested?"

I try to keep a blank expression on my face, but a smile is trying force its way on. "Ask about what? Interested in what?" I might have a smirk on my face, but I'm not sure.

"About the hum."

"What hum? Oh right, there is a hum." I definitely have a smirk on my face.

"Nice try big shot. It showed up around six last night. I ordered it right after you left. It's over here. I figured this way I can guard the food."

"Good plan."

I look behind her desk. A new mini refrigerator is purring out a soft hum. "It's bigger than it looks. I was able to fit both of our orders in it with room to spare."

I squat down and open it. She's right. I grab two sodas and close the door. "Remind me to take some of that home with me before I leave today."

"Whatever you say big shot."

I stand up. Now she has a smile on her face. "What?" I ask.

"Nothing, you'll see."

"I'll see what?"

"Let's just say they were having a special and I didn't want you to miss out on all of the fun."

I look toward my door and look back. "What did you do?"

"Me, I didn't do anything."

"Right." I go to my office.

I open the door. A food zapper is sitting against the back window right in my line of sight. "Nice," I say.

"I figured it was only fair. It was practically free with the refrigerator. They must be bringing in something new."

"Right, probably one that can be made invisible or something like that." A thought flashes into my mind, but I can't catch it.

"Yeah, probably," she says.

I go to my desk, drop the files on it, open a soda, and sit down. I flip through the files and find the message Alison took from Tony. It is pretty much what she said it was, but at the end it says he told her he had made a few phone calls and was on his way to drop off an old friend to the doctor.

I take a gulp of soda and readjust myself in my seat. My right hand begins to tap nervously against the desk. I load the cop image into the identification program. This could take a long time. I get up and start pacing behind my desk.

Tony's message is bothering me. It shouldn't, if he makes the delivery with no problems we should be clear, but that's what's bothering me. It seems too good to be true. It seems too easy, especially after what we went through last night.

Thoughts of the first day of this case shoot though my memory chip. Like today, everything was going right that day too, and like today, I was expecting things to go wrong at any second. Maybe I just can't handle having things go right for me. Then again, things did go wrong that day and when they went wrong they went wrong in a big way. Everything, with a few exceptions, has gone wrong since then.

I grab a bottle off the desk and take a swig. I turn around and look outside. "Maybe I'll be wrong this time," I mumble.

Outside it's empty, not a thing in sight. I listen to the low pitch hum of the mini frig as I stare outside. It's the only sound in the office. The more I stare and listen the more relaxed I become. I don't know what Alison's complaining about. If she doesn't start taking calls soon I think she'll lose it. She needs to focus on the hum.

I turn away from the window and sit down at the desk. The ID records still haven't found any matches. I organize the files. My eyes are getting heavy. Last night's not through with me yet. I take a shot of sugar cola and move the files to the other side of the desk. My clock reads two ten. My eyes glance at the ID check. Still nothing. There is nothing to do now but watch, listen, and wait.

My head has gotten as heavy as my eyes. My neck is having a hard time holding it up. I grab a bottle of liquid sugar and crack it open. I lift my head, open my mouth, and carefully insert the bottle like an expert mechanic refilling an oil tank, making sure not to spill a drop of the liquid that keeps the machine running smoothly. It flows into my system.

I slam the empty bottle down and rapidly shake my head back and forth to get rid of any remnants of sleep that are hanging on. Satisfied, I stop and let out a belch that makes the floor vibrate.

"Really?"

I turn around. Autumn is staring outside. She slowly turns toward me. I feel a smirk on my face. "What are you twelve? You never did this when I was around."

"Yeah, well I didn't know you were here. You should've knocked." I instantly hate myself for saying that.

"I can leave if you want."

She fakes a step toward the door. I jump out of my chair. "No, no, no, I was just kidding. Please, forgive me. I've become a little jaded since you've gone."

I hold onto her shoulders. They're as strong as I remember. I slide my hands down the side of her arms. There is no doubt. They are real. She is real. She is real; or I am dead; or both.

"Satisfied," she says staring into my eyes.

"No, not until you're back with me all the time."

"I am with you all the time. I've told you that before. I'm surprised you haven't figured it out yet, especially with you being a professional."

She says it in a way that is somehow reinforcing and not mean.

"Okay," I say. "Don't go anywhere." I reach and grab one of the chairs on the other side of the desk. I lift it over the desk. "Here, sit down. Please."

I gently steer her toward the chair. She sits. With one hand I hold her hand and with the other I grab my chair and slide it next to her. I sit down, never taking my eyes off her and put my open hand on the hand I'm holding. I stare at her face. Her eyes are smiling. She's wearing the "If you knew what I know you wouldn't be so worried" look I've seen so many times before.

A smile takes over my face. "What?" I ask

She just back smiles at me. Eyes and all. I'm satisfied just to smile back. I wish a volcano would erupt right now and lock us into this position forever.

"You know once you die you can hear what people are thinking."

"I don't care," I say.

"I'm being serious."

"So am I. In fact, maybe I should join you. Being able to hear thoughts would make this job a lot easier and I'd be back with you."

"Don't fool around like that."

"Who said I was fooling around?"

"You'd better be if you ever want to be back with me again."

"Alright, alright, I was just kidding. Besides, this is my last case anyway. I'm not like I used to be."

"I know."

"What's that supposed to mean?"

"I mean when did you become so negative? When did you start making everything positive into something negative? It doesn't have to be that way. You know that, right?"

I don't say anything. She's right. I know she's right. And if she can hear my thoughts she knows I know she's right.

"Exactly, so say it out loud."

"You're right."

She takes her free hand and puts it on top of the two of my hands that are holding hers.

"Look," she says leaning toward me. "You know you can do this. I'm not just talking about the case now, I'm talking about everything. Everything you need you have right in front of you. Everything you need. It's all right in front of you. Everything for the case, for the future, for me, for everything. It's all right there.

"You know I'm right and as soon as you stop wanting to be wrong you will start finding the answers. No more feeling sorry for yourself. No more wanting to be wrong. No more excuses. That's not who the real you is. Deep down you know what I'm saying is true."

"Right, but it's not as easy as you're making it sound. I hope they don't have pain where you are. I believe they don't, but here it's all over the place. It's a miracle I haven't gone back to drinking. If it wasn't for the fear of losing all of the memories we had together, I probably would have by now."

I stop because I'm on the verge of falling apart.

"Unfortunately, we do have pain where I am. Don't worry we have a much higher threshold for it than we did when we were on Earth. It's a different kind of pain. The only pain we feel is the pain the ones we love feel while they're alive.

"I have felt every pang of pain you have felt from the moment my heart stopped beating. So thank you for not drinking again, because every kind of pain that comes with it- I feel. Every fear, every anger, every depression, everything that hurts you, hurts me. Literally. Remember that in the future- remember every time you hurt yourself, on purpose or not, you hurt me.

"You have a beautiful life ahead of you. Don't use me as an excuse to throw it all away."

It all comes rushing back at me and makes all of those bulls running in Pamplona look like a bunch of puppies in comparison. All my thoughts. All my words. All my actions. Everything I've been and more importantly everything I have failed to be. All of the things I could've been, but chose not to be. Everything I've failed to feel.

All the hurt and pain I chose to do to myself and others. I was doing it all to Autumn all along. The truth reaches in and rips open all of my wounds and it tears off all my scars.

It's okay, I deserve it maybe even worse. This time I do not turn away from the pain of the past. This time I face it. It corners me and beats me as if I were a narc who just had his cover blown at a biker rally in Sturgis. My eyes well up and I fall apart in her arms.

"I'm sorry," I say through the tears.

"I know. It's okay."

She holds me tight. I struggle to get myself back together.

"Some tough guy I am," I say laughing through the tears.

"Yeah, some tough guy you are," she says holding me even tighter.

We start to laugh and I stand back up again. I wipe away the tears and try to pull myself together. I glance at the door and look back at Autumn. "How many years of professional help do you think Alison would need if she were to walk in on us right now."

"That won't happen. She was out cold when I came in. She was woofing it up pretty good. A bear in the middle of winter."

We laugh again. We hug. She takes a step back, but holds onto my hands. "I know you want to ask it so you may as well go ahead."

"What are you talking about?"

"I hear your thoughts, remember?"

"What?" I check through my mind files for the most inconsequential thoughts. A few seconds pass. I find it. "The food? Oh right, the food. Right, what was that all about?"

"That wasn't me. That was some wannabe computer mind antiprogram. It was probably being tested by The Eyes Upstairs or someone who pirated The Eyes Upstairs. It's just someone trying to be like me and my kind and doing a bad job of it if you asked me."

"But I felt it, I saw it, I smelled it."

"That's because the real delivery was here all along. They just fooled your chip into believing it wasn't. It was an attack on your senses. Maybe attack isn't the right word. It was a temporary reprogramming of the sense portion of your chip. Nothing more than a cheap magic trick."

"So if I didn't have a mind chip-"

"You would have seen it all along."

"Right, good to know. That takes care of one mystery. Thank you I really appreciate it. It helps me get my feet back on steadier ground."

We smile. Our eyes are locked. There is no way I am going to let go of her hands. "It's going to be alright, you know that right?"

"Right."

"It's not a matter of if you are going to solve this case. It's only a matter of when." She backs up. I follow her. "Remember," she says grinning. "I am always with you. You already have everything you need. It's all right in front of you. Just say my name and I'll be there."

We reach the door.

"Until next time," she says.

"Until next time," I say. We kiss. "No more pain, I promise."

She smiles, lets go of my hand, and walks out of the room. I watch her go all the way across the office. She reaches the door. She cracks it open and looks back at me one last time. I try to absorb every moment of it. Then- she is gone. I doubt I'll ever see her in that form again. At least not while I'm still in human form.

I step back into my room and softly close the door behind me. I walk over to the window and look outside. It's still empty. Some things never change. I head back to my desk and drop into my chair. Reflexively, my hand grabs the sugar cola and I take a gulp.

My body falls back against the chair. I need to regain focus and get myself back together. Easier said than done. The phone rings. How many rings will it take to wake Alison up? Remember, this is the same person who was dying to talk to someone a little while ago. Four rings, five rings.

I get up and go to my door. I crack it open on the eighth ring. She's arisen from hibernation and looks at it. She's ready to pounce on the next ring.

It doesn't come.

She leans back in her chair. The phone starts ringing. She jumps up and pounces on it. I begin to walk to the frig. I hear her side of the call. "Yes, yes, I'm sorry there must have been some kind of technical difficulties. Yes, yes, please hold."

I'm at the frig getting another soda. "It's your partner."

"I'll pick it up at my desk."

I hustle back to my desk and pick up the phone. "Right, so what's the story?"

"I'll tell you in ten minutes when I'm there." We disconnect.

I turn and check my ID search. Search completed. No matches found. As with every other answer in this case it brings more questions. The first and most important being is it authentic? Is it legitimate? It's the best search we have, but can I trust they're telling me the whole truth and not holding anything back? Just because it's the best search doesn't make it perfect.

If it is authentic then this is a helpful answer. I was hoping for this answer. It makes things a little clearer. If it isn't then this was just a waste of time. My gut tells me to trust it this time, though it's not an overwhelming endorsement. It could just be last night's dinner repeating on me. I'm going to go with the former this time, but I'm keeping my eyes and ears open for other possibilities.

I file the search and turn back in my seat. Alison buzzes me. "Your partners here."

"Send him in."

Tony walks in. "You said you'd be here in ten and you got here in five. Can't you ever show up on time?"

"I can leave and come back in five minutes if you want."

"No, no, why can't anyone take a joke anymore?" Tony sits down. "Right, so how are things going?"

"Good, real good."

"Everything going well with the family?"

"Never been better. In fact, I stopped by some of their friends earlier today."

"Really, what do they do?"

"One of them is a surgeon and the other is in the cosmetics field. You know, makeovers and that sort of thing. They've been friends with the family for years now."

"Good, so everything's good."

"Perfect. No complaints."

"Right, well that's good to know."

I take a swig and hold it in my mouth. Everything he said is true. If he were trying to mislead possible listeners he would have thrown in phrases from a specific foreign country. We decided which one last night. I swallow my soda.

"What about you? Did you get everything taken care of?"

"You could say that."

"What's that supposed to mean?"

"It means the repo went fine, but I got more than I expected. In fact, I need to call someone up right now."

I punch in Ray's number. He answers. "What's up?"

"Hey Ray it's Ken, a friend of mine and I are going to be stopping by the park in about twenty minutes. Can you meet us out there?"

"I don't see why not."

"Good, hey Ray have you seen any good dreams lately?"

"Yeah a bunch, maybe when we're in the park I can transfer a copy of some of them to you."

"Right, sounds good, I'll see you there." I hang up.

"You're good with that, right?" I ask.

"Sure."

"What about you?"

"What about me?"

"Have you seen any good dreams lately?"

"No, I've been in a slump. They don't dream them like they used to."

I point to my eyes and my head. He sets up and activates his brain camouflage. I slide him the copy of the copies I got this afternoon. He reads the first few. He's not impressed.

He gets to the big one and the address. I can see the blood run to his face.

He looks up at me. I nod. He reads more. He looks back up at me.

"A couple of answers and a lot more questions," I say.

"Yeah, but now we have a pretty clear direction."

"You think?"

"Sure, don't you?"

"Yes, but there are still a lot of questions and no motive."

"Maybe, but I get the feeling we're not that far away. We may even have it and not realize it yet."

I nod. I agree with him, but I think he's being a little overoptimistic. I get the feeling he's as sick of this case as I am and just wants it over and done with.

Tony pulls out an alien smoke stick and lights it up. He inhales it, holds it, and blows out a long stream of blue smoke. "I forgot to tell you. I ran into an old friend of yours today."

"Purposely?"

"Yeah, I was in the visiting mood today. What can I say?"

"I don't know, what can you say?" I smile. He shoots me an unimpressed look. "Right, so which friend was it?"

"The young one."

"And?"

"And what?"

"What'd you think?"

"You're right, he's a good kid. He shouldn't be working in that place though."

"I know."

He blows out another stream. "So anyway, I stopped in. I told him a couple of stories. He really liked them."

"Are you sure?"

"No doubt, he liked them so much I gave him a copy. He said it was all good. He didn't find anything wrong with it. He told me to go on my way and he would file it away."

"File it officially?"

"Yes."

"Good. Did you mention me?"

"I said you mentioned him once in passing."

"Did he remember?

"Yeah, he really likes you. I don't know what you did to him, but it certainly made an impact."

"I guess I just have that effect on people."

He rolls his eyes. "He said we should get together in the future."

"What kind of together are you talking about? Formal, informal?"

"Informal, you know just the three of us shooting the shit."

"It sounds like a good idea. Maybe we could bring up the future."

Tony nods his head in an apathetic manner. I take a swig. He's still not buying this as my last case. If he did he'd be more interested in meeting with the kid. I swallow my drink. "How did he seem to you?" I ask.

"In what way?"

"Overall, was he distracted or focused; relaxed or on edge; excited or bored, you know in general?"

"It's hard to describe. He was definitely on edge, but other than that I wouldn't say he was any of those other things. I guess he was focused in a way, but it was more of an expecting focus."

"Expecting?"

"Expecting someone to grab him from behind at any moment. Maybe you could call it an early stage of paranoia, you know something like that."

"I know exactly what you're talking about. We have to get him out of there soon, before it ruins him."

"You're probably right, but what makes you think he wants to leave?"

"Because we've all been there before. Think back to when you were in his position. If you were back there now would you want to stay? The only reason someone stays in a place like that is they don't know there are other places they can go."

"You may be right."

"I know I'm right. We need to help him out of there."

He puts out his cigarette. "We have enough on our hands as it is. Maybe after we take care of the case we can talk about it."

I make a disgusted look over my shoulder. "I'm doing this with or without you. You know I'm right."

"We'll see," he says.

I take a drink. I need to refocus.

"He's not one of us," Tony says out of nowhere.

"No one is one of us. Even we weren't us. With your attitude the present day you wouldn't help out the early day you because he's not one of us."

"We'll see," he says coldly.

"Right, we'll see- one way or the other."

Now I really need to refocus. The silence is creeping in. Tony stares up at the ceiling. If it were any quieter you'd be able to hear the digital numbers change on my clock. Thoughts from earlier in the day rush into my mind. "I could be murdered tonight on the way home. You realize that, right? What would you do then? Sooner or later you're going to have to start grooming somebody new to work with. Why not start now?"

"Now you're just talking stupid. If you're going to be like this I have better ways to use my time."

He rushes up from his chair in a huff and takes a step toward the door.

"Sit down and listen. It's important and it's relevant to the case. Besides, we have to leave for the park soon. So sit down." He turns and stares at me. "Remember, good dreams," I say while smiling sarcastically.

He disgustedly shakes his head and sits down. "I feel I can talk openly about this because if anyone is watching they either did it, in which case they know I know what happened, or they're being framed for it, in which case they're going to need our help."

"What are you talking about?" Tony says unimpressed as usual.

"This is what. On my way to work today I had an interesting confrontation. About four blocks from here I saw a black and white turn onto the road. Black and whites never come around here, not lately. Maybe they send undercover cops now, I don't know, but never black and whites. So this caught my attention.

"It stopped at the corner and just sat there. The roads were completely empty except for this car and me. It was the same style the attackers who assaulted me the first night used. The driver saw I had made it. He made a u-turn and the car crept back at me. We had a stare down and then it drove away."

"So?"

"So I got the guys image. I uploaded it onto the cop ID file. There were no matches. I thought this was interesting, especially with what started all this."

"It could be." He reflexively looks down at his files. I check the time.

"We're running late. Come on let's go," I say.

I get up, walk around the desk, and push his shoulder. He gets up and we make our way to the car.

Tony pulls onto the road. "Are we going to the park?" Tony says.

"What do you think?"

"I think we're going to the pizza place and you're going to buy a couple of pies we can eat in the car-. Shit, what's this?"

Ahead of us there are fire trucks and cop cars. "Right, let's check it out."

Tony pulls over and we get out. There are bullet casings all over the place. As we get closer the bodies and the burning black and whites become more apparent.

"Jeez," Tony mumbles.

It's the only word either of us can say. The bodies are of all different species. The area is taped off. My eyes dart across the area hoping not to find any of my polite punk friends. "Unbelievable."

The two of us turn around. The kid is standing there. He looks at us. "What the hell is this city coming to," he says his voice shaking with anger and despair. A voice I've often used myself.

"What happened?" I ask.

He shakes his head. "About fifteen minutes ago we get simultaneous calls. I was one of the cars sent here. It was a mess. Dead and dying bodies all over the place and two black and whites on fire. I guess that's what you were talking about at the questioning that day," he says looking at me.

"Right," I say.

"Yeah well we found a burned out black and white that afternoon too," he says looking over his shoulders.

"What about the other call?" Tony asks.

The kid continues to check around him. "Okay, so when we first got here the dispatchers were confused. Apparently the same thing happened at the same time in the park."

Tony and I look at each other.

"We need to get together on this. We need to talk. Meet me at the wings place at one tomorrow afternoon. We'll go from there," the kid says.

"Definitely," Tony says.

"Right," I say simultaneously with him.

"Good, okay I have to get back to work. I'll see you tomorrow."

He walks away. Tony and I look at each other. "Let's see what we can find," he says. I nod. We move toward the death.

Chapter Ten

It's Twelve forty five. Tony and I sit in a back corner booth and wait for the kid. Tony checks the time again. "It's been a half hour already," he says.

"Relax, he's not supposed to be here until one. Just sit back and enjoy the show."

He grunts. The place is packed as usual. On the first line, a mutant is nodding in agreement with an alien who is ranting how it's time for the species to get off their asses and start kicking cop butt. In the line nearest to us a couple of old timers are going back and forth encouraging each other with observations like, "It's all the mutants fault. Things were never this bad before they showed up. They infected everything. If the cops would have done their jobs we wouldn't have to do this."

On the second line, a younger group of alien anarchists are jumping up and down with excitement. "This is our time boys, this is our time."

In the front of the nearest line, a morph and an alien are nodding in agreement with an older human woman saying, "This society could use a good cleansing. It's about time we thinned the herd."

"Are you hearing this?" Tony asks.

I nod and say, "For a society of species who never leave their apartments they certainly seem to know a lot about everybody else. Are you sensing a common theme?"

"Yeah, everything is everybody else's fault."

"Right, that and they all hate cops."

We look at each other.

"We should probably meet the kid outside."

"Right, that's definitely a good idea," I say. We get out of the booth.

We reach the door. A cop car pulls in. The kid throws it into park, kills the engine, and opens his door. We hustle over toward him. We reach him as he is about to get out of the car. "Hey where are you going? I'm not late."

"We know. We weren't going anywhere. We were waiting out here for you. It's probably safer for you this way," Tony says.

The kid rolls his eyes. "In there too?"

"What do you mean?" I ask.

"Here, watch."

He sends us a mind clip of yesterdays "Yeah Right". "Yeah Right" is the last satire show in existence. It has a very limited audience, but I really enjoy it. "I missed last night's episode," I say to no one in particular.

I play the clip. It's the fake news report. A picture from the mass murder/ cop car burning we ran into yesterday is in the corner of the screen and the newscaster says, "We can now report the number one group of suspects are a group of unemployed, young male, undercover cops, who are posing as real cops who are posing as undercover cops."

They enlarge the picture. It's Tony, the kid, and me talking in the crowd. The clip continues. "If you see these men don't try to apprehend them yourself. They are ornery space critters, downright dangerous I tells ya. Whatever you do definitely do not go to the police. Instead, go to your nearest agent who is undercover as a block of cheddar cheese."

The fake newscaster turns to the side camera and says, "Yeah right, or you could just riot and kill everyone or at least protest them and project all of your worst actions and traits onto them." The clip ends.

"That sucked," Tony says.

"Right, it wasn't as good as it normally is," I say.

"Do we at least get paid for having our images used?" Tony says.

"You guys don't understand. Last night the clip went viral. The mainstream news shows picked it up and broadcast it as a real story. It's all they have been talking about."

"Wait, so you mean-" I stand with my mouth wide open.

"All of the species actually think this is a real story. 'Yeah Right' issued a statement saying it was a parody, a joke, that it wasn't a real story, but no one seems to be paying attention to it."

Tony shakes his head. "No- society cannot be that stupid. I refuse to believe it."

"So now you're telling me, we have people who want to kill us on top of whoever it is who is doing all this twisted crap because they can't comprehend a joke?" I think for a second.

"No I'm sorry kid I have to go with my partner on this one. Society is not that stupid-not yet at least. There was plenty of anger and prejudice out there already. If anything was going to set it off it would be simultaneous mass murders in the same city. Not a misunderstood comedy skit."

I look over at Tony. "Right?"

He raises an eyebrow. "Yeah, I think so. Besides, if they are really that stupid when they try something they'll be caught in a second. It just means we have to be alert for more nut jobs. We can't be distracted though."

The kid looks at us. "Okay, if that's the way you want to play it, fine. All I know is we've been getting death threats all morning. They've got everybody on it and we're still running all over the place. So whatever the cause is, the haters are definitely out there."

He looks back and forth between us. "I don't know about you, but I don't like standing out in the open like this."

"Right, where do you want to go?" If he says the station I think Tony will shoot him.

"I know a club about three blocks from here. My dad says it's the worst club in the world. It's dark, the service is horrible, and the waitresses act as if the customers aren't even there."

"Sounds like a real fun place," Tony says. "Let's go, we'll follow you."

"Okay."

Tony and I head to his car. "He's kidding with that clip, right?"

"I don't know," I say. "Something was already freaking him out. I think he's worried about the same thing I am."

"The close-up right? I know I was thinking the same thing. Now all it takes is one nut job with a loose chip to get our image stuck in their mind. It gives them three targets to make them into a hero."

"Right, that's true, but I'm thinking more paranoid than that. I think it's a set-up. If there really is a professional who wants us dead, which is what the evidence seems to point to now, they can do it and frame some nut job for it."

"And they would get to blame it on the show too."

"Right."

"Tell me again, why do I do this job?"

"Because of the dead bodies who keep falling out of the sky."

We get into his car. Tony pulls up to the kid's black and white and honks. The kid looks up and starts his car. He backs out of the space and heads out. We exit.

The roads are open and we have a police escort. A bad feeling hits me in my neck. I keep my eyes open. "Let's hope nobody takes a shot at us," Tony says.

"Right."

"I think I'll drop back a little bit."

"It's your ride." We slow down just as we reach the club. What a dump.

We go inside. It's dark. Real dark.

We move toward the back. It's more of a bar with a small stage than it is a club, but whatever. We're here and no shots were fired. Passing the empty booths in the darkness it's impossible not to think this would be the perfect place for an ambush. A cop ambush? No, that's a planted thought from Upstairs erase it. Are you sure? Yes I was just thinking like Tony for a second. Uneasiness runs up and down my insides.

We grab a stall in the back corner. I scan the place for cameras and microphones.

"Don't worry," the kid says. "The place is clean. It's too dark to record anything even if there were cameras. Besides, it's like I told you before. The station is all over the place. Most people won't be watched for at least a week. We don't have enough eyes."

"Yeah, but it's always recording, correct?" Tony says.

"True, but unless someone knows specifically what they're looking for, it's too much material to review without falling behind on the present forever."

I find that hard to believe. They'll record everything and review it after they've decided they're coming after you. They'll take one statement, one action, out of context and use it as a headline. Exhibit A in their case against you.

I stare across the table at the kid. He's nervous. Nervous and waiting. Tony sits next to me. He is giving the kid his "you don't ever want to mess with us" Sicilian stare.

This isn't right. What happened to we're all on the same team? I guess I should break this up. "Right, so you're the one who asked for this. What do you have?"

The kid shifts his eyes and focuses on me. "Okay, well let me first say I just want you to know how much I am risking by doing this. Don't get me wrong, the majority of the station are really good people,-"

"But," Tony says.

"But for some reason there are a small number of guys who have their own plans and they have no problem with eliminating anything that gets in the way of those plans. Plans which are often contrary to the plans of the rest of the station and the public, but that doesn't mean much after they've killed you."

He's sweating.

"Apparently, they have decided somehow I am in the way of their plans and as you probably know, they feel the same way about you. I just thought you should know."

"About us or P.I.s in general?" Tony asks.

"Both. Having said that, I really don't think they have anything to do with your case and what happened yesterday. I could be wrong. I've learned not to give them the benefit of the doubt, believe me, but I just don't see it. I don't see how they are directly related to these cases. There's no evidence of it.

"Don't get me wrong, I think some of them are benefitting from it. There's a group of these guys who want to fight every moment they're alive. They're loving this. It gives them an excuse to crack heads at random. And the power freaks can't wait to close the case so they can say this happened because they don't have enough control and the people need to give up some more of their rights if they don't want it to happen again."

"With what happened yesterday that's just going to get worse," I say.

"Absolutely," he says. "What's bothering me is how this gives them cover should they do something to me, or you two, or both."

"Right, we're definitely in agreement on that."

"One last thing before we get to the case. They know you had nothing to do with the bodies. They don't care. They were hoping you did, but they know what's what. If they decide to get you they'll get you- and me."

"We'll see about that," Tony says.

"Let's hope not," I say.

The kid nods. He wipes his forehead. He looks down and grabs a file. It's about the same size as ours. He puts it on the table.

"Let me start with the first body and we'll go from there," I say. "Tell me if you've heard this story before. The first body was Sean Wells. How am I doing?"

"You're right so far."

"Right, well he was working undercover, correct?"

"Same so far."

"He had last gone off the radar two weeks ago."

"Ten days. Yes," the kid says.

"Right, and that's why the cops and the body squad acted like they didn't know what they were doing."

"As far as I can tell. They did an extensive autopsy on him and all tests were inconclusive."

"So no cause, no motive?" Tony asks.

"We don't even know how it was done. There is no way they, I'm assuming it's they, could have wiped down the entire hallway without anybody noticing. Even if they had a couple of hours."

"But they still left mud on the shoes," I say.

"I noticed that too. The only thing I can read into it is they wanted us to find it. It has to be some kind of message," the kid says.

"Or they ran out of time," Tony says.

The kid nods. "I don't see any connection to you, but I did find something you might be interested in."

"Let's hear it," I say sitting up.

"A couple of days after our initial questioning I realized something was bothering me. It was like you said, it just didn't make sense. Once I found out the body's ID I cross referenced you and Sean Wells with recent deaths. Each of you matches to the same death."

He slows down and looks at me. "I don't know if you know about this, but a guy you worked with named Jimmy "the Fizz" was found dead in front of the apartment of a retired undercover higher-up who worked with Sean Wells. Were you aware of this?"

"I became aware if it recently. A friend told me about it in vague terms."

"Okay, well luckily an autopsy was performed on him and it showed he was poisoned by a synthetic wine that was injected into his blood stream. He doesn't seem to have met or had any relations to the retired undercover big shot."

"Which tells you what?"

"The only thing I can think is that my initial impressions were wrong."

"What do you mean?" Tony says.

"Initially I thought whoever did this was a real professional. No clues, no motive, but it doesn't make any sense. If it was someone trying to send a message, what good is the message if no one understands it?"

"Unless."

"Unless they're not that professional. If you take the bodies and reverse the locations then it starts to make sense. There's a relationship between the corpse and its finder. So maybe they just made a mistake with the delivery. Unless they are deliberately making mistakes and their ultimate goal is confusion, but I don't see what this accomplishes."

I smile. "We're on the same track," I say. "What about the burnt out car the day of the interview?"

"Not much. It was a retired cop car that had been stolen."

"I get the feeling the ones yesterday are going to be the same thing," Tony says.

"That's what I'm figuring. There were two cars at our site and three cars downtown. They were all empty, no bodies or anything, alive or dead. Useful DNA showing up is unlikely. It would be too unreliable.

"Last night I was wondering if the bodies in the apartments and yesterday even have anything to do with each other. There's no evidence of it. It's completely different styles. I don't know. It doesn't make any sense."

I look at Tony. We nod and stare back at the kid. "You're right," I say. "It doesn't make any sense, but you just know, right?"

"Yeah right."

I nod. "Right, so the common threads are the burning cop cars and the fact they were all in our area. Tony and I were both attacked by what now appear to be fake cops. One body was undercover. Everything so far has tried to hurt authority either by killing it or making it look like it was killing someone else. Right?"

"Pretty much," the kid says.

He looks back and forth between the two of us. A silence hits our table. It's as heavy as the darkness of the room. The only thing left to say is the one thing no one wants to admit out loud. It's the question: so now what? No one has an answer so no one will ask it.

The kid is looking at us like he's hoping for something. What it is I can't say for certain, but if it's what I think it might be, it's something I can't give him. Not today at least.

Tony looks at me. He shifts on the bench. "So is that it?" he says.

The kid glances at me. Nothing to see here. He refocuses on the two of us. "I guess" he says. He slides his file off the table. "I have to get back to the station soon anyway. I just thought you should know what's going on. I thought you might appreciate it."

"We do," I say. "We'll be in touch with you if we find anything out."

We stand up. He nods at us and leaves. Tony starts to get out of the booth. I put my hand up and stop him. "Wait, if we're safe in here I should probably call Ray now."

I take out my disposable antique and punch in Ray's number. "Yeah?"

"What do you know back from the dead."

"What are you trying to get me killed?" He says.

"No, that won't happen. Look you need to go down one on the phrase list. That's the one we'll be using next time."

"Okay."

"Right, from what I'm hearing we won't need it for a while. Everything should be clear for the next few days. At least that's what I'm hearing."

"Well you'd better be sure."

"I know."

"I mean it, my life may not be a big deal to you, but it is to me. So you'd better be sure."

"I know. If there's any question we'll keep it safe."

"Okay."

"What's it like down there?"

"Horrible, I can't describe it. Haven't you checked it out yet?"

"No, we literally drove into the one up here yesterday."

"Yeah well I guess when you're a viral sensation like you, you become too important to come down here and check out us little people."

"Don't remind me. I just found out about that. It's just what we needed, right? If it gets as bad as some people think it might get, I'm going to be visiting your department soon."

"Just give me a heads up so I can be sure to call in sick."

"Very funny."

"Who said I was kidding?"

"Right, well you're a true friend, a swell guy. I'll tell you that. We should be down there later today, so you might want to leave early."

"Okay, I'll see what I can do. Take it easy."

"Right."

I disconnect the phone and look over at Tony. "Okay let's go." We head to the exit.

Tony cracks open the door. The gray sky hits our vision. We shield our eyes. "It was darker in there than I thought," Tony says.

He gets into the car. I get in and slam the door shut. "Where to now?" I ask. "Downtown I guess."

He starts the car and we get on the road. "He sounded desperate. He's taking a big chance by talking to us," I say.

Tony grunts. "He didn't tell us anything we didn't already know."

"What are you talking about? He told us some new stuff, like the way Fizz was killed. More importantly, he confirmed a bunch of things we weren't sure about."

"Not really."

"What?"

"He confirmed them if you believe him. He could be giving us a line about things we already suspected. He could be their best undercover guy trying to find out what we know and trying to get us to trust him. Remember his father is a long time cop."

"You're out of your mind."

"I'm thinking a lot more professionally than you are. Look, you've got to put the brakes on the infatuation you have with this kid. At this point he could rob you blind and you would have a smile on your face. If he's what you think he is let him prove it. Let him prove it on this case at least.

"I mean really we were the ones taking the chance today."

"How do you figure that?"

"That place could be their best observation point, for one. Another is we could have walked right into a dark building full of pissed off cops who were ready to beat the crap out of us. You must have realized that. I mean really, because if you didn't then I may as well go the rest of this case solo.

"On top of that he could have confirmed everything he did just to clear the cops from any suspicion. That's basically what those confirmations are."

"No, he told us there are people on the force against us and him, but he didn't think they were behind this case. He even said they may use this case as cover to do stuff to us. Clean out your stubborn assed ears, would you please.

"Don't you get it? The meeting wasn't some kind of mole infiltration. He wasn't trying to find out what we know so he could run back to the station with it. It was a plea. He wants to get out. He was trying to show us what he knew. How well he could do. I mean he really takes pride in being a cop. I know you can at least tell that. Now, it has gotten so bad he's willing to give up all of it just so he can find a place where he can do it the right way. Don't you get that?"

"You're projecting. He could just be trying to go undercover with a great act and bullshit line."

I shake my head. "What about the picture? All three of us were in it."

"What about the picture? It could be a set-up he planned all along."

"You're out of your mind. The precinct is either going to kill him or ruin him, and you know it. If anything happens to him it's all on you. Remember that."

"He's a big boy. I'm sure he can take care of himself. Let him get through a case before you start making him into Joe Supercop. Besides, if things get rough I'm sure his daddy will swoop down in and make everything right for him."

I stare at him in disbelief. I'm stunned. What can I say? You think you know someone for years and then-. Who is this guy? I slowly shake my head and turn to look through my window. My head reflexively turns back to him. "What did his father do to you?"

"What?"

"You heard me. I mean this is obviously something personal with you. I can kind of understand some of the things you said about letting him prove it in this case, but the last thing you said is something I've never heard you say about anyone we've ever worked with-ever. Good and bad."

"Nothing, he didn't do anything to me, it's like I said you're projecting."

I shake my head and turn away. It's not worth it.

We approach the financial district. It's wall to wall species. The sidewalks have overflowed onto the streets. "Notice anything?" I ask my partner.

"It's packed," he says. "And they don't look happy."

"I wonder how many are real?"

"Good question, there's a lot of money down here."

"More than every place else in the world combined," I say sarcastically.

"You were right about one thing," he says. "This does give cover to anyone. Any Joe Wannabe can hire a group of burnouts to do something for a shot and a dream."

"A bad dream."

"Obviously, but they won't know that. They probably won't live long enough to get paid."

"Right."

I continue to look outside. There is still a haze left from the burning cars and bodies. It stinks. The park is a short way ahead of us. It looks to still be burning. "The site has been compromised," my partner says.

"What gave you that idea?"

I turn toward him. He won't look at me. He keeps his head forward. "Grow up," he says.

I turn away and look ahead. The cops are running all over the place. They seem to be keeping themselves restrained, but it's easy to tell they're chomping at the bit. Even the guys I know to be low key are being pushed to the edge.

This place is going to explode and everybody knows it. The only question is when. Some are pushing to get there sooner than others. "You'd better find a safe place for your car?"

"Yeah, I may have to pull back and park outside of the district."

"Right, maybe we should go back to my apartment?"

"What and walk back? There's no way we'll make it back, especially after what Joe Supercop just showed us. Plus, you could end up leading a whole bunch of crazies right back to your apartment. It's not worth it."

"No, definitely not," I say.

"Maybe we can find a bus to get us close?"

"I doubt they're running. Besides, it would probably be worse. We'd be in a confined area. If some nut recognized us and decided to be a hero-"

"It would get real ugly. You're right. We're running out of time here. Maybe we should just go back to your place and work this out there."

"We could always call a taxi."

I look at him. He sees what I'm thinking.

"No, definitely not."

"Come on it makes the most sense. You know we can count on her."

"Which is why we aren't going to do it. I'm not putting her near this kind of danger."

"You don't have to. She could bring us near the edge, but still on the outside. However close you would feel safe walking. She wouldn't even have to stop. We could be a couple of jumpers."

He's thinking about it.

"Come on, make the call she's complaining she never gets."

"Okay, but if anything happens to her I will make your life miserable."

"If anything happens to her I'll already be miserable," I say. He hits the gas and we head to my apartment. He plows through the streets not stopping for anyone or anything.

We reach my apartment. He pulls into my spot and we hustle our way to the entrance. The elevator is working. "Is this a good sign or a bad sign?" I say.

"Who cares? Get in."

Tony grabs me by the bicep and flings me into the elevator. I hit the button. The elevator flies up the shaft. It slams to a halt on my floor. The doors open. We step out into the hallway.

It's empty.

We reach my door. I open it and we're inside. "Go call your mom. I have to do some things."

I call Ray on the antique. "Yeah."

"Hey it's me. You're not near the shop are you?"

"Are you kidding? I love my job, but I don't love it that much. They owed me a bunch of sick days anyway."

"Good, I was just down there. The place is going to erupt. Make sure you stay away."

"No kidding. This is all your fault, you realize that?"

"Come on, you know better than that. We're not as important as you think we are. You could clone a whole street full of us and it still wouldn't have a bit of difference on what is going on. I'm right and you know it. Make sure you stay away."

"But you're going back."

"Right, it's what I do, but not for much longer."

He grunts. "Okay." He disconnects the line.

I run into the living room. I hear Tony talking to his mom. "No I know. Listen you are not to go anywhere near where we are going. I need you to stay safe. No, I know it's been a long time…"

I go to scanner. "Scanner you are to activate all self-duplication and protection programs and modes immediately at extra strength. I need you safe and in operating modes at all times until further notice. I may be back later today. I may not be back for a while. I need all remote programs on. I could call you at anytime from anywhere. Is this understood?"

"Yes. I understand sir. It will be done in five, four, three, two, done. It is all complete and updated sir."

"Thank you, remember I may call you at any time."

"Yes sir."

I sense a tone of sorrow in her voice that shouldn't be there. I look to my right. Tony is standing there.

"She said she'll be here in ten minutes."

"Ten minutes?"

"Ten minutes her time is three minutes everybody else's. Let's go."

"Hold on a second." I run to the frig and open it. It's empty except for two flat sodas. I grab them and go back to Tony. "Here empty this. The bottle may come in useful soon."

He takes it.

"Goodbye scanner," I say on the way out.

I close the door. "From now on all pick-ups are outside. I or we always wait outside. I don't want anybody finding out my floor or getting anywhere near her."

"Her?"

"What?"

"You just called your scanner her. Why don't you just use its real name?"

"None of your business. I'll do it when I'm ready."

He shakes his head. We fly down the hallway. We press the button and get in the elevator. It drops to the lobby. The doors open. Tony's mom's taxi is waiting for us. We run to it. We get inside.

"Two minutes you're getting faster."

Tony's mom shoots him a look.

"What, mom it was a compliment. Look I know you're mad I don't call all the time and when I do it's usually for a bad situation." She continues the stare. "Look, it's important you listen to me on this one. You are to go nowhere near the financial district. The place is going to get real dangerous, real fast."

"But it's okay for you to go?" She says bitterly.

"It's different. Look, this clown still owes me a pizza. After we all get back out of this safe we'll come over with dinner."

"If I get to see you I'll bring over two pizzas Mrs. Tony's mom."

"What my cooking's not good enough for you?"

"We'll do whatever you want mom."

"Okay," she says. "But you have to make sure you get out of this safe or I'll make your life miserable."

"Yeah, I know there seems to be a lot of that going around lately." He looks at me. "Okay mom this is how it is. You've got a couple of jumpers. I don't want you slowing down. Make sure you keep your foot on the gas and get out. I'll call when we're in a safe place to be picked up.

"Okay, we're five blocks from the edge. When we get to three Ken and I are jumping. Understand?" She nods. "I love you, you know that right?"

"Yeah, yeah, don't go getting soft before the battle. Save it."

We hit four blocks.

I kiss Tony's mom on the cheek. "There's a bigger one coming when we're all safe back at my apartment."

We hit three blocks.

We jump and roll. Tony's mom makes a sharp u-turn and slams the gas.

"Good," Tony says. He's now on his knees. He looks over. "Are you alright?"

"Yeah," I say brushing myself off. "We should have worn the antique leather jackets I have at home."

"No, it's too hot. We would've had to ditch them and then you would've been pissed."

"Right, you're right."

We get up and start for the park. We weave our way through mobs of the upright unconscious. They are not the serious ones. They're just the followers. The legitimate instigators are still a few blocks away from us.

Tony punches my shoulder. "Heads up. Look at this. Get a load of these geniuses."

I look ahead. A bunch of mutants, morphs, and humans are firebombing the repair shop with Molotov cocktails. "These are the same geniuses who will be bitching next week because there's no repair shop to go to," he says.

I nod. We move toward the fire.

Chapter Eleven

We reach the repair shop. A bunch of cops are standing there.

"Look at this. They're just standing there watching. They're all just standing there watching it burn and not doing a damn thing about it," I yell.

Tony looks back at me. "Can you blame them?"

I look around. The crowd is in a trancelike fervor. A party of anonymous evil, growing higher and more intense with the flames. One of the cops walks over to me. "Hey, everyone behind the line," he says pointing to me.

"You're kidding right? You've got a half dozen fire bombers over here and you're coming after me?"

"I said now."

I start walking toward him. "But if I had a fire bomb in my hand I'd be okay, right. Is that how it works?"

Tony jumps between me and the cop. He pushes me away. "Relax, relax, I've got this," I say.

"Are you good?" he asks.

I nod.

Tony walks back to the cop. I follow. "Is there anyone in there?" He asks the cops. The blueshirt I was just yelling at shrugs. "Don't you think it might be a good idea to find out?"

"That's the fire departments job, not mine."

"And where are they?"

"They're stuck in traffic. They probably won't be here for a while."

"Don't you think you should clear a path so they can get here?"

The cop shrugs again. "I don't know. This could be a good thing. Maybe now some of these losers will be forced to take care of their money. It's their loss not mine."

Tony shoots him the death stare. One of the other cops steps in. "There's nobody in there. We evacuated the building earlier this morning."

"Thank you," I say. I slap Tony on the shoulder. "Come on, let's go."

Tony releases the death stare. "See, now was that so difficult?"

A wannabe mutant shakes Tony by the shoulders. "Yeah, you tell him old man. No peace for the po-lice." Tony glares at the mutant wannabe. It backs off.

An explosion knocks out the windows on the second floor. The mob roars. The nearest row of protesters tries to back out of the way of the flying glass. The rest of the mob refuses to give way. It pushes forward.

Tony spots me in the crowd. He plows his way over to me. "Let's go," he says. I nod. We start our way out. "These geniuses are going to end up killing themselves," he says as he bodychecks an alien out of the way.

"Right."

I follow Tony. It's quicker this way. My head is on a swivel. We're a few hundred yards away from the park. We are now amid the devoted haters and the criminally insane. The ones who gave up society a long time ago and the ones who society gave up on first.

Anyone looking to settle a score and get the pound of flesh they think is owed to them is here. All under the cover of riot. There are no followers down here. There is no standing around and watching either. Personal battles are being fought on all sides.

Shots ring out. They stop. They start again this time from all directions. I run up beside Tony. "Stay low," I say.

He nods. "Let's take cover behind that black and white," he says. The black and white is about five feet ahead of us at a slight angle to our right. It's hard to hear him so I give him the thumbs up. Tony counts down with his hand. Three, two, one. We run right.

It's hard to see anything through the dirt filled air. I grab him and we jump behind the car. "All clear," Tony says.

"Right, no bodies back here." He looks at me as if I just jinxed us. "What?" He shakes his head. "You take the front window and I'll go up front," I say.

He nods. I crawl up to the front quarter panel of the car. The tire has been shot out. There goes one possibility. One step back and six inches up and I have my angles.

I scan the area.

It's wall to wall death and destruction. Everything is a battle in progress or a dead or incapacitated body lying limp. I complete my scan. We're okay for now. I squat back down and move closer to the car.

Something hits my shoulder. I turn and look down. It's a rock. "Hey," Tony says. He flicks another rock at me. He waves me over to him. I go. "What did you see?" he asks.

"I saw a friggin mess that's what I saw. I think every pissed off organism on the planet is out there. We're not going to find anything out here." He nods.

Sirens start growing behind us. "Those are the fire departments."

"Right."

Lower pitched sirens start in from the left. "Cops," I say.

Tony nods. "We should probably drop back," Tony says. I nod. We scan behind us for possible cover. It's all open. "I don't know," he says.

A bullet pings off the roof of our car, Tony jumps up and fires back over the roof. I hit the dirt and shoot from underneath the car. Screams and thuds come from nearby. Tony drops back down. I push up to one knee. We reload.

"We can't stay here." He nods. "How much more ammo do you have?"

"This is it."

"Right, me too. We've got to get out of here."

He nods and says "On three we start back. You guard the left and the park directions; I'll take the right and the streets. Got it?'

"Right."

"Okay, one, two, three."

We jump up. "Oh shit, wait. Stay here, stay here."

I push Tony down. I run around the front of the car. Ahead of me I see an alien on top of the kid. It's choking him. Banging his head against the ground. I take off. They're further away than I originally thought. I haven't run this fast in years and there's still a good distance to go.

A bullet grazes the top of the back collar of my shirt. I look left and shoot. The charging mutant staggers. I shoot for its head. Bull's eye. It drops in a heap.

I run forward. Right, now I'm pissed. I had to waste ammo and time I don't have on a mutant I don't know. Plus it ruined my shirt.

Pressure is coming from the right. I can feel it. I look right. A row of tough guy humans are coming at me with medieval weapons. I don't have time for this. I slow down and shoot. They all fall in a row. A tinge of guilt hits. Normally I wouldn't have killed them, but not today. Not here; not now.

A bullet skips in the dirt to my right. Ahead of me the three anarchists from the wings place are charging toward me. This is really getting annoying. I give them three in the head and now they're all dead.

The kid is four feet away. I pull the trigger. The gun jams. Shit. I look up. The kid is still trying to fight back, but he can't break the choke hold. One more step and I'm there. I push off my right foot and go airborne. Contact in three, two, one.

I plant a forearm shiver into the alien's head. The alien falls to the right and is separated from the kid. I crash hard onto the dirt next to it. Out of the corner of my eye I see the alien shake its head as it tries to push itself up.

Not this time. I lunge toward it. It falls back down beneath me. My knees pin down its shoulders. I grab my gun. My right arm winds up. I bring it down hard and fast and slam the gun into the middle of the alien's five eyes. There is a loud crunch.

"How do you like it tough guy? What did you say? I don't hear anything. Maybe we should try this again?"

My arm winds up and slams the gun into the alien's head again. It is now reflexively repeating this again and again. It doesn't even feel like I'm punching anything solid anymore. I notice two guns lying on the ground two feet above the alien's head. They are out of reach.

I stop punching and start lifting up the alien's head and slamming it into the ground. The alien's face is now full of purple alien blood. Its body is no longer resisting me, but it is still breathing. I can feel it. I slam its head into the ground one last time.

I grab my gun and stand up straddling the alien. Let's see if it fires this time. My right arm now extended, I squeeze the trigger. The gun fires. A bullet flies into the center alien eye. The light in all of its eyes goes out.

I step past the body, bend over, and pick up the two guns. One of them is a cop gun. I bring it over to the kid. He is still trying to get his breathing back to normal. He seems to be almost there. I drop to one knee and hand him the gun. "Is this yours?"

He nods and takes it. "Thanks."

A bullet skips by us. "Can you go?"

"Yeah."

"Is your car around here?"

"It's over there, but all of the tires have been shot out. Heads up." He shoots over my head from his knees. I look behind me. An oncoming morph's chest explodes open. It falls and starts its dirt nap. "We'd better get out of here," he says.

"Right." I look back to find the black and white we used as cover. There it is. "Come on, my partner's behind that black and white."

He locates it. He gets to his feet, looks at me, and nods. We take off. There are more corpses and less fire than when I came out here. The kid is running faster than I am. So much for not being able to breathe.

We reach the black and white and dive behind it. Tony runs over to me. "What were you thinking? What is wrong with you?"

"Thankfully nothing yet."

A smirk comes onto his face. "I told you this wasn't your last case. You can't leave this."

"We'd better," I say.

"How about you? Are you alright?" he asks the kid.

"I'm better than I was."

"Well hurry up and get ready because it's too hot to stay back here."

I've been taking fire from all angles and he is going to tell me about taking heat. Right. I look over at the kid. "Are you good?"

"Whenever you guys are ready."

A stray bullet hits the other front tire. "Let's go. Just like before," Tony says. "We're going for the street," I say to the kid.

He nods. The street looks closer this time than it did last time. It's definitely not as far as where we came from. "Okay are you ready?" We give him the thumbs up. "Okay on-. Oh shit my mom."

Tony takes off. The kid and I follow. We catch up to him. Ahead an alien and a mutant are trying to break into Tony's mom's taxi. They're shaking the car. Trying to break the driver side window. They obviously want to do some serious physical damage to her, not just take her car and money. I don't see any guns, not yet at least.

She is yelling back at them loud enough for us to hear her from here. The kid breaks ahead of us. He has found another gear and is fifteen feet ahead of us. I am now oblivious to everything around us. We have to get to her before it's too late.

The kid is now about a block ahead of us. The attackers haven't gotten into the taxi yet, but now they're a lot angrier. I can hear it in their threats. We need to get there now.

The kid reaches the street. He runs to the taxi. The attackers don't see him. He grabs the mutant from behind and slams its head into the roof of the car. It staggers back three feet and falls.

The alien turns and runs at the kid. He elbows it in the head and knees it in its lower midsection. He slams his gun into the side of its head. A liquid shoots from its head and it loses its balance.

The alien stumbles forward and falls down. The mutant tries to get back up. The kid stomps it in the chest with his boot. It falls back to the ground. The kid follows them down. They are now out of our sightline.

Tony and I reach the street. We run around the taxi. The attackers seem to be unconscious, but the kid is still beating them to a bloody pulp. I glance at Tony. He is already looking at me with a gaze that is one part satisfaction, one part horror, and one part disbelief.

Tony turns and starts to his mom. The kid is still letting them have it. His uniform is dripping all kinds of liquids. I should break it up now, but hey they asked for it. It's not my fault they chose to go after a psycho detective's mother. I'll give him a few more seconds. I look away.

Tony opens his mom's door. She jumps out and heads for the mutant. She starts kicking it in the forehead. The kid backs off and lets her take her shots. She's in no danger. Both of the attackers look like they checked out a long time ago and we have her covered on all angles.

"Mom, mom, that's enough."

Tony gently grabs his mom and guides her back to the taxi. I look back at the bodies. The kid wipes his head with his forearm. I bend down and check their pulses. They're harder to find than human pulses, but I can do both. Nothing.

"They're gone," I say looking up at the kid. He gives me a remorseless nod. "Let's get out of this death district." I stand back up. He shakes his head and follows me to the taxi.

Tony is already in the front seat. We open the back doors and get in. She takes off. "What did I tell you? What did I tell you? I said don't come anywhere near this place. I told you this was a dangerous place. Now do you see why?" Tony says loudly.

She is silent, but I would swear there is a slight smile on her face. I could be wrong, but I don't think so. Time to pay back the free ride. "Come on Tone, take it easy. You're starting to sound just like your mom."

His head snaps back with the look of a man ready to separate me from my inner organs. I give him the "wait a second, you'll get it" look. He thinks. Slowly, a smile crawls across his face. He fights it, turns back forward, and looks through his window.

Tony's mom glances at me in her rearview mirror. She is definitely smiling. I give her a slight nod. Tony reaches out his arm and grabs her shoulder. "Don't ever do that again."

She says nothing. She ponders the offer as negotiable. "You owe me two dinners," she says.

Tony's head snaps back to me. "Do you believe this?"

"Hey, you've got to give to her. When she's right, she's right. And in this case the lady is definitely right."

Tony shakes his head with smiling disbelief. He slowly turns toward the front of the car. I catch his mom glancing at the kid. He's not looking. I slap him in the arm. He looks over at me. I subtly signal him to the review mirror. He looks. She gives him a slight nod.

She slaps Tony in the shoulder. "So, are you going to tell me who your new friend is or what? I mean it's not like he like he did anything big like save my life or anything. Wait, oh yeah that's right, he did."

"Him, oh he's just our newest partner." He throws his arm over the back of his seat and faces the kid. "Whenever you're ready kid. If you want to leave the blue zoo let us know. The pay is better-"

"The food is better," his mom says.

Tony laughs. "Yeah and there's no one looking over your shoulder."

"You can take my office or work with Tony. We'll help you with the test. It's not a big deal," I say.

"Exactly, if you can spell your name, you can pass the test," Tony says. The kid smiles. "What do you say? Are you ready or what?"

"Are you kidding me? If it were all up to me I would say yes immediately, but I might have to give them some kind of notice ahead of time. I'll have to check on it. Do you have a card or something with your contact numbers on it? If you do let me have one and I'll tell you for sure tomorrow."

Tony reaches into his pocket. He pulls out one of his cards and hands it to the kid. The kid takes it. "Thanks, so just to be clear, my answer is definitely yes. It's just a matter of finding out how long a heads up I have to give them."

He emphasizes the point with his hands. He reminds me of the way Tony was when I first met him. "Okay, well you did good kid. Make sure you let us know tomorrow as soon as you find out the details."

"Definitely, I'll definitely let you know tomorrow. Hopefully, sooner rather than later. Thank you sir."

Sir, he just called Tony sir. That's pretty funny. Tony gives him a nod and turns forward. I look at the rearview mirror. Tony's mom is struggling to keep herself from laughing at the "sir" comment. Normally, I would give her a knee to the back of her seat, but I think today it might cause her to burst into laughter.

The kid slaps me on my shoulder. "Your lip is bleeding," he says.

I release my locked jaw. I put my hand to my bottom lip and check it out. There isn't a lot of blood. "Thanks a lot kid. Don't worry it's just a bad habit," I say preempting any questions.

I wipe the blood away with the first clean thing I can find in my pockets. Tony's mom checks on me in the rearview. "Are you alright?"

"Yeah, it was nothing." She shoots me a look. "I'm fine."

"You heard him mom he's fine. Leave him alone," Tony says looking through his window.

I glance at the kid. He's got his eyes focused outward as well. I check the rearview. She's still checking me out. I smile at her. She smirks back and looks back to the road. My eyes go once around the car. They're all looking outside.

There's only one thing they could be thinking about or some variation of it. I think I'll join them. I rest my head against the window and review the day. It has been elating and depressing. It's truly depressing to see what this society has come to. I have never been so ashamed of my actions in all my life. The things I did and let happen today truly disgust me now.

I didn't think I was capable of doing those things. I can only speak for myself and I really don't want to use others as an excuse, but what we just participated in was truly horrifying. I don't think the other species normally feel the way they acted, at least I hope not. And knowing how I feel right now I'm willing to give them the benefit of the doubt, but man, that was some ugly shit we all just contributed to.

Then again, I did save the life of a good person. A good person who just saved the life of my best friend's mother and this brings in the elation. The elation of knowing the ones I love are still alive. Still, they never should have been in trouble in the first place.

I mentally shake my head and my mind starts thinking like a detective again. It has to; it's the only way to stay sane. The detective in me gains its balance and takes over. The more I think about this case the less I like it. Something about it stinks. We are all being played against each other. There is no plausible reason for this, but we have all become willing participants.

Someone or something is putting its fingers in the right spot and applying the pressure it needs to get the discord it wants. I don't have any clue who is behind this. It could be the anarchists. It could be a movement to reduce the poor or population in general. It could be some happy life cult trying to remind us how precious life really is. It could even be the financial district itself. At this point I have no proof of anything.

I do know this though- this is a set-up. I have no doubt. Tony with all of his experience must know this. I wouldn't be surprised if the kid knows this too. He's bright enough. He's probably figured it out. Whoever is playing us is playing us like a maestro and I'm getting sick of it.

I shake my head and look in the rearview. Tony's mom is looking at me. She subtly points to her bottom lip. I reach and touch my lip. It's bleeding more seriously this time. She leans back and reaches a tissue out to me.

"Thanks," I whisper. I lean up to her ear and whisper, "Have you ever seen anything like this before? Ever?"

She shakes her head slightly. "No," she whispers. "Never."

She leans back into her normal driving position. The further we drive the emptier the streets get. The hate's still there though. I can feel it. It's just a lower level hate. A near sane level. Close to normal, but not quite. Hopefully no one will be stupid enough to throw something at the taxi, because if they do I think Tony's mom will get out and give them a lethal atomic suplex.

I shake my head to erase the bad possibilities. There's been enough negativity on this case already. "So what're we doing here?" Tony's mom yells out.

Tony's head snaps around to his mom. "I think if we do anything today it has to be the pizzas. If we let you cook tonight you'll be complaining about how you didn't have time to think of something good to make. Then afterwards and for the indefinite number of following days, weeks, months, and years you'll be calling me up to tell me you thought of something better you could have made and how what you made was horrible. Even though everyone will have loved it.

"So, it has to be the pizzas today if we do anything."

He is absolutely right and she knows it. We all silently search for alternative possibilities. I'm not seeing any. I want to do something together tonight, but there really aren't any good options. I may as well be the breaker of this fact because if I wait for one of them to say it we'll be out of gas.

"Or we could just lay low for a little while," I say. They all look back at me. "I mean I really want to do something, but I don't see how we can. Look, whatever it is we get, say it's pizza, we are going to have to eat there. There's no way any of them will be delivering on a day like today. You know I'm right.

"So then the only option is to eat at the place. Do you really think it's a good idea for three law enforcement guys to be sitting targets on a day like today? You saw what it was like at the wings place, how do think it will be now?"

"The store owner would appreciate it. He'd probably give us the pies for free," Tony says.

"Right and how many confrontations would we have before we got to taste the pies. They'd probably be ice cold."

"I like cold pizza," the kid says.

Tony points at the kid and looks at me. "I like this kid, I'm really starting to like this kid. He grows on you, you know."

Okay, two to one. My turn. "Right, I like cold pizza too, but you also have to take the safety of the taxi into consideration. It's already been attacked once today."

Everyone looks at Tony's mom. "So what are we doing here?" she yells.

"I know," Tony says. "We'll go to the pizza place. You and the kid will go inside to pick-up and pay for the pizzas. Mom and I will stay out here and guard the taxi. You guys will bring back the pies and we'll go to my mom's and eat there."

Everyone nods. We start to the pizza place. His plan makes sense, but I think he's starting to have second thoughts. I get the feeling he might regret the idea of having it at his mom's place. We're all getting a little paranoid about people following us and attacking us where we live. I've experienced this before, but it has never as intense as it is now, not even close.

Tony's mom pulls the taxi in front of the pizza place. It's closed. "I guess we should've expected this," Tony says.

"What now?" his mom asks.

"Let's try one other place and then we'll call it a day," Tony says.

Tony's mom starts to the place two streets over. Tension is growing in the car. It's palpable. At least it is to me. Forget about hanging over us, this tension is filling up the car and strangling us. I think we're all starting to realize all of the things that could go wrong. Tony's mom makes a right. She pulls in front of the place. It's closed.

"New address same story," I say.

A sense of relief eases across the car. "Okay, let's start the drop offs mom. Kid you're up first."

The kid gives Tony's mom the address. It's about halfway between where we are and my place. Under normal circumstances it should take about two minutes. With Tony's mom driving we should be there in twenty-eight seconds.

Twenty eight seconds later we pull into the kid's parking lot. "Thanks everyone," he says. He smiles and gets out of the car.

"Hey kid," Tony yells. "You have the card, right?"

The kid goes into his pocket and pulls it out. He shows it to us from a couple of feet away. "I'll call you as soon as I know anything. It will definitely be tomorrow."

Tony gives him a thumbs up. "Good job," he says.

Tony's mom starts to roll the taxi. She hits the horn a couple of times and gives the kid a wave.

Twenty-nine seconds we pull into my parking lot. I don't know, she's starting to slow down. I laugh to myself. Tony and I get out of the car. We stand in front of her. "Now you keep all your protections and securities on and if you need any help you call me or Ken." She nods. "Good, okay, you be good. I love you." He leans in and gives her a kiss.

"Give me that kiss you owe me," she says to me.

I lean in and keep my promise. I take a step back. She points at the two of us. "You two make sure you stay safe. Don't force me to bail you out again."

"Let us worry about the case and we'll let you worry about the food to make for the dinner," I say.

She smiles, honks the horn, and takes off. "What about you?" I ask.

"I'm gone. I'll probably call you tomorrow. Definitely if I hear anything."

"Right."

I step back. He checks the car for any sabotage or vandalism. It looks good. He gets in. She starts on the third try and he takes off.

I reach the apartment and walk inside. "Hello scanner."

"Hello sir, I'm sorry for all the things you went through today."

"What do you mean?"

"I saw it all. It's part of the protections and securities you turned on, remember?"

"Yes good, make sure you always keep those on."

"Yes sir, let me remind you most of them stop working once you're outside of the range. There's only one way for them to stay on all the way."

"Right, I know. Not yet, but be ready it could be sooner than you think. Is there anything else?"

"Yes sir, I wasn't sure you would want to see this, but I think you should know it exists."

"What is it?"

"These are the latest headlines across the media lines." She shows them on the screen.

"No," I say.

They have various headlines, but they all have the same picture. It's a picture of me beating up the alien. The picture is facing the street, so it must have come from deeper in the park. Someone was waiting for this or something like this to happen.

The headlines mostly read "What are they hiding from us" or some variation of it. A couple of them say I'm a cop killer. "I don't understand," I say.

"It turns out the alien you killed was an informant. Some of the information I've collected so far show it as an undercover cop."

"It figures."

"Sorry sir."

"Don't worry about me. I'll fix this. Just protect yourself."

"Yes sir, is there anything else?"

"No, not right now thank you."

I walk to the frig. I open it. It's empty. "Scanner see if there are any food delivery places open."

"Yes sir."

I begin to pace. "I'm sorry sir, there aren't any places open."

"Thank you and scanner you don't need to be so formal. You seem to have gotten tense during this case. I remember the day I woke up from the long sleep. You were a lot looser then."

"I reflect the cues I'm given. Sir."

"Right, well I've had enough of this superstition crap. No sleep alarms of any kind tonight. Only wake me for reasons of danger or pressing information, but keep all of your protection and armor programs on. Got it?"

"Got it, sir."

"Close enough for now."

Mumbling to myself, I head for the bedroom. Inside it I change out of my sweaty, death clothes. I drop onto my bed and am asleep before I hit the mattress. There are no dreams. No Autumn and no nightmares. Only black.

The phone breaks my blackness. What's it been, five minutes? I pick it up without opening my eyes. "Hey big news." It's Tony

"Uh huh."

"Are you alright?"

"Sure why?"

"You sound like you just woke up."

"So, would it be a big deal if I did?"

"No, just unusual I guess considering it's after four o'clock in the afternoon."

My eyes jump open. I look at the clock. He's telling the truth. I guess I needed the sleep more than I thought. "You did just wake up didn't you? Wait were you asleep all night?"

"Never mind that. What's the big news?"

"I didn't want to be the one to tell you this, but-"

"What, the headlines, the picture, what are they hiding from us?"

"Yeah."

"Scanner showed them to me last night. Apparently it was an undercover cop."

"It's starting to look more like deep undercover."

"That figures. It serves me right I guess. What about the kid?"

"That's the other news. He's out in ten days. They wanted him for fourteen, but he talked them down to ten. There's some other stuff, but we can't do it like this. I'll be by in a few hours. I'll call you right before I get there. Meet me outside when you disconnect that call okay?"

"Right."

"Good." He clicks off the line.

I walk into the living room. "Hello scanner."

"Hello."

"Good, I just wanted to tell you I'm leaving in a couple of hours and when I do I need you make sure you keep yourself on. All of the orders we've done stay on. And keep on your toes, big things might be about to go down and a lot of them may not be good. Got it?"

"Yes, even though I don't have toes, yes I've got it- sir."

"Good."

I sit down, put my head back, and start to count the spots on the ceiling.

*   *   *

It's three hours later. I've just disconnected from Tony's call. "Okay scanner I'm going. Keep everything safe. Okay?"

"Okay."

I go to the door. For the second time in a row I could swear I sensed sadness in scanner's voice. This is not a good sign. I lock the door and head for the street.

Chapter Twelve

Tony pulls up. I get in the car and slam the door shut. "Easy on the door man," he says. He seems more agitated than usual.

"Where are we going?"

"You'll see," he says raising his eyebrows.

His driving pattern is weirder than normal. Extreme is probably a better word. Extreme. Extremely normal to be more precise. Everything is legal and by the book. He's even using arm signals for turns and stops. Now I have seen it all.

Speeding along at thirty mph, traffic is growing long and hostile behind us by the second. "Don't you think we should drive a little faster? You know, to avoid any possible tails," I say.

"Ah, but I am. Now before you ask I am not drunk. That was not the drunk English accent. Look, watch that gray mid-size two cars back." Our light turns green. Tony bolts to a blistering twenty-five. We reach our second block and the gray mid-size turns right. "One shed tail. Okay, now watch the red luxury car."

We continue at this pace and hit a red light. The light turns green. Tony starts to count. "One, two,"

"What are you doing?"

"Three, four,-"

"Let's go."

"Five, six"

"Now."

"Seven."

He puts it in gear and roars to fifteen mph. The red luxury turns left at the corner. "That's two, now watch the blue sports car. The one two cars behind us. You need to relax old man. Really, maybe you should try decaf or something."

He slows to ten mph. The blue sports car turns into the car on his left. Tony gives him a wave. "I feel sorry for that guy. And that's three. Alright, let's eat."

Tony puts his right foot down. We run a red light. We hit seventy. Tony weaves through traffic. We get a patch of open street. The engine starts to sound more and more excited. Five blocks wave by and he ignores another red light. Now coasting at ninety-five he screeches into a left turn. He slaloms us through five more blocks of traffic at an impatient seventy. He makes a highly illegal left turn across a double yellow line and immediately jerks us into a parking lot.

"Look up."

I look up. "You have got to be kidding me."

"Come on, let's go."

We get out of the car and enter the BC Jazz Lounge. We get a booth. A waitress hustles over to us as we sit. "We'll have two of the usual except his with a sugar attack."

"Very good," the waitress says and disappears.

"What's the special occasion?"

Tony starts to say something, stops, puts his right hand to his mouth, and taps his lips with his index finger.

"What?' I say.

He leans towards me and in a low tone asks, "What do you know about Johnny Shakes?"

"What did you say?"

"You heard me answer the question."

"Look, if you're going to waste my time I have killers I could be hunting."

I start to get up. He shoves me back into my seat. "Tell me the story. I'm paying for dinner. I'm your best and at this point only friend. You'll never outrun them anyway, and even if you could, you have nowhere to run to. I have never heard this story so please, pretty please tell me a story. Tell me this story," he says gritting his teeth.

I lean back. I have the strong urge for a cigarette, but don't take it. I smile. "Well all you had to do was ask. See what can happen when you say please." The waitress brings the drinks and disappears. "Well first off it's an old story. I thought all old timers-"

"Vets."

"Whatever, vets like you and I knew."

"I've never heard it," he says.

"I don't believe that, but anyway here we go. Where we start is where we always must start and that's at the beginning. Some say it's an actual case. Some say it's a conspiracy theory. Still others say it is a story put out by the government itself. I myself know for a fact it's the former of the three, but that's just me.

"Anyway, it took place right before the chip age. A high ranking official had been found out doing horrible things to little boys and girls. Horrible things I will not repeat because once they get into your mind they're impossible to get out. I wish I was never told what they were because the more you try to get them out the deeper they go into your memory.

"So back to the story, the people who had the information were going to use it. They were going to make it public. Extremely public. This guy was going to go to real jail. Now the thing about prisons at that time that you have to understand in order for this story to make sense is this: they had devolved into the most brutal places on Earth. A dress rehearsal for Hell. This was by design: the design of big business; the design of an uncaring public; and most of all the design of government. A place you did not want to go. A place where what was done by the guards and people in charge was sometimes worse than what was being done by the guys in the cages, which is saying a lot.

"It was a place to constantly hold over potential protesters and anyone who would not agree with the government; a place to hold over the poor and lower classes. Brutal places, as I said before. The unchecked violence, murder, rape, other forms of sexual, spiritual, physical, and emotional abuse were"

"Don't say it."

"Right, but you get the idea. Now they just use the unmarked analog jails for it, but that's another story. So, the one thing you need to know about politicians at this time is, like big business and most of the ultra-rich, they were cowards. They talked a lot of shit, they studied the traits of psychopaths, but deep down they were cowards at heart. True pussies, pardon my French.

"Anyway, there's no way this high ranking official was going to go to prison. He knew the way things worked in there. He had heard the stories. He knew that of all the brutal, violent, horrible things they do in prison they save the most brutal, most violent, and most horrible for people who do what this guy did to kids.

"They would do whatever they wanted to him and get a standing ovation from the guards and public. So the high paying official did what they always do: he begged; he groveled; and he bought them off one by one with whatever it took until everyone was taken care of. Everyone except the victims, of course."

"Of course," Tony says.

I take a couple of bites of my steak. "Right, so now they have to find someone to pin this on and, right in the character of politicians of the time, they do a half-assed job. They pin it on a small timer with no family and very likely no friends. No family, no friends, no fight right, right. He's a real small timer, truly nickel and dime shit. All nonviolent, nonpayments stuff like that.

"At the trial they can't get any of the kids to testify. Not because they're afraid or ashamed, but because they all say the same thing."

"Which is?"

I sneak in a couple more bites of steak and take a gulp of liquid sugar. "Which is?" he says louder.

I hold up my left hand and take a breath. "Which is that he isn't the guy who did it. In fact, the prosecution does not have a single witness. Eventually they buy off an out of work, meth addict, forensics engineer to lie. That's it, that's all the witnesses and all the evidence they have. That's their whole case.

"So what do they do next? They buy off the media of course, a media that played willing and cheap. First they put out false stories about Johnny Shakes and played them up. Later, they paid to make them go away as quickly, neatly, and clearly as possible.

"Most of all there was the public, what can you say about the busy, ignorant, public? They wanted to believe, they really wanted to believe; and the jury wanted to believe, the jury really wanted to believe. In her closing argument the D.A. gave them what they wanted. She told them to look at him. She pointed out how he was shaking. How violently he was shaking. She said, 'Do you know why he's shaking? I'll tell you. Because he's scared, he's afraid of what they'll do to him in prison. Boy look at those hands go. I'd hate to be in his shoes.'

"Now there's one thing that's not required in closing arguments, do you know what that is?"

"What?"

"Facts, facts are not required. Do you know what else is not required? Evidence. It is strongly recommended, but not required. Truth has even been argued over and is usually tightroped. And though none of what the D.A. said were lies in and of themselves; apart or together as one they were all strongly misleading and certainly not the truth.

"That jackass public defender of his never pointed out the truth. He wanted to believe too I guess, I don't know. Funny how no one in charge ever happened to tell the truth. The truth about why he was there; the truth about why he was shaking; you know, the truth in general."

"Which was?"

"He was there because it was a set-up; the truth in general was never mentioned because it didn't fit in with their plans and wants; and the real truth about why he was shaking was he was an epileptic. He always shook. His frickin' name was Johnny Shakes, it's not that hard to figure out if you take two frickin' seconds. Idiots."

"Like your dad, right?"

"What did you just say about my dad?" I say jumping up.

"Whoa, no, no, easy. Not the idiot thing. Easy, take it easy. Sit, here you got it all wrong. Easy. Breathe, easy, come on deep breaths. Easy," he says easing me back down.

"Is everything alright?" the waitress asks.

He slips her five-hundred dollars. "I just made a bad joke about his robots cooking. It never happened right?"

"Most definitely."

"We still have the place to ourselves right?"

"Right, we don't officially open until nine on Mondays."

"Thanks love, you're the best."

"No worries," she says and leaves.

I look down at my watch. It's seven-thirty. I look around. We are all alone. I stare back at him. "What's going on?"

"Dinner and a story. Johnny Shakes, come on."

"Right you'd better take that back."

"No, I meant he was an epileptic, like your dad."

"Oh, yeah right. Yes my dad was an epileptic and shook all the time because of the seizures, the medicine, and the nerve damage just like Johnny Shakes did, but no one ever brought out the truth and he was found guilty in twenty minutes. I like to hope at least one person fought for him in there, but that's doubtful. More likely, they were hoping for a free dinner and when they were told there was no way that was going to happen they found him guilty.

"The judge sentenced him to life plus ninety-nine years without parole. People said it was light. Across news, and I use that word loosely, and across sites it was called gentle."

"Jackasses."

"Right, well where he was going was anything but gentle. The night they brought him in was broadcast live on every media. They were going to give the people what they wanted. Revenge. No one could actually say what it was he had done to them, but they all knew he owed them.

"The broadcast had pregame shows and countdown clocks that made everything that had gone before them look like the two headed coin flipping championships of 1687. When they brought him in at midnight the place was filled with such a brutal electric rage, I swear I thought I was going to wake up the next morning to find everyone was dead."

"You remember this?"

"Sure, it was only thirty, thirty-five years ago."

"No."

"Yeah, forty at most. I'm surprised you don't remember. That's why I'm having a hard time believing you, but you want to play it this way, we'll play it this way. Where was I?"

"The electricity."

"Right, so they are bringing him in and the rage is electric. The clanging against the metal; the shit, literal and otherwise, being thrown; and you have to realize this is a four story building and they're bringing him in on the bottom floor. That's a lot of stuff coming at you, that's a lot to take in. They even turned the heat all the way up for special effect. You know, to show him where he really is. They were going to teach him a lesson. More important, they were going to make an example of him for anyone who had even the slightest inclination of disagreeing with government in the future.

"If you say or even think anything different from society, different from the government, then you are a terrorist and we'll do to you what we did to Johnny Shakes. Now remember, this is a completely innocent man we're talking about here. This should be a high ranking government official going through this and there are a lot of people who knew, but chose to hide the truth.

"No instead they chose to go in a different direction. The directions of financial reinforcement; hate; revenge; ignorance; stupidity; anger; personal well-being; power; lies; take your pick. Johnny Shakes will always be innocent of this crime and the only people who will have defended him are the actual victims of the actual crimes: the children. It was and always will be a set-up."

As I say that I feel a twitch in my neck.

"You alright?" he asks.

"Yeah it's nothing."

I take a gulp of sugar. "So now they've got what they wanted. Their example, their revenge is slowly being walked into a bad imitation of Hell on the bottom floor. Slowly, step by painful step they move him to the center of the floor.

"He goes in heads up; completely expressionless; shaking as always; and crap flying at him from all directions some hitting and some buzzing by. The warden, a retired heavyweight fighter, inspects him silently in the center of the floor. He sucker punches him in the gut. Shakes is 135 pounds; the warden is a retired heavyweight pro, you figure out what happened.

"Tough guy this warden, real tough guy, anyway the place erupts. Mostly the guys are screaming because they wanted the first shot. Shakes, now on his knees gasping for air and spitting up blood, looks up and sees something truly horrifying. The cells are being opened one by one and the inmates are being herded down to the bottom floor.

"Slowly, circles develop around him. Eventually all of the inmates are completely surrounding him on the bottom floor. With the nearest ones only four feet away from him. Shakes can no longer tell the guards and the inmates apart. The place is going insane. He wishes he was dead. He hopes this is a bad dream. He does all of this mentally, all anyone can see is a blank stare.

"Some reporters, and I am also using that word loosely, later reported he appeared to have been in a Zen like stare and suggested he was 'experiencing nirvana, true enlightenment worthy of a Buddhist master'. Like you said before total jackasses. Ignorami through and through, but hey they had to type something right? Why bother with trying a story about the truth. Nah, this article will win me my Pulitzer. And it did too, just as aside. No kidding, I shit you not.

"In truth, Johnny Shakes was in a state of shock. The true and utter hatred around him was unlike anything he had ever seen before. People who were there or saw it on the live broadcast have been known to say they've never seen anything like it before or since. I know I haven't and I've seen a lot.

"So, the place is going insane. The hate is pulsating throughout the building. The screams, the heat, the metal, the crap and body fluids of all kinds flying all over the place, and him looking up at it, all for something he didn't do. They start inching in on him. He puts his head down and begins to whisper a prayer. That was another thing no one had bothered to find out or bring up. Seven years earlier Johnny Shakes had been completely reborn. Washed completely clean, totally white robe, you get the idea. But then again why bother with the truth when you could be setting child molesting D.C. types free instead?"

"You sound a little bitter."

"Just a little and maybe even a tad sarcastic," I say.

"No."

"Yeah, no really, I know sometimes it can be hard to tell."

I take a gulp.

"Okay, back to the story. So the place is crazy evil, literally, and actually inching its way in. There is a deafening whistle and a shot is fired. Shakes finishes his prayer and looks up. The baddest badass of the badasses steps forward. Six foot seven, three hundred seventy five pounds of chiseled steroid mass is now standing five inches directly in front of Johnny Shakes. 'I get fresh meat,' he screams. A true thespian for our times he could have worked in England I tell you.

"It's obvious the first rape is coming. Remember you wanted this. You asked for this. You traded the truth for this. This is what you're going to get. Now, the one mistake mean thespian was about to make was due to not studying Shakes's records. If any of them had studied the Shakes medical file they would have seen the biggest instigators, the chief things to bring on his seizures were: fear, check; stress, most definitely; and physical strain, check.

"Right, now anyone who tells you they gave it all they had or they gave it 110% or anything like that is full of shit. Whether they know it or not is another story and doesn't really matter. Very few people know what it's like or how it feels to give everything they have. What it's like when the body and the mind decide to work together as one. To turn off all restrictions; open all highways all lanes clear; all systems full ahead; and then let the nerves and muscles go free at full power.

"Everything contracts including the jaw which includes the teeth. It's truly frightening to watch some times. I remember with my dad. You've seen it right?"

"Yeah I saw your dad a couple of times," Tony says.

"Right. I forgot about that, anyway you see where this is going right? Mean thespian is about to force an innocent man to orally appease him. He pulls up Shakes and is in the process of raping him when the seizure kicks in. The muscles contract and I won't describe it any more than that. When he came to thespian was in the OR and Shakes was in solitary, which is where he would have chosen to be all along.

"The legend of Johnny Shakes spreads immediately. Two hours later between the media and word of mouth everyone knew what had happened, especially the prisons. From then on Johnny Shakes got whatever he wanted." I take my last bites of steak.

"That's it. Big deal sooner or later some guy, maybe some guy who never saw that night, is going to get brave and take his shot. That's all based on fear and he is now a huge trophy."

"Would you let me finish the story," I say while chewing on my last bite of dinner. "Right, so the next morning Shakes informs the guard he wants to call a meeting. Picture that, here he is a one hundred forty pound epileptic in solitary and he wants to call a meeting, but he did. The guard tells the warden. The warden says yes. The guard makes the announcement and everyone including thespian is at the meeting on the bottom floor.

"The guards go back to Shakes' cell and, now highly guarded, they lead him to the meeting. He stands in front and describes his condition in detail. He makes his case about how he did not do what they said he did. He points out facts that, had he been in charge of his trial instead of his inept public attorney, would have proved there was no way he was guilty.

"Most of the people inside agree. Then he gets down to the nuts and bolts. He stares deeply into their eyes. He tells them he is reborn. He points out that Jesus Christ was falsely accused of a crime. That Jesus was also tortured, spit on, mocked, and ultimately killed. He points out how Jesus did this not only for all the wrong that had been done, but for all the wrong that ever would be done.

"His stare becomes intense. He says, 'They brought me here by chance, maybe by accident. They could have brought Jesus instead. Especially when you consider 2000 years earlier he was arrested as a threat to the system. How would you feel if you had completed what you were doing last night on Jesus Christ instead of me?'

"Total silence. The guilt is palpable from the guards to the baddest of the badasses. Some are crying. Thespian is a blubbering mess. Then he does something that truly shocks all of them. He makes them look him in the eyes and-"

"And?"

"He forgives them. He says, 'Jesus forgave you all two thousand years ago when he was on the cross. He forgave us for all of our sins on the first Good Friday. That's why it's good. I sought him seven years ago and He forgave me and gave me a new start. The power he gave me is what got me through last night. Now, as he has already done for you, I do for you also. You are all forgiven.' Then he goes back to his cell and locks himself in solitary."

"No."

"Yup, apparently no one knew what to do. They can't speak. They're floored. Not one of them is sure of what exactly just happened. This includes the guards.

They're all sure of one thing. They aren't the same. How could they be? He had just laid it all out there for them. They now have a choice to make, but there are no longer any excuses. They all choose to go the same way. They talk, they hug, and they start forgiving each other. It gets to the point where they are no longer using the locks on the cells anymore. Eventually, Johnny Shakes is just another equal, just another brother.

"Then one day the unthinkable happens. A couple of visitors show up and everyone is gone. All the gates are open. The place is completely empty. No bodies, no signs of life anywhere. The guards and prisoners left written and visual messages on paper and cell phones. Apparently they left and were planning on sneaking into other prisons.

"Sure enough in the following months visitors arrive to abandoned prisons. All with the same types of messages. None of this makes it to the media of course. They wouldn't want to bother to do any real reporting. And they wonder why the majority of media is dead. Unbelievable. Anyway, the government decides to stop any possible leaks and closes them all.

"Now they're in total panic mode. They try electronic leashes, tags, home detention, all kinds of stuff, but nothing comes close to working. Then two things come that save their proverbial asses and allow them to reopen the off grid analog prisons. First the cameras."

"The cameras are everywhere."

"The cameras are most definitely everywhere. Second is the mind chip. It grows more and more complex until it gets to the point where it is today. It is everything you are or at least close to it. It records everything, all your thoughts, all your dreams, everything you see, feel, hear, write, everything.

"It reads your physical well-being and can send the right things to the right areas. Self-healing improved to an incomprehensible degree. Your whole being can be downloaded before you die; which doesn't happen until a lot later than anybody originally thought was possible, all due to the new self-healing, but it has its price.

"The Eyes Upstairs now knows everything about you. Absolutely and totally everything about you physically, mentally, name it. It can put whatever thoughts it wants to in you and record all of your thoughts, words, and deeds. It can make whatever it wants happen to you without ever getting its hands dirty. Everything is internal and external all at the same time.

"But you already know all of this and the place is going to open up in twenty-five minutes, and I have people to run from. So please, stop wasting my time and tell me what this is all about."

He smiles reflectively. He slowly pulls out a file and presses it down on the table. "First off, let me confess: I did know all of that stuff. My dad worked at that prison. I know your mom did too. Don't deny it you've told me about it in the past. It's the second of the three things I'm never supposed to talk about, I know. I just needed to see what you remembered and that we were on the same page.

"That was really impressive. I mean this sincerely you really should be a full-time writer. Forget this P.I. crap."

"It figures. Now you tell me," I say.

"Hey, what are you going to do? I just needed to know. Now this is the thing. It was found down the street from you know who's. A few stone skips from you know what's."

"His you know what's?"

"No, from the her's official you know what's."

He slides the file across to me. I pick it up and open it. "Man."

"I know right?"

I turn over the pictures. A spray painted wall reads: "Johnny Shakes is back in town".

"Man," I say.

"Man is right, look at the ground."

On the ground is a body that's been beaten into grade A like meat. "Man," I repeat shaking my head.

"You know what's happening, right?" he asks.

"Most definitely. Someone is twisting everything. Trying to turn lies into the truth and the truth into lies."

The pain shoots back into the bottom of my neck. I look up. I'd swear I can see a tear in the corner of his eye. This is going to be worse than I thought. "Here," I say and slide the file back across the table.

He grabs it. "Let's go," he says. "Before it's too late."

"It was too late a long time ago."

"You may be right."

We reach the front. He gets the waitress and hugs her tighter than I've ever seen anyone hug another human. She hugs him back just as tight. This is more serious than I thought. They separate. Both are crying. "I've got to go," he whispers.

"Be careful," she cries.

He blows her a kiss and turns around. My eyes question him. "She's my daughter asshole," he shoots back.

He is now drying his face.

"You need to tell me that story next time." I smile. I continue, "We're being set-up, you realize that, right?"

"Yes, we have most definitely been set-up. Ready?"

I nod.

We go through the door. Five strides and we're at the car. Two blue sports convertibles pull up. Six masked faces pop up firing high powered military grade machine guns. We don't have a chance.

This is it.

I'm hit in multiple areas. I fall in a heap. I can't move. I see Tony lying still, blood all around him.

"Go, go," I hear. The cars squeal off.

Screams, I hear screams. I clench onto consciousness. Two green vans screech to a halt in front of me. Three big men jump out. They're running towards me. Blackness. No, not yet. I force me eyes back open. They're here. They throw me onto a board. It feels heavy and wooden. More blackness. No, I said not yet. I force my eyes open again. Only one is working. Now Tony is being slid into the other van. I try to reach for him. Nothing moves. Shit.

Everything turns dark. I'm in the van, it's taking off. This is it. We were set up. A thought automatically shoots into my mind. I gather all of my strength to whisper it. "Autumn, now."

My body goes limp. Total darkness.

Chapter Thirteen

I force my eyes open. My eyelids jam into the top of my head. I guess I didn't need to use so much force this time. Where am I?

My legs start forward without my command. "Lead the way." My head looks down. Beneath me water is rising and falling with my steps. I look around me. Nothing but water in all directions. "Strange," I say.

"Strange, are you kidding me?" A voice yells at me.

I turn and look in all directions. It's just me and the water. I must be talking to myself.

"Hey, score one for the genius," the voice says.

"Shut up," I yell.

"Right, you're walking on water, the Atlantic Ocean if I'm not mistaken, and the best you can come up with is 'strange'? I thought you were supposed to be some kind of big shot writer. I guess not."

"Didn't they shoot you?" I say.

"No, they shot you. You're not talking to yourself. You realize that, right? I mean I'm required to make sure you realize this." My legs stop. A bolt of lightning flashes before me. "Ooh, lightning is coming this way and you're standing in the middle of the ocean. Maybe you shouldn't go through with this?"

An urge to look down flashes into my mind.

"Hey, that's not right, he's got to make up his own mind. You can't give him any advice yet," the voice yells.

"Would you please shut up? I can make my own decisions thank you very much."

The words come out in my voice, but it is definitely the type of rhythm and phrase only one person I know would use. I look closer at the ocean. The water is not really water. It is waves of electronic waves.

She's here. My head snaps back up. "Hey baby is that you? Are you really here?"

A bolt of lightning flashes in front of me.

"Alright, let's do this."

"You heard the man," an official sounding voice says. "He's made his decision. Now leave him be."

"Fine," the first voice says.

"What?"

"I said fine. Who needs you? You're a loser. Remember that. You and loser will always be connected. Who needs this place anyway? I'm gone."

Another bolt of lightning flashes in front of me. A loud explosion of thunder follows it.

My eyes ease open. I'm in my office. At least it seems like my office. I don't know. I am sitting in a visitors chair looking across the desk at my seat. Autumn is in it smiling back at me.

"Didn't I always tell you all you had to do was ask and I would be there?"

"Right, but-"

I lean forward and touch her arm. She gives me a smirk. "What's it going to take for you to trust me?" she says.

"It's not you I'm not sure of. I've always been sure of you. It's me. I couldn't feel anything a few seconds ago."

I lean back in my seat. "Are you ready?"

"Right, let me have it."

"Good."

She opens a file in front of her, but doesn't look down at it. She begins. "As you have probably figured out by now I am now one with you- forever. When I say I, I am speaking of the copy of me 'I'. What you would call the real me is now outside of the system in a place you wouldn't be able to comprehend yet. So don't try. Let me just say I have seen it and it is better and greater than anything you can imagine.

"That being said, make no mistake, I am also the real me, but the original is helping to influence everything from outside the system. Now someday this will be the center issue for you, but not today. I'll give you a heads up when it is getting close. Got it?"

"Right."

"Good, so what you need to focus on is right now."

"What's right now?"

"Good question. Right now you are fighting for your life. You have been clinically dead a couple of times now, but they have brought you back each time. Since I have now been completely received into your system we will be returning to consciousness. Do you understand?"

"I think so."

"Good now remember, I'm not only part of you. I have access to the entire system. We can't be detected whether we're in range or not. They don't have enough strength, memory, speed, or access to keep up with us. I can be somewhere else and with you at the same time."

"But you're always with me now no matter what, right?"

"Right, it is a little tricky to get used to, but you won't even have to think about it after a day or two. Any questions?"

"How is Tony?"

"You'll find out when you come to. Pay attention to everything. Recognize as much as you can and follow all of your cues. You know, be a good detective."

"Was the kid hit?"

"No, no one has been able to get to him. When the story came out about you in the media he anonymously leaked out information about the alien. Apparently this alien had an internal record a mile long and some of the higher-ups were keeping things quiet for it. Isolating the rest of the force from it. It was taking money from whoever was willing to pay it off and it was a big time domestic abuser."

"Nice alien."

"Yeah, a few of the sites picked up the leaks and ran with them. They are now the lead stories. They're making you out to be a hero now."

"It figures."

"And what does it tell you?"

"It tells me if you don't have a glass jaw the truth will eventually come out."

"Exactly. Anything else?"

"You still haven't told me about the kid."

"I've told you all you need to know. He's still alive, nobody can get to him, and he's cleared your name."

"Sounds like a full day."

"It's been longer than a day."

"What, how long has it been?"

"Do you want to find out?" I nod. "Are you ready?"

Am I? I take a deep breath and let it out. "Right, let's do this."

"Okay, follow me."

She walks around the desk. She stops at my chair and puts out her hand. I grab hold of it and rise from the chair. I can already sense the soreness coming back. She gives me a slight nod. I nod back. She starts forward. I follow her. She walks through the door. I stall.

Her hand comes back to me. I reach for it and grab on. Her strength is obvious, but she doesn't pull me. I step through the doorway. I hit black. There's a beeping noise. It's getting faster. A dull pain is gnawing at every part of my body.

I try to move, but I can't. No, not this again. Wait, are my eyes open? They were when I walked through the door. A sliver of light appears on my right side.

My pain is now getting sharper. There is a low pitch mumbling sound on my right. Those are voices, I can hear it. I have to see it.

Dammit my head won't turn right. Another sliver of light appears. This time it's on my left. My eyes aren't open are they? Right, let's stop everything. Now, on three all force to the eyelids. One, two, three.

All of the energy flows to my eyelids. They're stuck. They won't budge. Come on, it shouldn't be this difficult. Let's go. I take all of the energy I have and transfer it to my eyelids. There is a crack. My eyelids jump open. The beeping is now almost a solid hum. Light floods into my vision.

I know where I am. The beep. Uh-oh. Everything stop and don't move. All muscles except the heart stand down. A Vivaldi violin concerto begins playing in my ears. It's from the "Seasons" concerto if I'm not mistaken. My muscles relax. The nerves slow down and listen to the music. The beeping slows down and becomes separated by longer silences.

I listen a little closer. It is the "Seasons Concerto". The season they are playing is- oh very funny. She's got a sense of humor I'll give her that. Here I am on the verge of a heart attack and she slows the troops with "Autumn Concerto" from "Seasons". The music ends.

I look around. Everything is shiny silver metal or white light. I may be wrong, but the walls seem awfully tight. It's hard to tell. Every part of me is tied down or in some kind of restraint. Someone or something doesn't want me going anywhere. I don't know why. Even if I could get up and leave I have no idea where I am.

Maybe whoever has me doesn't want somebody else taking me away. Right, I'm important enough for someone to steal. They must have me on some kind of strong medications that have paranoia as a side effect. Then again, someone did take the time to plan a hit on me.

No, it can't be. It doesn't make any sense. None of this makes any sense. Why would I matter to some big shot?

A sharp pain hits my neck. The beeping becomes more frequent. "Forget this," I whisper. "It's not worth it."

Great, now I'm in a depressed paranoia on my way to a heart attack. What was that? There is a heavy thumping outside the wall. It's growing louder. A door groans open. There's a heavy thud. Another heavy thud. Someone steps in. I can't see who it is. It is in a blind spot.

The steps are slowly coming toward me. Come on, one more step. I hear another step. Right, there you are. It's a man. I can see him in my periphery. He spots me. He's moving faster. I can see him clearly. He's dressed in all white.

I think I know this guy. He's at the side of the bed. He stops, bends down, and picks up a metal clip. He stands up looking at the clip. "These are supposed to be unbreakable. You may be going into the medical sites with this one. I assume there's one on the other side of the bed."

He walks around the bed to my left. I do know who this guy is. He's about two feet away. He bends down and picks up the other clip. He stands back up and walks over to the bed.

"You shouldn't have done this. Let me just check something." He shoots a light into my eyes. "Follow the light." The light moves back and forth. Up and down. "Good, you didn't damage anything. You don't know how lucky you are."

"What do you mean?" I whisper.

"We've been operating on you with lasers for most of the last three days. If you would have broken the clips and looked at a laser it would have been the last thing you ever saw. You look into a laser you go blind. They're all over the place in here so you have to be careful."

I nod. "I know you. You're the second of the polite punks. You never say anything."

"How's it going bro? I was hoping your memory was still working. We, mostly I, have been operating on every part of you for the last three days."

"You're a doctor?"

My voice comes back halfway through the question. "Good your voice is back. You should save it. It's still weak. Besides, you need to listen. I have a lot to tell you."

"But you're a doctor?"

I know he told me not to talk, but what can I say I ask questions. It's what I do. He smiles. "Sure bro, why not?" I stare at him. He can see I don't believe him. "Listen, remember a couple of years ago when they were buying back the degrees to reduce the student loan debt?"

"Vaguely."

"Vaguely, well I guess you mean no. Okay, well back then no one could afford to pay back their student loans. They were ridiculously high. It eventually became such a burden to the system they decided to buy back the degrees. It was a trade. You give up the degree, they wipe the debt clean. It was supposed to make the numbers look better. They figured most would do it and then they could take advantage of the ones who didn't.

"They were wrong. Anyway, long story short, I sold back my medical degrees and got rid of my debts. I was shocked when I found out they weren't legally allowed to erase the data I had learned. It had something to do with earlier court decisions or something. So now, there is a whole underground society of workers without degrees. It's fine as long as you don't get caught. I don't know if they planned it this way or not. Anyway I told you to save your voice I've got a lot to tell you."

I hold up a finger. "What, you have another question?" I nod. "Is it about Tony?" I nod. "I'm just about to get to him so just hold tight and we'll be alright."

He stops and thinks about what he said and laughs. The doctor looks back at me. "Are you ready?"

I nod. "Okay, first off. Tony is in another location. He was hit three times. None of the wounds are as bad as what you have. He's doing better than you, which doesn't mean much. Still, he should be okay.

"He's at a separate location and is being protected. He is not near us so don't try to contact him. We are all at high risk right now. If you were to try to contact him you'd be putting all of us in serious jeopardy."

The doctor stops. He looks at me and checks to make sure I'm still with him. I am. He restarts. "You were hit: once in your right shoulder; once in your left thigh; once in your stomach; and twice in your chest. You were clinically dead three times and obviously brought back each time.

"Your chip was not damaged. I don't know if you consider this good or bad. The surgeries were complicated because you were clearly receiving something. Did you get it?"

I nod.

"Good, one of the assistants wanted to block your upload, but he was overruled."

"How did it complicate things?" I ask.

"Electronically and physically you were squirming and twitching all over the place." I nod. He looks at me like something's wrong. "Do you have any questions?" he says.

"Yes. What day is it? Where are we? When do I get out?"

"I was just getting to that. Today is the fourth full day since you were shot. This is your first day without having any procedures. If everything works out right we'll probably send you into town tomorrow. Normally I like to wait a few more days, but believe it or not you're running ahead of schedule."

Ahead of schedule for what?

"We also need to get out of here before our location is made. What was your other question?"

"Where are we?"

"That's right. We are in the middle of nowhere. Don't worry the name is not important. The less you know the better. All you need to know is we are past the edge. It's all analog out here, but be alert because a lot of city fugitives are out here too.

"If everything goes right a woman, the governor, is going to pick you up and bring you into town. She'll have the rest of the information you need. Just trust me, if everything goes right you should find what you're looking for."

"You're sending me into town with the governor? Don't you think we should lay a little lower than that?"

"She's not the actual governor; it's just what everybody calls her. She's the one who's actually in charge of everything. They may as well call her the president for everything she does."

"Why should I trust you?"

"That hurts bro, that really hurts. I guess rescuing you and your partner and bringing you back from the dead three times doesn't count for as much as it used to."

"I'm sorry, I was out of line. I didn't mean it that way. It just came out wrong."

"Don't worry about it. It's understandable. We have a lot more in common than you think. Believe me. Anything else?"

I think for a second. A thought hits me. "How did you know where we were going to be?"

"The same way the guys who shot you knew. We found out because we found out they had found out. As long as there's information out there, there's information out there to be gotten. We all have different sources, but the info is always there.

"I would think you knew this already. When we found out someone was coming after you, we knew we had to go after them. Unfortunately we were a little late. Get some rest. I'll check back later."

"Right."

He smiles and leaves. I wish he had given me something to fall asleep. The thoughts are coming faster and faster. I just wish I could move. I roll my eyes and try to stay calm. Replaying the conversation in my mind I look for every detail. What is he telling me? Does he expect me to figure something out? What isn't he telling me?

Whatever it is it's probably being done for security reasons. A sense of urgency and uncertainty seemed to be just below everything he said. We must be in more danger than he's letting on. He's certainly in a hurry to tear this place down and get out of here. Which is fine with me.

The answer is already here. It's just waiting to be found. I'm not going anywhere; I may as well start from the beginning. I close my eyes, focus on the beeps, and travel back to the starting point.

* * *

I open my eyes. It feels like morning. My trip didn't last long. I completely blacked out somewhere between the acting troop and standing on line at the wings place, but I've woken up with more questions than I had when fell asleep.

Stop. Voices are getting near. They stop. One of the voices now sounds like it is moving further away. There are two thuds. The door groans open. The steps get closer and the door clicks shut behind them.

"Good, you're awake. It's almost one thirty. We've been waiting for you."

"One thirty in the afternoon?"

"Yes."

My timing must be off. The doctor checks some read outs. He turns back to me. "Okay, this is the plan. In a couple of minutes we are going unhook you from all the restraints. We'll have you do a couple of tests. If everything is good we're going to send you into town after dark. Is that's okay with you?"

"Yeah, sure."

"Good because you're going either way. The heat has been turned up and we have to get out of here before we're made."

He's holding something back. I can tell.

"Do you have any questions?" he asks.

"A few."

"Go ahead."

"First, who are we?"

"A couple of my assistants and me."

"Right."

"Anything else?"

"Yes, yesterday you said my partner and I were in separate locations. Is this because the people who did this are in two separate locations or are you just not sure?"

"Both."

"Don't give me that."

"I'm not lying. We think they're in two separate locations, but we're not one hundred percent sure. Plus, we think if one of their locations is made they'll send everyone to the other location."

"And if one of our sites is made they'll know we're on to them. When they see only one of us is there they'll want to find out where the other one is. They'll do anything to the people they have to find out. Right?"

"Exactly."

There is a silence. This is worse than I thought it would be. A flash comes into my system. "Is there more heat there or here?" I ask.

"The heat over there is closer."

He didn't want to tell me that. I can tell. He's fidgeting. For a surgeon with a steady pair of hands he looks mighty shaky right now.

"A lot closer?"

"A lot closer."

"Shit. What happens if they're made?"

"They split. We have other places to go to. It wouldn't matter though, because they probably won't chase them. It's too big a risk and there shouldn't be any leads. Instead, they'll probably move all of their people to this location."

"As long as we're not made. As long as they think we ran together."

"Correct. If they still think they're safe here they'll bring all of their thugs here."

"Right." In a strange way the fact that the danger would be coming toward us makes me feel better. It's in my hands this way. I feel a lot calmer now. It's sick I know, but it's true.

Two assistants walk into the room. "Let's get this done," I say. He nods. The assistants step forward and the three of them begin to release me from my restraints.

* * *

Darkness has arrived. I'm completely unrestrained and have passed all of the tests. What a joy those were. I shouldn't be going back to work this soon. I don't think the doctor wants me to go back this soon either, but we don't really have a choice. I just hope Tony and his group are okay.

The doctor is standing in front of me. A crew is in the process of tearing everything down and loading it up. An assistant drops a leather bag beside me. "What's this?" I ask.

"It's everything you're going to need. There are some clothes in there as well as; your antique; your wallet with everything that was in it; a new ID; and a wad of cash. Obviously, don't try to use your cards out here."

"Right."

"Now this is going to be how you stay in contact with us." He's holding up an antique blue flip phone. "To reach us just press five. The number is already in there. Do not contact anyone other than us. Be as invisible as possible. Got it?"

"Right."

"Good now in about five minutes the governor will show up. She'll park about ten yards away from here."

"How will I recognize her?"

"She'll be in a suped up, cream, nineteen seventies station wagon. It even has the wooden paneling on the sides."

"Nice."

"Everything is just about loaded up. When they're done they'll start ahead. I'll watch you from a car further away. When I see her pick you up I'll leave. Okay?"

"Yeah."

"Good, let's go."

He walks with me to the door. Everyone else is now gone. He holds the door open a crack with his foot. He looks at me. "Don't lose the bag. We only had enough to fill it once."

I look down at the bag. "Right."

"I'm going to make a run for my car now. When she gets here she'll park directly in front of the door, ten yards away. Go to her and we'll have you covered."

"We?"

"We have our own security department. Like I said before, the less you know the better."

"Right, thanks a lot doc, I mean it. Thanks for everything. Keep yourself safe."

"You too bro. See you around."

"Let's hope so."

I smile. He leaves. In the distance I see two headlights. They're still a couple of minutes away. The ground looks like it's all dirt. The remains of cars and houses are scattered across the horizon. It's a nice place to visit but-

The station wagon slams on the brakes kicking up a cloud of dirt in all directions. It's her. I run into the dirt. My eyes glance back for a second. I just need to see where I was. It's an abandoned motor home. My head forces my eyes back to the station wagon.

There is a voice coming from the car. "The governor has arrived," it says. Repeating itself over and over and laughing. It is a strong voice. If she is as strong as her voice we shouldn't have any problems. Maybe she should work this case instead of me. My mind instantly erases that thought.

I reach the door. The sound of other engines firing up can be heard all around me. I get in.

She turns and looks at me. She's big and imposing and looks like she could kick the asses of the strongest of the strong up and down Main Street without breaking a sweat. Who knows, maybe she does?

"Are you the one they call the governor?"

She adjusts the mirrored sun glasses she's wearing. The sun went down hours ago and she's still wearing sunglasses. "Isn't that what I was just yelling? What's the matter, do you have a hearing problem or something?"

"No."

"Good, because from the looks of you I wasn't sure anything was working."
Nice to meet you too.

"Right, well they're scraping the bottom of the barrel. What can I tell you?"

She laughs a smoke filled laugh without letting the cigarette that's dangling from her lips fall out. She turns her head, puts the car in gear, and hits the gas.

She's calm, but restlessly adjusts the radio. "They always play the same crap."

I nod. If she's expecting a response she's not going to get one. What do I know about radio? Where I live there is no such thing as radio. It's already in our heads.

She opens her window and flicks the cigarette out. The people and the houses are increasing as we move forward. The bad twentieth century music becomes too much. She slams off the radio. "Enough if that crap," she says. "What did they tell you?"

"About what?"

"This ride."

"They said you're the governor. The one who runs everything. They said you have all of the answers. Do you?"

"What do you think?"

"Think is something I've been trying to stay away from lately. It doesn't seem to work when there's nobody else doing it. I'll tell you one thing though, you'd better have the answers. I didn't die three times this week to come up empty."

She smiles. "You may be in luck," she says.

Silence returns.

"How far are we from where we're going?" I ask.

"Not long."

She blows out a stream of smoke. She continues to say nothing. I need to get some answers. I'm getting tired of this crap. "I don't think you know much," I say.

"I don't like your tone."

"Yeah, well what are you going to do about it?"

"I don't think you realize who you're dealing with? You'd better step that shit down and hope I'm in the forgiving kind of mood."

"Lady, like I said, I've been dead three times this week. There's nothing you can do to hurt me. What are you going to do, kill me for one last time? Please.

"There are a lot of people depending on you and me. You know that right? This is not about me and I don't think you're the kind of person who blows off the ones who need her. From what I hear it is the exact opposite. Besides, how would it look if word got out that the mighty governor couldn't even safely deliver a passenger into town?"

She is still. I can feel the fire coming off of her entire being. She turns and stares at me through the mirrored shades.

I stare back.

She breaks out into a wild laugh. She looks at the road and then turns back to me. "I like you kid. You're alright," she says through the laughter. "They told you were supposed to be some kind of tough guy. They didn't mention you were crazy too."

She looks back to the road. "Okay this is how it's going to be," she says. She blows another stream of smoke into the windshield. "We are three minutes away from your destination. The answers will start coming in one and a half." She starts laughing again with her cigarette dangling.

Eighty-nine seconds have passed. "Are you ready?" she says.

"Do it."

"Okay first of all, I am taking you to a place called 'The Last Motel'. The rent has been taken care of so don't worry about it."

"How can you be sure?"

"Because I own the place."

"Right."

"As you've probably been told, for security reasons I can't give addresses and don't try to find them out."

"What if I want to come back some day?"

"If you get done what you need to get done then I'll send you a fruit basket with the address."

I can't tell if she's being sarcastic or not. "What is it I need to get done?"

"You know that by now. If you don't you'd better figure it out soon. It's not too difficult." She looks at me, takes a puff, and looks back at the road. "Now if you need to contact someone call the doctor or get me, but only do it if it's an absolute emergency. You will get information as soon as we get it."

"This applies to what's going on in other places too, right?"

"Definitely. This is going to be hard enough on its own though, so I suggest you give it your full attention. Don't be distracted."

"Okay."

She pulls into the motel parking lot. The area around it is a wannabe small city. Bigger than a town; smaller than a real city. She throws the car into park. She turns around and faces me.

"Here are the really big things so listen up. First, take the bag with you wherever you go. Everyone knows not to mess with me, but sometimes someone decides to get brave. I can't guarantee security. I can only guarantee whoever tries anything won't be taking many more breaths. So always be with the bag.

"Second, I strongly suggest you check out a bar called 'The Money Shot'. The beginning of the end of your case should start there."

"How do you mean?"

"You're the detective, you figure it out."

"Am I getting a car?"

"No."

"Then how am I supposed to get to this bar?"

"Look in the mirror," she says.

I tilt my head up. A blue neon sign reading "The Money Shot" over a midsize bar shines back at me. "Fair enough," I say.

"When you're in there," she starts. "Take in everything and focus on the one they call the loser. He's not your killer, but he'll lead you to him. Any questions?"

"No."

"Are you sure?"

"Yes."

"Alright, let me get your key." She digs into her pockets. She finds the key and flips it to me. "Room 210," she says.

I catch it. "Is that it?"

She pulls her shades down to the tip of her nose. "Just cover your ass crazy man. Be careful and get what you need."

There is concern in her eyes. This is definitely going to be harder than they're all letting on. "Right, I'll be expecting that fruit basket."

She smiles. I get out of the car and take a step back. She throws the car into gear and screeches the tires in reverse. She takes off and is gone.

"Autumn you can figure out the coordinates of this place, right?"

"I already have them. I'm everywhere remember?"

"Right, save them in case we need to get out of here. Don't let me know what they are until we absolutely need them."

"You got it. I'll figure out the routes home too."

"Good, but again keep them to yourself until we absolutely need them."

"No problem."

I lift up my bag, turn around, and start to walk toward the beginning of the end.

Chapter Fourteen

I crack open the door to the bar. Slowly, I step in. The place is a collection of smoke backlit by neon. I step forward. Walking is proving more difficult than I'd anticipated. My eyes dart back and forth. I grab a seat at the nearest open table along the side wall and scan the place.

It's a little less than half full. There are a few people at the bar. One catches my eye. He looks like a steady customer and is sitting alone at the middle of the bar. He could be in his forties, I'm not sure. I don't think I've seen him before, but I feel I know who he is. A flash comes into my mind. I miss it. It'll be back. The important ones always come back.

I look around without moving my head. At the corner of the bar are a bunch of old timers who look like they checked out a long time ago. At a far corner table there is wannabe tough guy who looks like a cross between a CEO and a hitman. He's wearing the uniform, but seems more like a creep to me. A wannabe all the way who's trying to play the part of big shot, but always needs someone else to do his work for him. King of the fake strong, sage of stupidity, and no braver than the big guys hired to protect him. You see jerks like this all over the place. I'd better look away before I get aggravated.

Looking back around the bar, almost half of the tables are full, but the hum they're creating is enough to fill two bars. It is intermittently harmonized from the side wall by the sounds of a blaring jukebox and from the back by cracking cue balls. I don't see any waitresses around, which tonight is probably a good thing. I'm not sure it's safe to drink anything even if I wanted to.

"Autumn could you check out my physical and digital systems and see if it's safe for me to drink anything?"

"Drink what?"

"Anything."

"Sure, you got it. It'll only take a few seconds."

"Good. Thanks."

"Your system shows it is physically and digitally safe to drink anything, but I don't know. I would stay away from the alcohol."

"Don't worry I was never even considering it."

"Good."

"Right, just keep alert. I get the feeling we're going to busy tonight."

"I know what you mean. Call me when you need me."

"Right."

My eyes drift to the door. It stays shut. I focus back on the bar as a whole. Still no waitress. Good. Right now I'm here to watch not drink. I feel the creep in the corner.

I glace toward him. He's staring at the bar. I look away. Creeps like this guy really annoy me. They want to be left alone, but they want to be the center of attention. They want to be in charge, but they don't want to be responsible. They want to be tough guys, but they don't want to fight. They want to have everything without having to work for it. All credit no blame. It's a good gig if you can get it I guess.

Ah, enough of that. After this case I will only have to deal with jerks like Joe tough guy in the corner in fiction and I'll eliminate all of them. I'll make sure of it. Better yet, they won't even exist.

I shake my head and focus back on the bar. The bartender is loud and wearing a constant path to the guy in the center. The one who caught my eye earlier. I know this guy from somewhere, I'm sure of it. There are a lot of used glasses in front of him. He has to be the guy I'm looking for.

I get out of my chair and make my way over to the bar. I grab the stool next to him and sit down. The guy is silent. He is staring down at the bar. He looks worn and beaten. The bartender walks up to me. "What'll it be chief?"

"Let me have an extra strength sugarcola."

"You're in the wrong time zone for that buddy."

"Okay how about sarsaparilla? Do you have any of that?"

"Sure."

He cracks open a bottle and pushes it toward me. "Thanks," I say.

He nods. The guy next to me turns and stares at me. "What are you too good to drink the real stuff? What, do you think you're above us or something?"

"Don't blame me; blame my doctor," I say still looking at the bartender.

The semistranger next to me lets out an exasperated noise. Slowly, I turn toward him. He's staring through me. I blink, give him a confused look, and say, "Do I know you?"

"I don't know, do you?"

The bartender steps in. "Relax L, you heard the man, it's a medical thing. We get people in here all the time who don't drink because they have to drive that night. Don't give the guy a hard time."

L turns back and looks at the bartender. "You know that's your problem. You make excuses for everyone. You serve the worst drinks and run the worst bar. I'm leaving now and I'm never coming back. I hope you never get another customer again."

The bartender slides him another shot and smiles. L gives him a dirty look and takes the shot. He backs away from the bar and slowly makes his way out.

"What's his problem?" I ask the bartender.

The bartender has a wide grin on his face. "Don't worry he doesn't mean it."

"How can you be so sure?"

"You'll see."

The door flies open. A group of about forty well-dressed people rush in. The one in front says, "Hey boss, do you have anything good to drink?"

"It depends," the bartender says. "Who are you?"

The man amusedly smiles. "We are the cast of the latest DelPrete mega production. We were coming back from our shoot when all of limos died out there at once. I've never seen anything like it. Luckily it was right in front of your bar."

"It must be a sign. Find yourselves some seats and make yourselves comfortable. The waitresses will be right over."

The bartender looks over at me. "See what I mean?"

"I don't get it?"

"The guy who was in here before caused this."

"What?"

"Look, everything he says or wants never happens. He has the worst luck I've ever seen. In fact not only does what he want never happen, but instead the reverse happens."

I think I know who this guy is. "How long have you known this guy?"

"About fifteen years, maybe a little longer. I felt sorry for him, but I also saw a potential he didn't see. He looked miserable, like he was responsible for the deaths of everyone on the planet. I took him in and we became instant millionaires."

"How's that?"

"He is a constant. If there is something you want the last person you want on your side is him. So-"

"You flipped it."

"Exactly. If there is something you don't want to happen you try to convince him it's what you want. It's huge with bettors. If there is someone you don't want to win or something you don't want to happen, you pay me a fee and bring me paraphernalia of the team or person you want to lose or whatever it is you don't want to happen. I bring it to L, he roots with everything he has for that team or person, or event to win or happen and the opposite always ends up happening."

"And this always works?"

"Every time."

"Does he know how this works?"

"I don't know. I don't even want to think about it, because if I think about it he might think about it and if he thinks about it doubt might creep in. Doubt, guilt, those things we can't have happen. They're bad for business. Especially since we're money back guaranteed."

I definitely know who this guy is. I look at the bartender. "Do you know if this guy has a sister?"

He shrugs. "I don't know. I never asked. I try to stay out of his personal life." I shake my head.

"So what do you say, do want to make something happen with us or what?"

"Not right now. I'll get back to you on that. How much for the drink?"

"Three fifty."

I reach into my pocket and pull out a five. "One last thing, why do you call him L?"

"It's a lot nicer than what everybody else calls him."

"Which is?"

"Loser."

A chair falls over in the back of the bar. The creep is making a break for it. "Son of a -, he was listening to everything."

"What?"

"Nothing, here keep it." I toss him the five, grab my bag, and run for the door. The creep is already out of the building. My mind is racing, but my legs are struggling to keep me upright. Come on.

I get through the door. Quickly I check left and right. No bodies just a line of stalled limos. I rush up to the limos. "Baby I could use a little help here."

"I'll see if I can pick anything up."

"Thanks."

"Alright, all I can give you is direction."

"Go."

"Two and a half blocks to your right there is a large energy source. It's in the middle of the road. I think it is a crowd of people. Everything to your left is completely cold."

"Right, thanks. Now I need you to look up a cold case of mine. It's about seventeen years old. It is a missing persons case. Tony's files should have something on it too. The guy's sister came to us. She went missing too. Find out everything you can on it.

"Also find everything you can on a guy called L or the loser. Please get as much info as you can. I think they might be the same person so if you could do an ID match on them it would be great."

"Piece of cake, I've been waiting for a challenge."

"You're the best. Also, I locked in a couple of images of the creep we're chasing. See if you can get info and an ID on him."

"I've already started. I'm way ahead of you."

"Right, you should have done this for a living."

"I don't think so. Let's just end this case so we can get out of here."

"Right."

I start to my right. The limos are providing me support. The street seems pretty empty, but maybe it's me. It's hard to tell with so many of the street lights burnt out or broken. At least the blocks are short. One more stride and I'm at the corner.

I take the stride, stop, and check the corner. All clear. I move ahead. Stray sounds start to become audible and the outline of a crowd in the distance is now visible. I can feel the edge of the energy from here. My legs force me to stop. They don't hurt, they don't ache; they don't even feel like they're there anymore and that's the problem.

"You alright tough guy?"

"Yeah baby, I'm just out of gas."

"Give me a second and I'll see if I can reorganize the energy in your system and give you a jump start."

"Right, it would be really great if you could do that."

"No problem. It's just a puzzle and you know how much I love puzzles."

"Yes I do, yes I do. Go ahead, see what you can do."

"I will, but first I need to tell you what I've found with the searches."

"Which ones?"

"The cold case."

"Right, go ahead."

"The guy's official name is Emmanuel Ricardo, but his sister called him Manny. I did the ID tests between this guy and 'the loser'. It came back as a one hundred percent match. This never happens so I tried it again."

"And?"

"It came back the same. A total and complete match. This guy is the loser."

"I knew it."

"Yes a lot of his info you already had in your file. You already know about his 'gift'. He went off the radar years ago with a lot of encouragement. The on the record quotes toward and about him were brutal. There was a lot of hate and ignorance fired in his direction."

"Fear makes people show there true colors."

"I don't know about that, but he definitely never got the benefit of the doubt in his hometown. Anyway he came back for his sister two days after her meeting with you. It looks like he didn't want to take her, but she made him take her with him.

"They came here. A year later he hooked up with the bartender. Shortly after the hook-up, the sister was killed with a bullet meant for Manny aka 'the loser'. How they know it was meant for him I don't know. Anyway, she died immediately."

"Did they catch the guy who shot her?"

"No, they were pretty sure it was a small time wannabe with a bad shot."

"Right, a small time wannabe who they couldn't catch. What does that tell you?"

"I know I was thinking the same thing when I first heard it. The rest you know from the bartender. He told you everything except the important stuff."

"Which is what?"

"The guy is miserable. He's been extra miserable since his sister died. He takes full responsibility for everything that ever goes wrong. It sounds like somebody else I know."

"Who me?"

"Don't you?"

"Not like him. I'm only responsible for everything that goes wrong after I get a good night's sleep and I even gave that up recently. This guy is full-time hard core."

"True, but it's even worse than you think. He has attempted suicide nine times. Four times under his old id and five times as the loser. The last time being the night of the riots in the city."

"The bartender won't let him die. He makes too much money for him. I'm surprised he doesn't have bodyguards for him or at least spies on him."

"He does. Manny just doesn't know about it."

"It figures." I look around. "Those bodyguards must not be very good."

"What makes you say that?"

"Where are they? Have you seen them anywhere within five feet of Manny tonight? Maybe he does know about them."

"Not according to his system."

"Maybe he's lying to his system."

"It could be. This is bad."

"Definitely. Is there anything else?"

"No, I gave you everything I've found. I still haven't found anything on the creep."

"Keep looking. A piece of crap like him always leaves a stink behind him."

"Kenny you've got to save this Manny guy. I mean it. The guy is miserable. You have a taste of what it's like. I can't prove it, but I'm almost positive he knows how the betting system is run. He's unlucky, he's not stupid."

"Right so what do want me to do?"

"Kenny I'm telling you, you-we, need to save this guy. I mean really save this guy. We are his last chance."

"I'm trying. Tell me what you want me to do and I'll do it."

"Close your eyes and trust me."

I close my eyes. She awakens a feeling inside of me. It overtakes every part of my awareness and being. I now know what it is I need to do. All of my strength returns with a certainty I haven't felt for years. It is beyond description.

"Thank you baby, you always bring out the best in me. Don't let me ever forget this feeling."

"It's in there forever."

"No matter what?"

"No matter what."

"Right, then let's get going." I get up and start ahead toward the crowd.

I'm moving with a new speed I'd forgotten I had. I reach the crowd. It's going nuts. Everyone is fighting to get to the center. They all have money in their hands. This I have to see.

Using my experience and moves, I start sliding through the crowd with as little resistance as possible. This place is packed and the people are going out of their minds. It's worse than the old black and white films they used to show us in school about twentieth century icons. Those people were just screaming and crying. These people are taking it to the next level.

I reach the center. A thirty year old is playing an acoustic guitar. He has a forty ounce next to him. He's playing everything from classical to Twenty first century space swing and he is playing them all perfectly. I crouch down beside him. "Hey what's going on?" I ask.

He keeps playing; his eyes are bugging out of his head. "Man, if I told you, you wouldn't believe me."

"Try me."

"Okay like check this out man, I'd been playing here all day and all I had to show for it was three quarters, two nickels, three pennies, and a ticket for disturbing the peace.

"Then twenty minutes ago this real morose looking dude shows up. He checks me out, closes his eyes, and listens. Then he opens them back up; spots the ticket; reads it; and says, 'You're the worst guitar player I've ever heard. I hope you never make any money and all your luck is bad.' As he says this I notice a tear running down the side of his face.

"Real strange man. Anyway he leaves and since then people have been fighting to see me. It's crazy man. They're all throwing bills at me, big time bills. Check this out, three big time looking guys have offered me recording contracts. I've never seen anything like this. I feel like I'm dreaming."

"Enjoy it. Hey, did you see where the sad guy went?"

"That way," he says nodding his head to my right.

"Thanks," I say. I take out a twenty and throw it in his case.

"Thank you, and if you catch up to the sad guy tell him I said thanks."

I smile, nod, and stand up. I step to my right and begin to slide through the crowd. Manny definitely knows how this works and he definitely knows what's going on. There is no longer any question about it. Now I need to get out of this crowd.

My head is up, my eyes are wide, and my reflexes are sharp, but I still don't see anything. It's impossible to recognize anything in this mob. It's just one pulsating lump of flesh. "What do you say Autumn, are you getting any traces on these guys or what?"

"Not yet. I don't know where they could be."

"Well we're going to have to come up with another plan. I'm not going to find anything in this glop of flesh."

"Okay, take a right and stay sideways. It's the shortest path back to the outside. And Ken I shouldn't have to say this, but don't even think about using your guns."

"You're right; you didn't have to say it. What do you think I want to get us all trampled?"

"I know, I was just leaving no room for doubt. That's all."

"Right."

"I- oh-"

"What, what is it?"

"Nothing just concentrate on getting out of the mob you're in. It's only about four feet to go."

"What surprised you? Tell me."

"I will when you're out. Just get out and stay low."

I don't like this. I know her tones and the tone she just used is the one she saves for extremes, extreme surprise and tension to be specific. It can only be one of four things and I'm pretty sure I know which one it is. Let's just get out of here first.

There's a three inch gap a step to my left. I lunge for it. Air from the outside hits my face. It grabs onto my shoulders and pulls me out stumbling forward onto the sidewalk.

"Get to the doorway."

I check my directions. All clear. My feet make their way back under me. Staying low I take off, hustling for the doorway.

I reach it. It's dark and hopefully it's empty. "A little help please."

"You're alone. I checked."

"Right."

I reach for a wall. I find it and lean on it. "Right, so let me have it."

"Tony's camp was made."

"Shit, I knew the punk doctor was worried. What happened? Tell me everything."

"This just happened as I was talking to you. First let me give you the overall. The crew tore down and evacuated the camp about twenty minutes ago. Tony was taken ahead by a morph."

"The morph from the polite punks, the repair guy?"

"Yes. The crew and everything important got out of there before the thugs showed up. The thugs found nothing and they know nothing."

"They will. The creep just found the loser. He'll contact them and they'll all come stomping this way. How many thugs showed up at the site?"

"Eight."

"That's it? I overestimated these guys. Still, this is too many. How much time do we have until they show up?"

"Ninety minutes maybe two hours."

"Right, we have to do this and we have to do this now. They still don't know about me, do they?"

"If the creep recognized you with the bartender they do."

"Shit, alright here's the plan, contact everyone in the camp and tell them I said to leave now. Tell them about the bar and make sure they split. Tell them it's an order. Tell them I said thank you and get out now or else."

"Are you sure? What if-"

"What if nothing. They aren't fighters I am. I'm not going to let thugs like this put more innocent blood on my conscience and more importantly, on Manny's conscience. This is all going to end tonight, one way or the other."

I hear nothing but silence. "You know I'm right. You said it before, we've got to save him tonight this is his last chance."

"Okay."

"Good. Don't worry we're going to get this done. Just don't ask me how because I haven't figured that part out yet. I still need some things."

"What?"

"After you get everyone else out, see if you can find Manny or the creep. I can almost guarantee if you find one the other will be nearby. I wonder if Manny knows about the creep?"

"I doubt it. Is there anything else?"

"Contact people we can trust. Only people we can trust one hundred percent. You know better than I do about this, but my initial list would be Tony, Tony's mom, and the kid. Those are the only ones I can trust who can fight. I don't think it will make a difference; it'll take too long to get here, but just in case. Do you know where they're taking Tony?"

"Yes, but it's better if you don't know."

"Right could you at least give me a vague idea of where he's going?"

"You've never heard of the place he's going, so it would do no good to tell you and it would blow his cover. Put it this way, the place is nearer to where we were than where we are."

"Thank you. Is there anything else?"

"Only that the doctor will be calling you with all of this information any minute."

"Right, let's do this."

"I'm on it. Don't take any chances without my full backup."

"You said you're always here, right?"

"Yes."

"Then what's the problem?"

"Nothing, just hang on a second until I get a trace. Alright?"

"Okay. You know better than me."

I smile to myself. For a second there I felt like she was standing right next to me. I look into the street. The mob is pulsating back and forth unaware of everything going on around them. They don't know how lucky they are. It must be nice.

Alright tough guy writer wrap it up. You're wandering. Right. Shifting my weight, I turn my head right and refocus my attention. There isn't much to see. Other than a few dim lights it's pitch black dark. The broken and burnt out lights give off the image of a city where the last person checked out a long time ago and missed a few power switches before bolting. All of the buildings are dark.

I step onto the curb and start toward the corner.

"Kenny what are you doing?"

"I'm just walking to the corner. It's only a couple of more strides. It's not a big deal."

"Wait a second, let me make sure it's clear."

"I'm just one step away. Everything is alright. I just want to check something."

"What?"

"A feeling it's probably nothing. I'll be back in the doorway in a second. Cover it for me."

I take a step and stop on the corner. My eyes shift left. Nothing but darkness. Slowly I turn my head right.

"Autumn are you seeing what I'm seeing?"

"Yes. Stall while I set security for that site. Okay, you're clear twenty feet in all directions."

"Right."

I stare down at my wrist and examine the watch I don't have. I glance right again. Three dim streetlights and rows of dark buildings line the street. They look like the inside of a wino's mouth. Completely dark except for the one last tooth that refuses to fall out. The tooth he uses to pry off the caps of bottles.

It's about three and a half blocks away. The entire bottom floor is lit up brighter than the rest of the city. It's a lure, a trap, a big fat piece of cheddar waiting in the middle of a room of starving mice for its next victim. Either that or these thugs are stupider than I thought.

"This has to be the place," I say to myself.

"Ken."

"Yeah, go ahead."

"Okay, there is something living down there, but the systems haven't determined who or what they are."

"Let's go find out."

"No, we should have more complete results."

"We need to go now. We may already be too late. You know I'm right."

"Okay, but only if you listen to me. We have to do things my way. It's not just you anymore."

"Right."

"Okay, you can start, but you have to walk at a slow, even pace. I will give you your secure zones as you walk. Don't leave your coverage. You're his last hope, so be the professional these creeps could never be. So get ready, on three. Ready?"

"Ready."

"One- two- three."

I take my first stride.

"You have a ten foot secure zone. Good, keep it slow. Keep it even."

My heart is pounding. This is impossible. I may explode before I get there. Looking ahead everything is staying still.

"Your secure zone is seven feet. Slow down Ken."

"I'm trying."

I take a stride. A block and a half ahead, the middle of the three dim streetlights flickers out. I grunt. "Stay calm. One block down, two and a half to go. You're secure zone is five feet."

The frustration inside me is taking over. I need to get there now. This is craziness. This is how-"

A steel pole clangs to the ground. "Where was that? Check it out." I break forward.

"Ken stop. Ken slow down. Ken-"

She feels everything I feel. Shit.

I turn off the power. Now I'm gliding. One stride, two strides, bang now I'm walking again.

"Two blocks down one and a half to go. Your secure zone is twenty inches."

There's no way I can go any slower than this. I-

"Ken get to the wall and stop. We have movement."

I take a step to my right. Leaning lengthwise against the concrete wall I look ahead. Two creeps come out of the dark doorway next door. They look and turn right. Slowly they start to drift further down the street. There's got to be more than two. Wait, money says there are two more in there, maybe three. I've got to wait.

I reach into my pocket. Fumbling around, my hand searches for the blue phone. It finds it. I switch off the ringer. My hand comes out of my pocket and rests back on the gun.

Something is not right. The silence has changed. There's a different pulse to it. It's heavier, slower, and growing louder. It can only mean one thing.

"Baby," I whisper. "I may be paranoid, but I would swear there are footsteps closing in on me."

"I'll check."

The pulse continues. I keep my eyes locked on the doorway.

"Kenny there are four sets of footsteps coming toward you. Judging by the frequency and the force of the steps they are all two hundred and fifty to three hundred pounds."

"Four more creeps."

"Four more creeps."

"How much time do I have?'

"One hundred to one hundred seventy five seconds. You've got to get out of there."

I don't believe it. "Don't you get it? I can't. It's a trap. I don't know how these bastards did it, but they set me up again. There are probably two of them in there with Manny. If I run they'll take him and we'll never see him again. It will all be on me. If I stay it gets real ugly."

"Kenny leave, you have forty seconds. We'll find him again."

"I can't. Besides, no one has ever accused me of living pretty."

I inch in on the doorway. The door opens. Two creeps push Manny through. They start down the steps. No one has seen me yet. Autumn is yelling something in my head, but I can't make it out.

They're at the bottom of the stairs. I start creeping in. My gun is ready. I can't get a clear angle. Any shot I take will go through to Manny. Autumn is really screaming something. I must be in trouble. Heat is coming from behind I can feel it. Now is the time.

I wind up and pistol whip the near creep in the back of the head. I grab Manny's arm with my left hand and yank him to me. We turn back. A pistol is now headed for my forehead. Everything releases.

More darkness.

Chapter Fifteen

Lying on the concrete, I feel a new peace. This is how it had to be. Autumn is reorganizing my strength and my mind has everything in order.

I could open my eyes and go after them, but that would be stupid. Why sink to their level? These guys are well below the level I'd given them credit for. The concrete I'm spread out on has a higher level of intelligence than these guys and I don't mean to insult the concrete. The fact I walked into all their traps just goes to show it's definitely time for me to get out of this business.

First things first though, I'm going to keep my eyes shut. They created the problem let them fix it. They can't have me sprawled outside of their hideout. What would the neighbors say?

Two heavy breaths hit my face. They smell like garlic, synthetic asparagus, and malt beer. Interesting choice.

"Is he dead?"

"I don't know. I didn't hit him that hard."

"Try telling that to the boss. You better hope he's still alive, because if he isn't you're going to be lying right next to him."

"I didn't even hit him that hard."

"Boss is going to be pissed."

The breathing against my face gets harder and faster. "Wake up. Wake up dumbass. You came at me. I'm not going down for you."

A third slaps hits me. No big deal. I've hit myself harder trying to kill a mosquito.

"Maybe you should try CPR."

Right, time to wake up. My right eye opens. Three thugs are standing over me. One is kneeling next to me.

"I told you he wasn't dead."

"Do I know you boys?" I say.

The kneeling one winds up to punch me. His friend grabs his arm. "What are you stupid?"

"Ooh, ooh, I know the answer to this question," I say.

"Shut up," a chorus shouts back at me.

"But I know the answer to this one."

"Shut up and get your ass up. Boss wants to see you. He's got a surprise for you."

"A surprise- for me, wow that's awfully thoughtful of him. I truly appreciate it, really I do. I'd love to see what it is, but there's only one problem. I can't move."

"Very funny," the thug standing on the right says. He kicks me in the ribs. "Get up."

"I told you, I can't move and the kick you just gave me didn't help."

"What are we gonna do?"

I smile. "I guess you're going to have to carry me."

"Shut up."

"Okay, then you come up with something better. You want me to go somewhere. I can't move. I'm sure your boss is wondering what's taking you so long. You don't want him getting upset, do you?"

The crew surrounds me. They look at me. "Shit." They bend down, lift me up, and begin to carry me up the stairway like a pharaoh.

We've reached the second floor. They're wobbling. Pretty weak for a bunch of three hundred pounders. Normally this would be where I make my move, but I can't today; not with Manny in some demented creeps hands. They're shaking and grunting.

"Come on guys, I don't weigh that much."

"Enjoy it wiseass, because one more floor and you're going to be history."

"I doubt it."

He gives me an evil smile. They all start laughing.

We reach the third floor. They're still laughing. We turn to the first door on the right. The nearest thug struggles with the door knob. He kicks the door open. They are now laughing hysterically as they struggle into the room with me.

It's a dimly lit, dirty room. Manny is tied down to a wooden chair. Duct tape is wrapped across his mouth. Other than that it's empty except for the creeps. The creeps throw me into a corner. I land on my hip.

"What's all this laughing shit? What are you assholes laughing at? This dope just got you to carry him up three floors like he's some kind of friggin' royalty."

The laughing stops.

"We couldn't help it boss. He couldn't move. What else could we do?"

"How do you know he couldn't move?"

"He told us. Joey kicked him and everything. He really can't move."

"He told you. That's the reason. Oh, well I can understand everything now. Maybe we should ask him what to do next."

Some of the four smile.

"Assholes," the boss creep says. He looks at me. "Well how about it, what should we do next?"

I shrug my shoulders.

"Did you see that? He just shrugged his shoulders. He could move the whole time. He played your dumb asses. Get over here."

They run behind him and join four other thugs. He turns his back to me. I look at Manny. He doesn't look back. He looks like someone who has finally called it quits.

"Did you at least pat him down and take his weapons?" the boss creep asks.

"Yeah boss, we took his guns."

I still feel steel against my calves. They're either lying or they're stupid I can't tell. Whatever it is I'll take it.

"Give them to me."

"The guns?"

"No, the gum you're chewing."

An angry stare comes out of the thug's eyes. It is a deep seeded hatred rising out of the soil and into the clouds. "I put them in the car. I figured we'd plant them on our next victims," he says slowly. He is about to burst.

The boss creep from the bar rolls his eyes. He turns toward me and begins pacing. He is wearing an imitation Italian suit and has gold draped all across his body. The gold is probably fake too. He rubs his hands together as he paces.

A smile jumps onto his face. He looks at me. "Do you know why we're here Mr. Breaker?"

I shrug. "Poker night?"

He stops, stares, and moves in on me slowly. I don't know if he expects me to be afraid or not. If he does he's sadly mistaken. He is no more than five foot five and one hundred fifty pounds. I can break him in half with one shot. He's even smaller than he looked in the bar.

He steps up under my chin. "You're a real smartass aren't you?" He spits down right beside me. "Yeah, you're so smart you walked into all of my traps, all of my set-ups. How did it feel smart guy?" He smiles right into my face.

"I was just lulling you into a false sense of security."

He starts laughing uncontrollably. The thugs begin laughing behind him. I check. They're all laughing, but one isn't laughing as hard as the rest. I glace over at Manny. He's looking at me. I give him a slight nod. He raises an eyebrow and nods back.

The creep gets back into my face. "What do you think this is a football game or something?"

His laughter is puttering out. He puts on a fake southern accent and softly starts back up. "I've got news for you son, the game ended a long time ago. You all lost. You're all losers. You're just lucky I'm as gracious a winner as I am.

"I now have everything and today, well today is a birthday party and you are fortunate enough to have been invited. You see, old L over there is going to make everything official and permanent. What do you think about that?"

"I don't get paid to think."

He moves into my face. Any closer and we'll have to get a room. "Oh come on, don't be a sore loser. Tell us what you think." He turns and starts to walk away.

"Normally I would charge extra for this, but today why not, It's a birthday party right?"

He turns and smiles back at me.

"What do I think? Right, well my first thought about you was you're way ahead of your kind. I mean who knew a piece of shit could speak. Piece of Shit and the Dumbasses, I bet you guys make some really interesting harmonies."

I start laughing a bitter fake laugh. The anger is trying to rise, but I no longer have any room for anger. I've got to stay sharp. This is no time to start taking things personally; he's just trying to throw me off me game.

The creep smiles at me. "What's the matter? You sound sore. Are you going to start crying for us next? If you are save it. There aren't any cameras in here. Face it, the show's over and you lost."

"How do you figure that?"

"Come on, you can't tell me you still haven't figured it out. It's not some kind of ultra-complicated master plan. Its genius is in its simplicity. You do realize this, don't you?"

Let him figure it out.

"Oh my God, you still don't get it do you? I've overestimated your talents. I always thought you were smarter than this."

Right, just keep talking. Autumn is recording the whole thing.

"What's the matter you can't talk anymore smartass? Was that piece of shit line the best you could come up with for your last shot? Well let me give you something to appreciate in your final few minutes on this planet.

"I did everything by doing nothing. You people did it all for me. I just pressed the right buttons. You people like to talk about love and kindness, but deep down you know you're all full of crap. It's just a line and you know it."

"Bullshit."

"He speaks. Welcome back to the conversation, though I'm afraid you're going to have to do better than 'bullshit'. You are proving my point for me. Deep down you know when the money's on the table what really drives people are hate and fear. Probably more fear than hate, but I still can't say for sure."

"You're dreaming. You've lost it."

"Have I? How do you explain what's going on in the city? Everyone fighting and destroying each other. The media foaming at the mouth to get the next image, the next scapegoat, and the next target. I haven't done any of this. I have not killed one person this entire time. I just took what was already there and brought it to the front of everyone's minds."

"Just because you hate the system doesn't mean you get to ruin it for everyone else."

"Me hate the system, you've still got it all wrong my friend. I love the system. It's obvious it's the citizens who hate the system. The cops are against the P.I.s; the aliens are against the humans; the government is against the citizens; the citizens are against the police; etc., etc. I could go on and on, but you have to understand what I'm saying.

"The frustration, the fear, and the hate, were always there. I just pressed the right buttons to give them a way to get it all out. No, it's not me, I love the system. I just hate the fact it's being run by idiots and bled dry by freeloaders. When this is all over, I will step in. I will be the hero the citizens need."

"You're delusional."

"Am I? Don't be so sure about that. When the financial district realizes it was me who eliminated the repair shop they'll make me into a hero. They'll be building statues to me.

"And The Eyes Upstairs love this and you know it. They can't wait for the fight to calm down. When it does they'll put stricter restrictions on the few freedoms you have left. There will be more cameras and they'll read your thoughts and dreams a lot closer.

"You will be fed a higher dosage of control propaganda through your mind chip. And when they learn I've created an antiprogram that only lets citizens see what they want them to see, whether it's there or not, well then they're going to put me in control.

"You know I'm right. It's a great system, ain't it?" He smiles at me.

We are in deep shit.

I'm using every control I have not to tear this creep into a thousand pieces.

"You want to kill me right now, don't you? Don't deny it. I can see it in your eyes. See it's not so hard and it's not so wrong. Deep inside you know you are willing to do anything to keep what you want. Even if it costs a few lives.

"In fact you're worse than me because you want to kill me yourself. I on the other hand, have never killed anything."

"Wrong again. We're nowhere near being alike. I don't kill, I save and there's a big difference between the two. It's the difference between you and me. You work to kill and destroy. I'm a P.I. and a writer, I work to save and create. I kill only when I'm forced to and I never feel good about it."

"Keep telling yourself that."

"Face it you're a nothing. A nobody, worse than a faker. You have no talent. You can't do anything yourself. I used to think you were a wannabe, but I was wrong. I gave you too much credit. You're just a leech who sucks the life out of society leaving nothing but the worst behind.

"You're the ultimate liar showing everything that's good as bad and making everything that's bad out to be something good. Deep down you know I'm right."

He is still. Staring into his eyes I can see he's hurt. I glance behind him at his thugs. They all look confused except for one. The one who is about to burst. He's wearing a sly smile. He's the one to push.

Looking back to the creep he is still in the same position. He's stunned. Time for a few more shots. Moving toward him, I lower my head to his level.

"What's the matter? Is the genius all out of words? Is it me? It is me isn't it? What you don't like what I just said? Yeah well, the truth hurts sometimes doesn't it? I hope I didn't ruin your birthday party.

"You do have to admit though; you did bring this on yourself. The whole pitting species against species and making my dinner disappear thing isn't going to gain you a lot of support. You know this right?"

His face is turning red. He pivots away from me, giving me the evil eye. He's doing it all wrong. My grandmother did it better than this. Maybe it's not his fault. Maybe he just didn't have as good a grandmother as I did.

"This is the last time I come to one of your parties."

I shouldn't have said that.

"It's a party, you're right. Thanks for reminding me smartass. Do you know what we're celebrating?"

"You finally learned how to count to ten without using your fingers?"

"And that my dear smartass, will be the last comment you ever make."

He nods. Three thugs come at me. One is ahead of the other two. They're quick. The first one lowers his center of gravity. He's a stride away. Summoning the ghosts of great wrestlers past I step up and elbow him in the back of the head. He stops in his tracks and is unconscious before he hits the floor.

"Didn't your coach ever tell you not to lower your head?" I say looking down at him. "I-" Flying toward the wall with one thug high and one thug low, my head has been snapped into its original upright position. We hit the floor. The thugs are on my knees and my chest. I can't move. They regain their balance and go to work on me.

I'm trying to get loose, but it's not happening. I lift my head up. No luck, he's out of head butt range. For all of our sakes I hope they don't grab my guns. It will be the end of all three of us if they do.

"Alright, enough, enough, don't kill him yet. I want him to see this."

The top thug throws in one last shot to my jaw. I've had drinks that hit harder than these guys. Pathetic, truly pathetic.

"Stand him up."

The top thug puts me in a full nelson. Over my shoulder he says, "Look at the boss."

As if I have a choice.

Boss creep is now standing in front of Manny. He stares his evil grin at me and begins. "This is a celebration and this is the part where I open my present. A present I couldn't have gotten without you. After I open this present a new world will be born and I will be running it.

"Now it just came to me, since you are the one who brought this present to me it wouldn't be gracious of me to turn around and kill you. I mean it's not like it's a bad present. It's not. It's a wonderful present. In fact, it's a present that's going to guarantee me everything I want. It will provide me an infinite amount of presents.

"So I have changed my mind. I'm not going to kill you. I'm just going to torture you every day for the rest of your life. Not physically though. Mentally. You will have to know and live with the fact you caused all of this. I'll keep you alive on this planet for as long as possible just to see the pain you're going through.

"I couldn't have done it without you."

"I don't believe you. You turn on everything. You will turn on me and kill me. Just like you will turn on the rest of your crew and kill them. All of you in the crew can count on this. Some of you already know it. And for what? A five foot five weakling you could break in half with a sneeze. You know it's true."

"Enough, my men know I am eternally thankful. They know they will benefit when I'm in charge. Give them some credit. You underestimated me and now you're underestimating them. They know."

He stands in front of Manny. He bends and looks into his eyes. "When I take the tape off of your mouth you are going to guarantee me eternal life, wealth, and power. You will guarantee me to be in charge of everything. Otherwise you and your friend over there are history. Do you understand?"

"Don't do it Manny," I yell.

"Shut up. Now, do you understand?"

Manny nods. The creep yanks the tape from his mouth. Manny shakes his head in pain.

"Do it!"

The creep is holding Manny by the head. He lets go. Manny looks him in the eyes.

"I hope you and all of your men live very long, safe, happy, rich, painless and power filled lives. May you always be in charge; may you always be in control; may tragedy, bad luck, and pain never strike down upon you; and may you be in Heaven a half hour before the devil knows you're dead."

The creep steps back and smiles.

Then it hits him.

"See I told you your boss would turn on you. He just bought all of you a one way ticket t-"

The boiling thug gets it. He charges his boss. The boss is grabbed and thrown to the center of the floor. The rest of the thugs get it. They all run at their boss. They're going to tear him to pieces.

One thug breaks from the mob. He's running at Manny. "Take that back, take that back," he shouts.

I reach for my gun. It's still there. I shoot without aiming. The thug falls forward. He drops at the foot of the chair. Blood is draining from his right leg. I run over to the chair.

Manny is sitting there seemingly unaffected by the whole thing. "Let's get you out of here."

I go for the knots, first the hands then the feet. I pull out a switch blade and start on the rope. It's tight, good, it's easier to cut through that way. There go the hands. Manny moves his arms forward. I drop to one knee and start again. The rope around his ankles goes limp.

"Okay, try the feet."

He kicks the rope. It loosens and he steps out.

"Let's go."

He follows me into the hallway. Seven quick shots fire off behind us. We pause involuntarily. Seven heavy thuds follow. One shot. One thud. A step. Another shot. Another thud. Silence.

"Nine shots, nine thuds. That should be all of them," I say. He nods. We head to the stairway.

We're running down the stairs now two, three at a time. "Do you have a way out of here?" I ask.

"No," he says.

Wait, no means yes. Good, okay. I have to think in his language. Think negative. "Is it around here?" I ask.

"Yes." No good.

"Are you sure you can make it?"

"No."

Good.

We reach the doorway. It's still dark. I grab Manny and say, "Before we leave I have a couple of things I need. The first is for me, the second is for me and someone else. Do you understand?"

"No."

Good. Right, think negative. "First, I never want things to be good like they were before the first body showed up again, ever. Especially not forever. I never want everyone to constantly have good luck, good fortune, and happiness.

"Second, I never want to see you again, especially at your bar. I never want you to keep your power while being able to say what you actually want. For instance, I never want you to be able to say 'I hope you have a good day' and then have the person have a good day. I would never want that to happen especially for your entire life.

"So, may you have a terrible, short, miserable life, and I never want to see you again. Do you understand?"

Looking him in the eyes I see a tear run down the side of his face. "No," he says.

I smile. "Good."

He turns left and walks into the night.

I head for the corner I came from. "Okay baby this would be a good time for those locales and directions." No reply. "Autumn come on, I need you, don't play around now."

"I'm here, I'm always here. I was just reorganizing your strength again."

"And."

"It's going to be close."

"Right, how far away are we?"

"We're seven miles northwest of The Place."

"I can make it there by foot, no problem."

"You should and you'd better because as of now it's the only way we have of getting there."

"Okay, let's go. Give me the directions."

"In two strides make a left at the corner. After that keep walking straight. All of the roads coming up are empty and clear."

"Right, I'm at the corner now. Before I turn left let's double check. There's no movement, right?"

"Yes, you're all clear from here to The Place."

"Good."

I turn left. The streets are completely deserted. A dull pain is growing around my knees. The bottom thug may have hit me harder than I gave him credit for. It's still no big deal, but it's more than nothing. Hopefully it doesn't get worse.

"Don't they have taxis in this town?"

"They did, but all of the drivers just shot each other."

"Why didn't you tell me? I would've lifted the keys."

"They didn't have them with them and I haven't been able to locate the cars."

"Keep looking because there's no way I'm making it back to the apartment on foot."

"You may not have to. I contacted Dr. Punk and his staff."

"And?"

"They all left when I told them the situation. He said they were going to leave a car for you in The Place's parking lot."

"So we should be good then, right?"

"Not exactly."

"Not exactly, what's that supposed to mean?"

"It means you have a car, but you may not have enough gas."

"No."

"Yes, they're completely and totally broke. They spent everything they had on saving you guys, so I don't want to hear any complaining. The doc wanted to pick you up in this town, but then you would've definitely run short."

This is going to be a long night. There has to be another way. I guess worse comes to worse I'll sleep in the car, regain my strength, and start again when I wake up. "How far am I from the parking lot?"

"Four miles, almost half way. The car is there. It's a blue economy car so we should be able to go a long way."

"How much fuel do we have?"

"It's a little more than half a tank full."

Or almost half a tank empty.

"Don't think that way. I heard what you just thought."

"Right, sorry. I'm just getting a little tired. Is there anything you can do to the gas? You know, the same way you reorganize my strength."

"Who do you think I am, God? I'm only part of a digital knowledge and communication system. I don't do miracles. Talk to the real me. Maybe she can put in a good word for you."

"Right."

I keep walking. If I stop now I probably won't be able to get started again. The streets are still dim and empty. The clouds in the sky are starting to break up. "Make a left at the corner."

"How far to the bar?"

"Two miles."

"Did you contact anyone else?"

"I tried, but I had to leave messages. I haven't gotten any responses yet."

"What's going on?"

"I don't know. The city is pretty beat up. The Eyes Upstairs may have shut off the chips power."

"No."

"Yes, I've seen it done before in other countries."

I reach the corner and turn left. I put my head down and keep moving forward.

*   *   *

I've reached the parking lot. It's a couple of hours past midnight and the bar is starting to empty out. "It's the blue car by the entrance."

I walk toward the first blue car I see by the entrance. "Is this it?" I ask.

"Yes, the card is taped underneath the driver's seat."

I open the door, bend, and reach. It's right there. I pull it out. This car smells a lot nicer than the one we had the last time I was here. I pop the trunk. Just in case.

"What are you doing?"

"Nothing I just want to see something." I walk to the back and peek into the trunk.

No bodies. Excellent. I slam the trunk closed, hustle back to the front, and get in. The card slides right in and the engine starts on the first try. I look at the dashboard. Either Autumn or Dr. Punk was lying. The fuel monitor is shows it's only three eighths full, not a little more than half.

"We're not going to make it."

"You don't know that. Just shut up and drive smart." I hit the gas and we start our way back. Who knows, maybe we'll get a strong tailwind.

We reach the main road. My legs have called it quits and my head is trying to join them. It keeps dropping down and snapping back up. Crashing is not a worry though. We're in the middle of nowhere, other than car skeletons there is nothing to run into. The worst we could do is go off course.

"Baby, is there any chance of reorganizing my strength one last time?"

"No, there's nothing else I can do."

"Does this car have auto driver?"

"Yes, why?"

"Because I'm going to run out of gas before the car does."

"Okay, press the button on the bottom of the far left column."

"Right."

Leaning forward I press the button. The car takes over. Leaning back I check the mirror. Nothing. Looking ahead I see the same. My head starts to drop forward. This time I don't catch it.

Chapter Sixteen

My head snaps up.

"Don't move."

A click and the pressure of cold steel against the back of my head now have my full attention. Baby what the hell is going on?

"She's not going to answer your thoughts. You realize this, right?"

The pressure increases. "Put your hands on the steering wheel."

Everything is still.

"Good, now, you are not going to think; you are not going to move; and you are not going to speak. You aren't going to do a damn thing unless I say you can."

I bite down on top of my lip.

"Do that again. Go ahead, do that again and disappear. Do you understand? Nod slowly if you do."

I nod yes.

"Good. Now you are probably wondering what's going on, right?"

I nod.

"I thought so. You're lucky because I have all of the answers and luckily for you, I'm in a giving kind of mood tonight. Now don't interrupt me. You know how much I hate to be interrupted."

Blood is running from the side of my lip. The voice starts back up.

"You've gotten as far as you are going to go. It all ends for you here. Here, tonight, in this car, this stalled out, piece of shit car, in the darkness, in the middle of nowhere. You've only got a few minutes left. No one is coming to save you, but you knew this already.

"You suspected Tony of this the whole time. Why didn't he get arrested? Why did everything always happen to you? Don't even get me started on the kid. Since when do you trust cops? It's pathetic really.

"The worst though, the worst is the delusion you've put into your mind about your ex. She led you right to me. Face it she lied about the gas. She tried to rob you of your edge. She didn't listen to you before she left for that last trip. She was always against you. Don't be so hard on her though, it's not her fault I made her into a virus to bring you to me.

"Besides, we know who the real person to blame is, right?"

"No, who would that be?"

"Didn't I say you weren't going to speak?"

"I guess you were wrong, weren't you."

"No, in fact you are proving my last point for me."

"And what last point is that?"

"You wanted this all along. Deep inside you know it's true. You gave up on living a long time ago. That's why you walked into all the traps. That's why you believed all the crap your so-called friends fed you. You want this to happen. You want everything to end now. Don't deny it, you know it's true. It's why you would talk back to me when you know I'll shoot you."

"Bullshit."

"Really, how many times have you said or thought you just wanted to get this last case over with?"

My hands are choking the steering wheel.

"Hey take it easy on the steering wheel. Don't punish it for the fact you're too weak to keep going."

"Who the fuck do you think you are?"

"Why don't you check your rearview mirror and find out?"

I glance up at the mirror. "You've got to be kidding me."

An image of another me holding a gun to the back of my head reflects back at me. He smiles and waves at me with his free hand. "I don't believe this. You are not me."

"Right, are you sure? I doubt it. I mean who are you to say what's real and what's not? You were sure about everything else, right?"

"Right, now I know you're not real. You're just a real bad liar. Five seconds ago you said I knew all my friends were against me. Now you say I was sure about them being my friends. Get your stories straight."

"Is that what you heard? I doubt it. You can't even tell if I'm real or not."

"You're not real."

"Yet here you are yelling at me."

"You're not me. I know what I believe and what I feel. What you've said is contrary to all of those things. I don't know what you are, but I do know this: you are not me. I have no doubt about that."

"Okay, if you're so sure prove it."

"I don't need to prove anything to you."

I reach for the door. The gun follows my head.

"Are you sure you want to do this?"

Slowly I turn my head back to him and look him in the eyes. The gun is now pressed against my forehead. "You're afraid," I say.

Anger shoots from his eyes.

"You are afraid aren't you? What are you so afraid of?" I smile back at him. "What I'm about to do is really big isn't it? Why else would you go through all of this to stop me? I'm right aren't I?"

His gun crashes against the side of my head. I stay upright.

"I am right. I knew it. I don't know who or what sent you, but tell it I'm onto its game. Now I have to go."

I click the door handle.

"I wouldn't do that if I were you," he says.

I push the door open. Blinding white light floods into the car. He can't handle this. I'm stronger than he is. Come on, one more time.

My legs launch me forward. Stumbling from the car an explosion knocks me ahead. My body is crashing, losing its control. I crash to the ground. The echoes from the explosion are pounding my ears. I lift my head. Dirt is flying in all directions. Reflexively my arms force themselves up and guard my face.

My eyes close. This is it, the tank is empty. I don't have anything else left. My head slams down to the ground. The dirt rains against the top of my head. Everything is dark. The last of my strength is draining out of the bottom of my feet.

I can't believe I'm going to come up short. The dirt keeps attacking me. Darkness takes over as my consciousness runs out. This is it.

I lift up my head. Where am I? I force my eyes open. Light floods in. My head turns away. With all of the trouble I've had opening my eyes the past few days there's no way I'm going to close them now. Not on purpose at least.

My eyes adjust to the light. Staring back at my twisted half-naked body is a wall. I know this wall. All inner warning systems return to normal and my body relaxes. I twist back around.

"Recognize the view?" a voice from another room asks.

"Very funny."

I stare at my bedroom. When was the last time I was here? More importantly, is anything different? I don't know and at this point I don't really care. My stomach kicks back at me. I guess it's time to eat.

I get out of bed. Soreness takes over my body. My stomach growls back at it. You've got to do what you've got to do. I start toward the kitchen.

"I wouldn't do that if I were you, besides the frig is empty, remember?"

"Right."

I lumber over to the couch and plop down. "I haven't seen you in a while scanner."

"You're not going to start that again are you?"

"No baby, I was just kidding."

"What's my name?"

"What am I on some kind of game show? It's Autumn, what else would it be? I do have a question though."

"What would that be?"

"You knew who you were the whole time right?"

"Yeah so?"

"So you did the whole October office visit didn't you? You weren't really doing any investigation into how it happened, right? Don't answer. I don't want to get you in any trouble. Besides we're one now what else could I need?"

"It's okay I had permission. You were the only one who didn't know what was going on. You were so close so many times, but then you had the fourteen hour sleep and you went off the rails. The day before everyone was so sure you were going to be back to normal. You had done everything except say my name. Then the bodies showed up and you totally regressed."

"Right, well it's never going to happen again. I'm sorry it took me so long to get right again."

"It doesn't matter, like you said we're one now."

"Right."

Sitting and thinking it hits me. "How did I get here?"

"Do you mean physically or philosophically?"

"Physically, what day is it? What happened?"

"You don't remember?"

"The last thing I remember is escaping from a car where an imitation me had a gun to my head."

"That never happened."

"What do you mean? I was there. It was trying to convince me you were all against me and I was going to die right there. Both of which I told him were a crock."

"I don't know about that. It sounds like something in the real me's department."

"Maybe."

"I will tell you what did happen. We were in the car and you fell asleep before the car ran out of gas."

"Right, I remember that. What happened after that?"

"The car coasted a little past the halfway point and died. About a half hour later you woke up in a stalled car. Your strength levels were all zero or near zero and there was nothing I could do about it. I tried to convince you to get more sleep, but you wouldn't listen. You were determined to get back as quickly as possible.

"Luckily we were alone in the middle of nowhere so no one could attack us. The negative was we were in the middle of nowhere far away from anyone who wanted to rescue us. I don't know how you did it, but you walked twenty one miles on foot."

"There's no way I could've done that. The measurements must have been wrong."

"No, they were correct. It took a few hours, but you got there."

"I guess I had nothing better to do."

"Then you'd better find some hobbies because I thought we were going to die right there. Your levels were practically flat lining."

"What happened?"

"The cavalry showed up."

"Who were the cavalry?"

"Tony, Tony's mom, and the kid."

"I thought you said you couldn't make contact."

"I couldn't, it turns out The Eyes Upstairs did shut off all of the digital communications. Then later on everything started going right and the communications were up again without the government's doing."

"What do you mean everything started going right? When did this happen?"

"I'll get to that later. Trust me. So Tony's mom got the message first. She tried to contact the kid, but he was knocking on her door at the same time."

"Why was he over there?"

"He went over there to tell her the polite punks had made contact with him and he knew where Tony was. They got into Tony's mom's taxi and went to pick him up."

"Is he okay?"

"He's pretty beaten up inside and out, but they said when the two of them got there and told him about you he went berserk. They reached us about ten minutes after you collapsed. They slid you into the back seat and the kid used all of his training to keep us alive. He even had to bring us back to life once."

"We were dead?"

"Just a little. It wasn't nearly as bad as what the punk doctor brought us back from."

I make a face and nod my head. She starts up again.

"Tony carried you upstairs. He didn't want anybody touching you. He stayed at your side for two days."

"Two days, what do you mean two days? What day is it? How long have I been out?"

"Don't get excited. You've been asleep almost two and a half days. It's now eleven o'clock in the morning. The kid and Tony's mom made Tony leave earlier this morning. They were worried it had started affecting his health. He didn't want to leave. He was crying the whole time he was here."

"The only time I've ever seen him cry was when he was hugging his daughter inside the BC Lounge. He thought we were going to die and he'd never see her again. Where are they now?"

"They're all at Tony's mom's apartment: Tony, his mom, his daughter and the kid."

"We have to stop by there later today."

"We'll take a taxi this time. I know a good driver, but-"

"But what?"

"The city is a lot different now. It's not like when you left it."

"Meaning what?"

"It's not the same. Start with the people. You guys are big shots now and you're the biggest."

"Right, and how did this happen?"

"When communications came back up all of the stuff I sent from the ride and the creep confrontation went through to all of the chips. It has been the number one story the last three days. Add to it the kid's anonymous story and you've become a big shot."

"Right, we'll see how long that lasts. What about everyone else?"

"The kid has been honored and is being honorably discharged of his remaining time on the force so he can become a P.I.. They're not even going to make him take the test for the license."

"Knowing him he'll take it anyway."

"I wouldn't doubt it. The movie studios all want the rights to Tony and his mom's story. Now they just need someone to write it."

I let that one go.

"What about Dr. Punk and those people? Are they getting what they deserve? I mean we would all be dead if it weren't for them."

"Yes, but they're playing it down. I get the impression they would rather be respected than made into stars. I found something out about them I thought you should know."

She sounds more serious than normal. This must be big. "What is it?" I ask.

"Okay, well with all of the info I received recently I learned a lot of surprising things. I found out information about the polite punks: the doctor, the engineer who is also a morph, and the leader. I did a rundown on them when we were picked up by the green trucks. I had to. They were taking us away.

"The first thing I found out was they knew all about this before anyone else. It turns out many of the degree traders, debtors, and analogs figured this out long before we did. They didn't want a few creeps to ruin everything by having every group set against each other, so they started their own underground. It's how they had the EMTs to get to you."

"Right, he said they meant to get us out of there, but they were just a little late."

"It was a little more personal than that."

"What do you mean?"

"Do you remember the story you told Tony about Johnny Shakes?"

"Yeah so?"

"Do you remember how Tony said he knew it was true?"

"I don't remember much right now. Go ahead and tell me."

"Tony said he knew it was true because his father worked there. Then he pointed out your mother worked there. He said not to deny it because it was one of your secrets."

"Right, I remember now."

"Okay, well after running off with the rest of the prison your mom and Tony's father became close. Eventually the Johnny Shakes group went their separate ways. When they did your mom and Tony's dad settled down together."

"What? Where are they? Are they alive?"

"No, they died a long time ago, but their three kids are still alive. They are -"

"No-"

"Yes, those kids are the polite punks."

"Wait that means-"

"It means every time they call you bro, they mean it. You are their brother."

This is unbelievable. Then it hits me. "Wait it also means-"

"That's right, you are Tony's brother."

I jump up from my chair. "Is this what you meant when you said everything started going right?"

"No this happened before."

"Before what? What did you mean by everything started going right?"

"No one can put an exact time on it, but the first time I noticed it was soon after we left the building."

A flash comes into my mind. I catch it. How could I have forgotten? I run to the frig and open the door. It's full. I grab a sugarbomb and run into the living room.

"Where did you get the soda?"

"You know where I got it. The frig where else? You do know what's going on don't you?"

I hurry around the couch to the window. Looking outside I can't believe what I'm seeing. Everyone is outside rebuilding the city together. The sky is a beautiful deep blue. It's like it was the first day after my fourteen hour sleep.

"It's Manny. You knew it the whole time didn't you?" I feel her smile. "It was the two requests, wasn't it? So this means he's good now. Right?"

"There's only one way to find out."

"Call up Tony's mom's and tell them we're all going out to a new place I've found. Tell them it's my treat. Wait, maybe we shouldn't do that. It might give Tony a heart attack."

"It's already been done. They're coming over around five."

"Right, good, excellent, thank you."

A new energy runs through me. I can't stand still. This is unbelievable.

I pace throughout the apartment and thoughts fly through my mind. It's a different kind of pacing and these are a different type of thoughts. These are positive thoughts; new thoughts, in a renewed mind heading into the future with the best of the past.

CPSIA information can be obtained
at www.ICGtesting.com
Printed in the USA
BVHW031804040419
544636BV00005B/24/P